# A SMOLDERING FIRE

So Edward thought she was willing, but afraid. She stood where she was, frozen by the realization that he might be right.

"Come choose a table, Mrs. Whitlow."

She came into the room and walked past him. There were five tables, each with four chairs, the cards in place, and a table set up for refreshment. Except for them, the room was empty. She surveyed the arrangements and spoke without turning to look at him.

"Mr. Hadley, I came tonight because I received your note."

"What note?"

She whirled back, shocked at her mistake, and he laughed.

"Oh, I love the way you do that. That gorgeous red silk swirls in such a way that you look like a smoldering fire bursting into flame."

"You did send that note, did you not?"

"Of course I did."

"Would you stop teasing me!"

"Never." He was in front of her. Very close. So close that his one word was a whisper. He leaned even closer. "I sent the note." She was pressed against the back of the chair behind her. "For I will not leave everything to chance."

# BOOK YOUR PLACE ON OUR WEBSITE AND MAKE THE READING CONNECTION!

We've created a customized website just for our very special readers, where you can get the inside scoop on everything that's going on with Zebra, Pinnacle and Kensington books.

When you come online, you'll have the exciting opportunity to:

- View covers of upcoming books

- Read sample chapters

- Learn about our future publishing schedule (listed by publication month *and author*)

- Find out when your favorite authors will be visiting a city near you

- Search for and order backlist books from our online catalog

- Check out author bios and background information

- Send e-mail to your favorite authors

- Meet the Kensington staff online

- Join us in weekly chats with authors, readers and other guests

- Get writing guidelines

- AND MUCH MORE!

Visit our website at
http://www.kensingtonbooks.com

# THE PLEASURE OF HIS COMPANY

*Mary Blayney*

ZEBRA BOOKS
Kensington Publishing Corp.
http://www.kensingtonbooks.com

ZEBRA BOOKS are published by

Kensington Publishing Corp.
850 Third Avenue
New York, NY 10022

All Kensington titles, imprints and distributed lines are available at special quantity discounts for bulk purchases for sales promotion, premiums, fund-raising, educational or institutional use.

Special book excerpts or customized printings can also be created to fit specific needs. For details, write or phone the office of the Kensington Special Sales Manager: Kensington Publishing Corp., 850 Third Avenue, New York, NY 10022. Attn. Special Sales Department. Phone: 1-800-221-2647.

Zebra and the Z logo Reg. U.S. Pat. & TM Off.

First Printing: November 2003
10 9 8 7 6 5 4 3 2 1

Printed in the United States of America

# One

"The first time I saw him was in a graveyard. And he was laughing." Mariel had hoped to amuse her grandmother but had forgotten how easily shocked her companion was.

Mrs. Dayhull gasped and reached for the vinaigrette that she kept close by. It was at hand ostensibly for the dowager duchess, but Mariel had never seen her grandmother use it.

"Oh, I am so sorry, Mrs. Dayhull, but, you see, his laughter was quite understandable. He was standing in front of Miss MacMann's marker. It makes everyone laugh."

Mariel turned from her grandmother, folded her hands in front of her, and recited: "'Here lies Maudie MacMann. Lived an old maid but died an old Mann.'"

Mrs. Dayhull smiled politely, which was as close as she ever came to laughter.

"Look at me, Mariel. I have a hard enough time hearing when I can see your face."

Mariel turned back and then sat in the chair next to the bed.

"Did the laughing man see you?" Her grandmother brought her back to the subject with her usual tenacity.

"Yes, Grandmère, he did see me and bowed in apology."

"Why was he in Cashton?"

Grandmère's curiosity was encouraging. If she was still this interested in the world around her, then perhaps she was not as ill as Mrs. Dayhull's letter had intimated. Tucked into the giant bed with the opulent ocean-blue hangings and the grandiose murals on the wall, Mariel decided that the Dowager Duchess of Hale looked as imperious as ever.

Could boredom be as much an illness as true disease? When was the last time she had had a caller other than her physician?

"I have no idea why he was in Kent, Grandmère. Most likely he was visiting the Harbisons, for they had a house full of guests in anticipation of the Season. Our Polly and Georgie had been helping in the morning with breakfast and making up the rooms. I would have asked one of them, but all they could talk about was the one hundred guineas that the maid at the Crown had been given as a tip for nothing more than serving dinner."

Her grandmother snorted at that.

"I think it must be true, Grandmère. For the Burketts are a very staid, churchgoing family, rigid in their moral sense."

"You would know."

"Yes, thank you, I would. Ten years in Cashton married to the vicar gave me a thorough understanding of human nature."

"You had that before you ever married Charles."

"An understanding, perhaps, but not a thorough one. My life was much too protected at Braemoor to understand all of man's vagaries."

Mariel was pleased with her composure and even more pleased that it was not an affectation. Charles was dead. She made herself say the word. Charles was dead, not passed away, gone from her, or gone to God, but dead. He had been so for two years, and she had come to terms with that and her widow's life. Not that she knew yet exactly what "a widow's life" would entail.

"I would have forgotten all about the gentleman, but then I saw him again not a week later in Dover at the recital I attended for Marcus Ponto's most promising pupil. This time he was standing at the back of the room, looking as though he were trying to decide whether or not to stay. At the first intermission he approached Signor Ponto, and though we exchanged a few words, we had not time for introductions."

"Ponto never did understand even the most rudimentary etiquette."

"Yes, Grandmère, music is everything to him. It is what makes him such a wonderful teacher."

There had been few words, but they had been charming. Mariel could still recall them exactly. Ponto had welcomed him and turned to Mariel and said, "He has a true appreciation of the cello."

The man had bowed to her, his eyes twinkling, and added, "And for beautiful women."

Then before she could respond or he could say his name, Signor Ponto had rushed them back to their seats and begun the second part of the program.

"And you had no chance to meet him at the reception?"

"No. He did not stay or at least left before I reached the receiving room. It was quite irksome, for I had no expectation of ever seeing him again."

"And you want me to tell you his name based on a sheepish smile and the most simple of flirtations? I know the ton, but even I am not that observant. Exactly why are you so interested in this graveyard-loving, musically inclined gentleman, Mariel?"

Whether he was graveyard-loving or musically inclined hardly mattered. She knew this man was about more than laughter and flirtation. How to explain that first moment of shared understanding among the headstones? It was a communion without words. A gesture that encompassed the markers and a slight sigh that asked if she, like him, understood how fragile life was. She had answered the gesture with a nod. Oh, yes, she did understand. She would never have forgotten him even if she had never seen him again.

"But there is more, for I saw him again today. When Mrs. Dayhull and I were at the bookseller's. We were waiting at the carriage, as I had sent the footman back for a package we left behind. Who should appear but my mysterious gentleman."

Mariel smiled at her grandmother's skeptical look.

"Yes, it is amazing, is it not? He opened the door for me and took my hand to assist me into the carriage."

"And said nothing?"

"How lovely to see you again." A conventional phrase, not nearly as meaningful as their wordless exchange in the grave-yard but equally unforgettable. Or maybe the indelible memory came from the touch of his hand on her arm as he assisted her into the coach. How could a touch as conventional as his words convey sympathy and caring?

"And you still did not meet him?"

"No." Mariel said the one word with sharp exasperation. "He was gone into the shop as quickly as he had appeared and, besides, I had no one to ask for introductions except Mrs. Dayhull."

"And you know, your grace, that I hardly ever go out in society anymore. And he was with a group of men." Mrs. Dayhull spoke the last as though it were an insurmountable barrier.

The old lady nodded from her bed. "Again I ask, Mariel, why are you so interested in *your* mysterious gentleman?"

Mariel noted that her grandmother quoted her exactly with a distinct emphasis on the pronoun. "Does it not seem unusual that I would see the same man three times in three different places in less than a month?"

"Such meetings happen all the time, my dear. It is only that you have allowed yourself to become so reduced in acquaintances that even the chance met is fascinating."

"Grandmère, 'fascinating' is doing it too brown. I will concede to intrigued and curious but hardly fascinated."

"Can you describe him to me?"

"Of course. I have, after all, seen him three times. He is not much above thirty years. Tall, but not so tall he would stand out in a crowd." She considered a moment and realized she had quite a good mental image. "Broad shoulders, but that could be padding. Dark eyes, brown, with hair equally dark and worn slightly longer than is fashionable. Not because he needs a haircut, but by choice, for it was very artfully styled. His laugh was the most distinctive thing about him. The very sound of it made me smile, as though he were inviting the world to share his joke. And perfectly dressed but with a very simple knot to his cravat, so not a dandy. Oh, and he has a small scar above his left eyebrow and wears no jewelry."

"The charming laugh does reduce the numbers somewhat. I can think of a few who might match that description." She considered the possibilities, "Tall, broad-shouldered, brown hair, dark eyes, and well dressed." The duchess gave her an arch look. "With a small scar?"

Mariel nodded.

Her grandmother abandoned her speculation and gave her granddaughter her complete attention. "All those details on three brief glances? 'Fascinated' is exactly the word, my dear girl." The dowager duchess looked at her companion, who nodded back with an apologetic glance at Mariel. "And that is precisely why I called you to London. It is time for you to rejoin society. What does it say about your friendships that the only people you know to ask about this man are your servants and your grandmother?"

"You make me sound pathetic. I have been in mourning. My circle is understandably limited. And I am content with that."

"Pish tosh! What nonsense. And there is Anna. She is ten years old now. The perfect age for an introduction to town."

"Yes, I do agree with you on that." What a relief to get off the subject of her future. Anna's life was so much more promising. "It was another compelling reason for the visit. She is such a poor student, both Miss Weber and I have hopes that seeing sights of historical consequence will awaken some interest in learning."

"What does she need learning for? Reading and writing and the ability to carry on a clever conversation is all she needs to get on in the world. I was thinking more of Astley's Amphitheatre." The acerbic bite to her grandmother's words made her feelings clear.

"Yes, that too. I daresay even I would find some amusement

there." She would let Grandmère win that one. She was determined that Anna would not be a source of disagreement between them.

"Mariel, you are meant to mourn for a year, not a lifetime. Charles is dead and you are alive. There is no reason to live as though you are with him in spirit if not in fact."

Mariel flushed. "I am not playing the martyr." Why was it all right for her to admit in her private thoughts that Charles was dead, but when someone else said it so starkly, it made her bristle?

"You never had a true Season. Charles was all you could talk about for the few months you were here, and music was the only thing you paid any attention to."

Mariel stiffened but did her best not to let her irritation show.

"You will have a Season now, my girl. I will not allow you to come to London and do nothing more than play the harp."

"I no longer play."

"You no longer play?"

Her grandmother spoke with such shock, one would think she had announced that she had abandoned her child. Mariel shook her head, not inclined to explain.

"There is an instrument in the music room."

"I no longer play, Grandmère." She said it as gently and as firmly as she could.

Her grandmother was silent, but her expression spoke volumes, echoing at first surprise, then sympathy. When she did speak it was with a satisfied sniff. "If you no longer play, then you will have even more time to enjoy the Season, or at least the version of a Season that a young and lovely widow is allowed."

"I will not. I came to further Anna's education and to keep you company. I came because you said you needed me."

"Oh, my dear girl, as much as you try to hide it, you have a very healthy dose of Braedon arrogance in you. All those years of Charles's humility, and still it surfaces." She laughed, but the laughter became a coughing fit. It was an awful insult to her aging frame. Her whole body shook with the convulsive spasms. Mariel looked at Mrs. Dayhull aghast, but the other woman remained calm and merely shook her head.

In a few moments the dowager duchess was calm again, and she went on as if nothing had happened.

"I do need you, Mariel. I need you to be my eyes and ears in the ton. This is the first year I will not be there to see who flirts, who falls madly in love, who dances well or badly, and who makes a complete cake of themselves. I am relying on you to give me every single detail."

Mariel reached over and took her grandmother's hand. Not so long ago her grandmother's hold would have been firm, demanding. Now it was an old lady's grip. The cold, fragile hand that lay in Mariel's brought a real fear to her heart. "But do you not see that rounds of parties and entertainments would be even more meaningless now than they would have been ten years ago? And you know how I detest that gossip." She could hear the pleading tone that had edged into her voice, all but admitting defeat.

"Gossip is nothing more than an amusing exchange of information. You were too serious then and you are worse now." The duchess squeezed Mariel's hand with some effort. "I will not allow you to say no. Some fun is exactly what we both need. And you need it far more than I do."

Arrogance was not the Braedons' alone, Mariel decided, but the charge was so mixed with loving concern that she found herself agreeing. "I will do it for you, Grandmère."

The Dowager Duchess of Hale leaned back against her pillows and closed her eyes. Mariel stood and then paused as the duchess roused herself. "For me and for yourself. How else are you to meet your mysterious gentleman?"


"The first time I saw her was in the graveyard at Cashton in Kent." Edward Hadley looked at the painting on the wall above his fireplace and compared the grace of his great-aunt to his unnamed lovely. "She looked quite ethereal, dressed in some shade of gray that made her merge with the shadows of the trees that grow between the chapel and the graveyard. Do you know that particular church?"

Gerald Lockwood sipped his brandy and nodded. "Been to Cashton to one of the Harbisons' house parties but not the church."

Edward sipped his own brandy and decided that "quiet" was his mantra for tonight. All he wanted this evening was conversation, a friend, a warm room, and some brandy.

"The Harbisons' house party was exactly why I was there." He eyed the empty chessboard between them. A game of chess would not be too taxing.

"I tell you, Hadley, the Harbisons have been doing those parties for so long, I fear they have become a trifle routine."

"This one was anything but. The whole neighborhood was agog at the tip some waitress had received—a hundred guineas or some such absurd amount. That prompted Harbison to suggest an entertainment where each guest would give a hundred guineas to someone to whom it meant a fortune and come back in a year and report on the consequences."

"Did they agree to it?"

"Of course not, Lockwood. Why part with that much money and get nothing for it? When there was obviously so little enthusiasm for the idea, I suggested that they write a theatrical with that as the plot instead. It was quite amusing and with a very proper moral theme as well."

"Will it make its way to Drury Lane?"

"Hardly. But it did entertain us for near a sennight. I had no idea that Miss Harbison was such an actress."

"I suppose we will come to know all her talents before the Season is over. She is the last of their three to make her bow, is she not?"

"Yes, her name is Laurinda, and she is easily the prettiest of the lot."

"I see. Has she caught your interest, then?"

Edward raised his glass to toast the absent beauties. "All the Harbisons are lovely but not nearly as appealing as the woman from the graveyard."

Lockwood picked up one of the pawns and looked at him. Edward nodded and his friend began to arrange the pieces. "Did you meet her?"

"No, but I asked Harbison. Apparently she is a Mrs. Whitlow, in mourning for her husband, who was the vicar."

Lockwood grimaced.

"Yes, rather unappealing." And a complete waste of a beautiful face and elegant carriage. The eyes. So grave and searching. Looking, asking, but for what? "She was even lovelier the second time I saw her."

"Do tell."

"In Dover. At a music recital."

"What in the world were you doing there?"

Edward waved a hand dismissively. "Don't ask. I stayed only to the first intermission. The cello really has never held my interest. She was the only reason that I stayed as long as I did."

To see her sitting there in that lilac gown, he would never have guessed she was the widow of a staid country parson. He had been entranced by the way she lost herself in the music. He watched her as she closed her eyes and let the melody wash over her, through her. He kept that memory to himself.

"And you watched her, never mind the music, is that it?"

Edward nodded. She was the muse herself and her wonder aroused him as thoroughly as an exotic perfume. "Most music is wasted on me."

"So you still have not been introduced?"

"No." That brief exchange at the intermission could hardly count as an introduction. "Then today at Hatchards, there she was again. She was with an older woman, the one who companions the Dowager Duchess of Hale."

"Good God, Hadley, do you remember everyone you have ever met?"

Edward considered the question as though it was more than rhetorical. "One of my gifts, I do believe. From my mother's side of the family. She recalled every of the servants' names. My father called them all Harry."

"Better than what my father called 'em."

They were both silent a long moment. Edward wondered what had ever become of the chamber nurse who had cared so kindly for his mother and, years later, his father. The bequest must have given her some independence. What had Bertha Wichanson done with it?

"It will take you all of an hour to have me in checkmate, Hadley, then what shall we be about?" Lockwood considered the board and his first move as he spoke.

"My mantra for this evening is 'quiet.' "

"Your what? Mantra? Can I have one too?"

Edward laughed. "If you would open a book or pay attention to worlds beyond our own, you would know what a mantra is."

"Never been as intellectual as you, Hadley. Why not tell me and spare me the effort."

"It's an instrument of thought. If I think on it, then it will happen. Tonight my mantra is 'quiet,' for I have no wish to go anywhere. I read of it in one of Colebrooke's books on Hindu. Though I am not sure I have the best understanding of it."

Lockwood whistled. "Not a word I'll ever use. People would think I made it up. Not so sure you didn't. Spending time and money at Hatchards is one thing but actually reading the stuff . . ." Lockwood left the sentence unfinished as another thought occurred to him.

"What was the widow reading?"

"No idea. I saw her only outside. I handed her into her carriage. It hardly seemed the place to seek an introduction."

"Let's hope she is more intrigued by novels than by biblical tracts." Lockwood grimaced. "No matter how much she reads, I doubt she is your sort, Hadley."

"Is that a warning or a challenge?"

Lockwood held up his hands as if to ward off an attack. "Neither. Nothing more than an observation. I know better than to wager with you. My pockets are still to let over that last bit of nonsense."

"Your mistake. It was so obvious that Gordon knows nothing about horses and would easily be duped by the gypsy woman. Her looks only helped. How could you fail to see that?"

"If I could see through it, I was sure that Gordon would too."

Edward Hadley shook his head. "Gordon was thinking about more than buying a horse when he agreed to her price."

"Did he get her in the bargain?"

"No, her people made their own fortune that day and were gone before nightfall."

"Picking pockets?"

Edward shrugged, not really interested in the gypsies who had so entertained him last week.

"A vicar's widow is no gypsy, Hadley."

"Yes, much more inclined to clean hands and feet."

Lockwood chuckled and reached for the pawn and his first move: pawn to king's four.

Edward had known Gerald Lockwood since before they were sent down from Oxford for some nonsense that was ancient history. He was not the most intellectual of his friends, but Lockwood had known him longer than any outside his family.

He was right when he said that a sober vicar's widow did not seem his sort, but there was no denying the appeal of those grave brown eyes. If she was in London, and an intimate of the Dowager Duchess of Hale's, Mrs. Whitlow would be easy enough to meet. And he would meet her, he would be introduced, for he had a prodigious longing to see her laugh.

# Two

Mariel lingered over her chocolate and her dressing and then stopped in the nursery to speak with Anna and her governess.

Cecilia Weber greeted her as warmly as Anna did, the two engrossed in a familiar well-read book of Bible stories. Mariel had always thought the tales did not perfectly reflect true Christian charity, but Charles had valued them. Now Anna insisted that they were what she wished to learn from. Miss Weber had reassured her that such an attachment was not unusual, and Mariel had bowed to her wisdom.

The governess might be well into her sixties and insist that one child was all she could now manage, but Mariel could tell that she still enjoyed her work. She left them laughing over some silly poem they were concocting to entertain the duchess.

With an hour to spare before her grandmother would be ready for company, Mariel paused at the music room door and then, with more courage than should have been necessary, she went in. There was no fire, and the curtains were drawn, leaving more shadow than light. The instruments were all uncovered though, and she walked toward the harp. She stared at it a long, long while with her hands behind her back.

Slowly she sat on the chair and reached for the instrument. It came into her arms like the lover she had lost. Without touching a string, she set it upright and stood abruptly. Tears came from some well of pain still hidden somewhere close to her heart. He was dead. She was not. And someday she could play the harp again. Someday, but not this morning.

The light in the hallway and the footman at the head of the stairs each did their bit to push her emotion back down to its hiding place. Would it always be like this? Were unbidden tears a part of her life now, like the half-empty bed and quiet breakfast table?

*Oh, nonsense. I am behaving exactly like those parishioners that so annoyed Charles. Think about today and not what is gone,* she reminded herself. It was only that she had too many idle hours here, which left too much time for thought.

If she were at home, there was so much she could have done. Cashton was small enough that each effort made a difference in people's lives. She had hoped to do the same here, but London was so vast, it was daunting. And now, at her grandmother's insistence, her only duty was to enjoy herself. At the moment it seemed a monumental task.

Mariel settled on the sofa in the salon used for callers. Not that there would be any. She had a novel from Mrs. Dayhull that the lady had promised was quite entertaining. She would read that until her grandmother wanted company and then she would consider how to make the most of her time in London and still keep her grandmother entertained with tales of the Season.

No sooner had she read the opening sentence, "The family of Dashwood had long been settled in Sussex . . ." than the butler tapped on the door and stepped into the room. "The Lady Morgan Braedon is asking if you are in, ma'am."

"Oh, do please show her up, Spreen."

Mariel set the novel aside and tried to recall the last time she had received visitors. She resisted the vanity of stopping before the looking glass but did smooth the skirt of her light gray gown and straighten the fichu that filled in the décolletage.

Christiana burst into the room and brought sunshine and

some sweet perfume with her. They embraced and then stood an arm's length apart.

"It has been three years, Mariel." She hugged her again. "Much too long!"

"When did you arrive in town? You look wonderful, Christiana. Marriage and motherhood suit you." Mariel was only being honest. Christiana's good looks came from more than the fashionable dark green dress she was wearing.

"We arrived yesterday afternoon. And most days marriage and motherhood suit me beautifully, thank you." Christiana stepped back and began to draw off her gloves. "The last time we saw each other was in this very house."

Mariel noticed that Christiana had not returned a compliment about her looks. But they never had been an important part of her life, she reminded herself.

"So much has changed, Mariel. So much."

Her sister-in-law nodded.

"I am so sorry that Morgan and I did not hear of Charles's death until so long after."

"There is no need to apologize." Mariel took Christiana's hand in hers. "Morgan explained all that when he came to see me. Who could have known that my letter would be lost with the burning of Braemoor? So much was lost forever."

"Your letter was by far the most important. It meant you had to face all of it alone."

"My dear, even with a house full of people you must face it alone." She let go of Christiana's hand and gestured for her to take a seat.

"I suppose that is true, but how we who love you wish it could be different."

"Thank you, dearest. Your letters have been every comfort."

"How is Anna?"

"Very well. She and her governess came with me. Perhaps you can make time to meet her later."

Christiana clapped her hands. "Oh, I should love that above all things."

Someone opened the door, and a maid came in bearing a tea tray and some biscuits. It was the break they needed. Now perhaps they could go on to some other subject. The maid placed the tray on the table between them, but Christiana refused both tea and treats.

"And will you stay in Cashton, Mariel?"

"Where else would I go?"

"Have you thought of writing Braemoor again?"

Christiana's voice had an unusually tentative quality, and Mariel did her best not to bristle.

"Mariel, the marquis is ill and far away in Wales, and the estate is in James's hands now."

Mariel only shook her head. "It has been ten years. And each year makes it more difficult. The James I knew was cut from the same cloth as Father. It was always my explanation for why they so irritate each other. He never once made the overtures that Morgan did. He never once ignored Father's edict."

"But he is so different since he fell in love, since Marguerite came into his life."

"It will take more than your word on that to make me write again."

"You do not believe your letter was lost in the fire?" Christiana asked the question as if trying to find an explanation for her inflexibility.

"The truth is that I do not know whether James saw the letter or it was destroyed. But I do know that I have built a life without Braemoor and most of the Braedons."

When Christiana looked as though she would press her, Mariel did not give her a chance. "I will be content in Cashton, Christiana. I have a small house in the village. The Harbisons have been kind enough to include me in their social world. It is where I belong, where I am needed, and where I am comfortable."

Christiana nodded.

Mariel reached over to touch her hand. "I am sorry if I sound disagreeable."

Christiana smiled a little. "You sound like James."

"Grandmère calls it Braedon arrogance."

"Yes, and when I hear it in your voice, I know that it is too soon to be talking of reconciliation for all that it has been ten years."

Christiana toyed with her gloves and then looked up. "And then there is the duchess. How is she?"

"Failing but cheerful." Mariel spoke with some relief. At least this was a subject upon which they shared kindred thoughts. "I truly think visitors revive her. I have been here only two days and she has already moved from her bed to the chaise longue in her boudoir. And today she is going to dress, though I did urge her maid not to attempt anything that would tax her strength."

Christiana nodded, not smiling now.

"She is as acerbic as ever, still pretends to be deaf, and has dreadful coughing spasms that frighten all of us."

Christiana closed her eyes on a sigh. "How could we have let so much time pass between visits?" Before Mariel could speak, Christiana gathered her composure. "She seemed well at our wedding, but still I am appalled that Morgan and I took that so for granted and have not been to visit in almost two years."

"It is hardly convenient to make the trip from Wales on a regular basis, and your own lives have made demands." That made them both smile. "How old is Andrew now?"

"Close to a year and walking."

"Oh, my."

"Exactly. We left him with his nurse at my sister's home. Her son is just enough older to be a good influence. Monksford is not as far away as Wales, but still I worry about how long it would take to reach him if something were to happen."

"Nothing will." Mariel spoke with the complete certainty of a more experienced mother. "And this spring promises only rain. The country air is so much better than the London damp and fog."

"So I keep reminding myself. As for the duchess, distance is the only excuse we have. But"—she said the word with emphasis—"now that Morgan has acquired the property near Bath, we shall make that our principal residence and be much closer to town for whatever reason may arise."

"It sounds ideal. Where is Morgan?"

"With his man of business, finalizing some part of the land transfer." Christiana shrugged. "I did not want to put off this visit another minute."

Mariel smiled as Christiana stood up.

"You must know how dear she is to me. As dear as if she were my own grandmother." Emotion filled Christiana's eyes. "Will you come up with me?"

"No." Mariel reached for the teapot. "You should go alone, though I expect that Mrs. Dayhull will be with her. And do not show your sadness. She is not in pain and she is still quite sound in her mind, which is a true blessing." Mariel did not have to mention her father, the quite mentally unsound Marquis Straeford, for Christiana to understand that reference.

With a firm nod of agreement, Christiana left the room.

Mariel blew on her still-hot tea and took a small sip. There was only a few years' difference in their ages, but Mariel felt ancient compared to her sister-in-law. Was it because Christiana was still convinced that life could be lived according to her script, that each step she made would move her closer to what she longed for instead of accepting the fact that what you longed for might never be?

It was Mrs. Dayhull who came to the salon a while later to invite Mariel to join the others for tea.

Christiana was seated near the chaise longue, where yet another teapot awaited their attention.

Her grandmother looked a little tired, but her face was wreathed in smiles, as though she had some secret she could hardly wait to share. She gestured for Mrs. Dayhull to pour, pointed to a seat, and when Mariel was settled, she announced, "You are going shopping, Mariel!"

"Shopping?" Visiting shops hardly seemed to warrant such ceremony.

"Yes, shopping for clothes," Christiana added as though it were half her idea.

"It is what one does in London," Grandmère said.

"Oh, but I have not come to London to shop." Mariel grimaced. "I don't even like to shop."

Mrs. Dayhull passed cups, and the other two looked at each other as if this were the exact answer they expected.

"I came to entertain you, Grandmère, not to traipse around Bond Street."

"And the first step in entertaining me is to bring more color and beauty into my life."

Mariel looked at her gray gown.

"Exactly," Christiana said. "That dress does little more than meet the needs that modesty demands."

"Is it that bad? Surely you are exaggerating."

Mrs. Dayhull cleared her throat, and Mariel suspected it was not because she had drunk her tea too quickly

"I suppose that deep whitework border around the hem is the latest style?" Mariel hurried on, hoping to distract her sister-in-law with a discussion of current fashion. "You look adorable in that dress. I would look as though I were aping a debutante."

"No, you would not. Your shoulders are so elegant. The new, more elaborate sleeve design will show them to perfection."

Mariel shook her head. That had been the wrong tack to take.

"When you have a good seamstress, anything is possible." Christiana picked up one of the iced biscuits and took a small bite. "The true test of a modiste is her ability to make one appear perfect. I have discovered the most wonderful woman in Wales. To find someone with real talent that far from London is amazing." Christiana sighed. "I have tried to convince her to move to Bath, but she says the expense is too great."

Christiana gave her full attention to Mariel. "If you were dressed in a deep blue with just the slightest exaggeration to the sleeve, you would make every man stare."

"Oh, dear, I have no wish to make men stare." The gentleman in the graveyard had not stared. Was that because of her mourning clothes or his lack of interest?

Her grandmother's "Harrumph" was the nearest she came to a comment.

"Your mourning period is technically over." Christiana spoke with gentle insistence, and Mariel wondered if she and the duchess had rehearsed the familiar argument. "You have even exceeded the further half-mourning. I understand that your loss will be with you forever, but Grandmère deserves all the little pleasures we can bring her. It would cheer her so."

"I should never have left the two of you alone." Mariel glanced from one to the other. "It sounds like a plan the two of you hatched while Mrs. Dayhull was distracted."

"Oh, no." Mrs. Dayhull spoke up. "I quite agree. A companion is supposed to blend in. A beautiful young woman is not."

*I would prefer to blend in myself, but it appears that Grandmère and Christiana have different ideas. Oh, where is my supposed Braedon arrogance now?*

"I have never liked shopping, Christiana. You will forgive my frankness, but it seems so self-indulgent. When we have clothes that are perfectly serviceable, why should we buy more? Why not give the money to charity instead of furthering our own vanity?"

"Mariel!" Her grandmother's voice was laced with shock. "When did you become so evangelical? That is nonsense."

"Oh, no, Mariel, that is not true at all!" Christiana spoke over the duchess's objections. "You must see that buying clothes is nothing less than a more subtle form of helping the poor. Really, it *is* a kind of charity."

Mariel looked dubious.

"My sister and I have discussed this, and surely you will admit that Joanna has a superior intellect."

Mariel nodded.

Christiana put her cup down.

"You see, by choosing gowns with fabric made in England, we give employment on many different levels. Not just to the modiste but to the farmers who raise the sheep for wool, and to the weaver, to the seamstresses who work for her, the men who deliver the goods, and to the staff that support the modiste and her family."

"Oh, very good, my dear." Grandmère sounded quite impressed with the argument.

"Hmmm." Mariel considered it. "It sounds a trifle self-serving."

"Absolutely not." Christiana wrinkled her nose. "Or perhaps only a little. But Joanna has convinced me that it is so much better to help people find success in supporting themselves than to give them money because they have failed."

"There must be a flaw in this somewhere." Mariel thought a moment and looked at her grandmother. She should know better than to seek help from that quarter. "I know," she said. "What if the business owner is not generous, keeps more than her fair share of profits for herself?"

"Mariel, you cannot control every aspect of the mercantile system." Her grandmother spoke with impatience.

Christiana was more amenable. "I promise you we will not buy from any milliner, draper, or seamstress who does not seem worthy. And you can give your gowns to a charity that will appreciate them."

Mariel nodded, considering the last. "I think I know exactly the group that could benefit from them. There is a new organization that is attempting to find employment for prostitutes who wish to change their lives."

"Good. You can consider that after you have your new gowns in hand." Christiana shook her head in some consternation.

"Honestly, Mariel, you must at least attempt to think like a selfish sybarite, or London will not be entertaining at all." Her grandmother laughed. "The only thing we have said that truly caught your interest was when Christiana mentioned donating your old gowns to charity."

Mariel shook her head and let her own smile escape. "I will do my best to put my years of training as a vicar's wife aside, but the need here is overwhelming."

"And always will be." Her grandmother obviously spoke from long experience.

Christiana nodded her approval. "Then this will be your first step in doing some small part to ending poverty. It is what Charles would want and is certainly what Grandmère wants."

"Charles would. He always said I had too much concern for the poor." She turned to her grandmother. "He would agree with you that we must accept that the poor will always be with us."

"Poverty is their lot in life." Her grandmother nodded.

"That may be true," Christiana temporized, "but surely he should have nothing but admiration for someone who tried his best to improve those less fortunate."

"Not when I insisted that he ask for more help." Mariel felt a blush heat her cheeks.

"He was completely right," her grandmother said. "His role was to see to their souls, not empty their purses."

"You sound very like him, Grandmère. He insisted that giving money away was not the answer. That they must refrain from drink or pray more or, well, any number of things that were within their power and not at all within mine. He would say it was not our role to meddle. He called it 'playing God.'" Finally she admitted, "There were occasions when I was much too insistent."

"Then, a London Season is exactly what you need. It will either convince you that life is meant to be celebrated or shock you with its excessive self-indulgence."

"And to hear Grandmère's stories, it may do both at the same time."

Christiana clapped her hands. "You grasp the challenge

perfectly. We will set aside tomorrow for the draper and the modiste."

Christiana rose. "Shall we let Grandmère rest and go see Anna now."

Her grandmother shook her head. "You go on, girl, I want to talk a moment more with Mariel."

Christiana looked from one to the other.

Mariel shrugged and the duchess nodded. Christiana left the room when Mariel promised to join her shortly.

The duchess wasted no time.

"Christiana tells me that you have refused to see James."

"Oh, dear, Grandmère, why did she feel the need to discuss that with you?"

"Because I asked her," the old lady responded testily. "You have a responsibility to see him. And not only to mend the family break but to tell him about this supposed long lost brother of his."

"William."

"Is that his name?"

"It is the name Mama gave me. And she made me promise that I would hold the secret unless William should appear. Do not make me feel more responsibility for this than I already do."

"It is a shared burden since you chose to confide in me so soon after your mama's death."

"I was confused. And you gave me wise advice then. With the whole family sunk in grief, it was hardly the time to announce it." She shook her head recalling the horrid pall that hung over all of them that winter. "And after I was disowned, the opportunity was lost. Grandmère, don't you think that if he was still alive he would make himself known?"

"Yes, I do. I suspect he is long since dead."

Mariel nodded. "So you see, that is hardly a reason for me to approach James. It would only confuse an already awkward situation."

"Stubborn." The duchess breathed the word and made it sound worse than "arrogant." "Kiss me and let me rest. I can see that you have a long way to go before you can think about this clearly."

She did look tired now, exhausted by the emotional discussion. Mariel looked at Mrs. Dayhull with some apology, and her companion did no more than give an encouraging smile.

Mrs. Dayhull escorted her to the door. "It has been bothering her since you agreed to come. She did not want to distract you from town pleasures but felt she must at least try."

Mariel left the room, praying that this was the last of her efforts to bring them together again. She and James had each found their place in life. And like the poor, they would not be made any happier by outside interference.

Christiana was on the floor with Anna, the two of them and Miss Weber considering the fashion dolls that she had brought from Wales.

Anna called her to join them.

"I think that Anna and Miss Weber should have new gowns as well," Christiana declared.

Mariel was sorry that she had not thought of it herself. Miss Weber tried to disclaim the treat but was easy to persuade.

"We shall bear you in mind while we are shopping tomorrow." Anna nodded with some excitement at her mother's promise and with a glance at Miss Weber added, "Thank you so much, Mama."

"Wonderful." Christiana clapped her hands. "I personally prefer to have the fabric in hand and then decide on a design. Though there are times when I see a charming pattern and then must reverse the process."

"My head is spinning and we have not yet left the house."

"I have so selfishly missed Joanna since she married. Morgan is wonderful but does not quite understand as a sister would. I will rely on you to remind me of what is truly important. In turn you must admit your need. There is something I can teach you."

"What is that?" Mariel asked with caution and curiosity.

"Why, how to have fun, of course.

# Three

"Feel this, Christiana. Does it not have the most lovely texture? It's like liquid in your hands. To wear something made from this would be like being wrapped in pleasure. I prefer this silk to the satin."

Christiana looked at Mariel with some surprise and then at the clerk attending them. "We will consider both."

"But we have already made our choices, Christiana. And I have no need of so much."

"Any fabric that will cause you to wax poetic is a fabric we must have. The color is excellent and it does feel wonderful."

"It is a lovely fine net silk, madam. It is called malines. It would look lovely as an overdress of off-white silk like this one." The shop assistant handed Christiana the sample.

"You must have it, Mariel, and this warp-printed silk as well. It is an English silk, is it not?"

The clerk nodded and held up the length of deeply colored material. "The softened edges of the print ease the boldness of the blue and will be perfect. On you it will look deep and rich and elegant. Everyone will notice."

Mariel stroked the malines one more time, then dropped it with some impatience. How foolish, she thought. *The only reason I keep thinking of him is that I am so curious about our chance meetings.*

The clerk abandoned the warp-printed material and picked up the malines again. "This is not to be missed. Indeed, if you were dancing the waltz and a gentleman felt that beneath his fingers, he would never want to let you go."

"I do not want to be the target of gossip any more than I want to spread it." Mariel took the fabric from Christiana and handed it back to the assistant.

"Of course not, but what does that woman know?" Christiana whispered as she moved closer to retrieve the rejected material. "Men wear gloves when they dance, just as we do. If it feels good to you, that is all that matters. No one will notice anything but how lovely you look. And that is a perfectly acceptable subject to comment on, is it not?"

Mariel could see that Christiana was in earnest.

"Besides, Mariel, it is surely behavior as much as appearance that brings unwanted attention."

She handed the fabric back to Mariel, who was once again struck by its texture. It invited a caress as she considered Christiana's suggestion. "I think the two must have equal weight. I have seen ladies dressed in clothes of shocking décolletage and they are surprised when it draws comment. On the other hand, in Kent, Charles had occasion to help fallen women, and I can tell you that appearances count for more than we know. When they were seeking honest employment, it made all the difference in the world to have them dress soberly. No one thought to question their intentions. Especially when they were recommended by the vicar."

She put the malines down with some regret. "I think we will leave this for someone more daring than I."

Christiana bore the disappointment with good grace.

Mariel gave her a little smile. "Everyone is influenced by appearance. Would this clerk have waited on us so patiently if you were not dressed well and I did not look so needy?"

Christiana laughed. "It satisfies me that you at last agree that some changes are in order."

"You can share your triumph with Grandmère when we return to Hale House." Mariel reached for Christiana's hand. "Thank you for insisting on this. It has been wonderfully entertaining." She looked down at her black bombazine. "How could you step into this shop and resist the appeal? I cannot imagine a place that would excite the eye more. All the color, and the texture, the feel and the weave." She smoothed the wrinkles from a bolt of heavy red silk. It would make the perfect evening gown. "Having all these choices is nothing less than exhilarating."

Christiana did not try to hide her satisfaction.

"Now I have ten choices here and I am determined on no more than five gowns." Mariel considered the selections. "I must decide what five fabrics I can bear to part with."

"I think six or even seven would meet your needs better, Mariel. And remember, every purchase you make supports workers who are struggling to provide for themselves and their families."

Mariel rolled her eyes. "Oh, I love the concept that indulging myself is good for England."

"Well, it is. Indeed, it may even contribute to the war effort." Christiana went on to explain. "We are buying only fabric woven in England. None of this was smuggled into the country."

"Ah, I see. Then clearly seven dresses it will be." She stood tall. "For England." Christiana laughed, as Mariel intended.

They stood aside while the clerk organized the bolts of fabric.

"You know, Christiana, there is more to life than shopping and parties."

"Not for the next few months." Christiana spoke as if self-indulgence were as much a duty as church on Sunday. "London is the world capital in pleasurable excess. I think at one time Paris held sway, but since the revolution, no one would argue for it."

She held up one finger at a time as she counted the list: "Flirting, riding in the afternoon or being taken up in someone's curricle, perhaps a bit of gambling. Oh! And dancing." She paused. "You have denied yourself the simplest pleasures for too long, Mariel."

Flirting? Was that how to describe his reactions to her meetings with her mysterious gentleman? Of course that is what it was. Oh, dear, she had indeed been too long away from society. It meant nothing to him. He merely had more sophistication at his command.

"There are endless balls and endless rumors and perhaps a bit of scandal." Christiana sighed with evident satisfaction. "But in order to do any of these, one must first have clothes." She gestured to the counter before her, where the clerk waited, smiling and patient.

"Christiana, you must go give Mrs. Dayhull some assistance while I eliminate three of these wonders."

Mariel turned her attention to the fabric, trying to look at the choices with the perspective of the insight she had gained today. Surely she had not completely abandoned pleasure. Later she would sit down and make a list of the things she enjoyed doing. There must be more than listening to music.

Christiana's lengthy list of entertainments was not truly meant for her. She was a widow. Based on her tears in the music room that morning, she was a widow whose heart was not yet enough her own to consider anything more than the lightest of amusements. She would be content to observe the Season from the edge of the beau monde, as much by choice as social dictate.

That did not mean she had to be badly dressed. She turned her full attention to the fabric.

Her decision took longer than she thought it would, but only because she found two more swatches that had to be considered and then, of course, each of the ten samples had to be fingered again. Finally, she made her choices. She purchased all of the first ten after having decided at least one would be a gown for Anna's governess and the other a gift to her grandmother. If she could bear to part with them. Silly, she thought. How completely frivolous to be so entranced by the thread and texture of a silver-gray wool that was no more than a sheep's fleece well handled and colorfully dyed. Silly and frivolous and thoroughly delightful.

Mariel directed the delivery of the fabric to the modiste that they had decided on and went in search of Christiana and Mrs. Dayhull. The shop was divided into three sections, so that several customers could be privately accommodated at the same time. There was a small waiting room at the entrance. Mariel could hear Christiana talking to someone.

She stopped in the shadow, taken quite by surprise. Mariel had only to hear the voice to know who it was.

*Her* gentleman? Here in a draper's shop on Bond Street? This counted the fourth time in less than two months that they had chanced to be in the same place at the same time.

How could all these meetings be accidental? As she listened to Christiana tell him about her seamstress in Wales, Mariel considered the idea. Perhaps in London they could be explained away, but the occasion in Kent and Dover were not so easily understood. Was he following her? And why?

Mariel moved closer to the doorway but still stayed in the shadows, and their conversation drifted back to her.

"Why do you not ask Lord Morgan to subsidize the modiste's move to Bath?"

"Oh, I could not do that. If the people in town were to hear of it, the Braedons would most assuredly be persona non grata. I am not the only one who appreciates her skill."

"I can see what you mean." It was the gentleman speaking now. "Preserving a good understanding with your neighbors is a more important concern. Especially when you now have all of London at your service."

They were not even talking about her. Mariel straightened, determined to finally affect a meeting. Her steps were slowed by another voice, a woman's.

"I am so sorry, Lady Morgan, but Mama is expecting us. We are to discuss wedding plans." She laughed a little, as though she could not contain her pleasure at being able to use those words.

They were going to discuss wedding plans? Her mysterious gentleman was engaged? Mariel reconsidered her intention to present herself, caught between surprise and disappointment. She peeked around the corner.

"How lovely for you." Christiana was all understanding. "Then surely you must hurry. You can meet my sister-in-law at the Westbournes' ball."

Mariel could see them now. The woman, a girl really, was lovely. All blond and dainty, wearing a china-blue pelisse and chip-straw bonnet that made her both young and sophisticated, which she undoubtedly was.

He looked amused. The way he had in the cemetery. There was a patient tolerance there too. The way he had looked at the concert. Then he took the girl's arm with the same gracious comfort he had used when helping her into her carriage. It was her mysterious gentleman; there was no doubt of that. But the news of his engagement shaded all their previous meetings, reducing them to meaningless. How could she have thought otherwise?

Mariel waited a moment longer, until he was handing his fiancée into their coach, and then joined Christiana in the receiving room, trying for a look of unconcern. "Where is Mrs. Dayhull?"

"I sent her home in a hackney. She was quite tired and was happy with the idea of going for fittings one day later in the week."

Mariel drew on her gloves as they waited by the door. A light rain had begun, and so they waited for the coachman to move the carriage a little closer.

"Who was that gentleman you were talking with while you were waiting for me?"

"Oh, a friend of Morgan's. And newly engaged. I can hardly wait to tell Morgan." The last was said as though exchanging the latest *on-dit* were a game they played. Indeed, it was a game all London played. And she was so on the fringe of this game that she did not even know this player's name!

A name was all she wanted. Hopefully it would help her understand why he was so interested in her. To avoid any further embarrassment, any further flirtation. If flirtation was all that it was.

Christiana was already out the door the Hale House footman had opened from the other side.

Once they were settled in the coach, Christiana returned to the business at hand. "Now, Mariel, we are agreed that we will go to Madame Morisée, are we not? She is hardly the most popular of stylists but only because she charges more than some of the others." Christiana looked over her shoulder at Mariel. "Her sisters and cousins are her employees, and she must pay them a generous wage."

Mariel did her best to banish the nameless man from her thoughts. She could hardly bring herself to call him a gentleman now. "If Madame Morisée is that expensive, then it is just as well that I have spent hardly any money these last two years."

"You do know that the dowager duchess would be happy to gift you this wardrobe?"

"But it is not at all necessary." Mariel turned from her consideration of the roadway and looked fully at Christiana. "Indeed, my father may have refused his consent, but Charles's family is most generous and have treated me always as though my portion did in fact exist. And I have money from my mother. To this day I think the money she left us was her way of protecting us from the marquis's wrath after she was gone." Mariel smiled, pushing the sadness to a far corner of her mind. "Indeed, my dear, I am a comfortable if not precisely a wealthy widow."

Christiana nodded her approval. "Then I am leading you to an indulgence that will leave you lighter in the purse but will most certainly add to your comfort."

\* \* \*

"Please hold still, madam. I have no wish to stick you with the pins, only the fabric."

Mariel stood as still as she could, but if this took much longer, she would most likely start crying from sheer boredom.

"I can tell without asking that you preferred the draper's to this part of the process." As she spoke, Christiana paced around the needlewoman, bending close to examine her pins and stepping back for an overall view of drape and style.

Mariel started to shrug, then stopped at a harsh click of the tongue from the seamstress fitting the fabric to her.

"Talk to me, Christiana. The seamstress is very capable, talented even, and hardly needs your supervision. Tell me about that friend of Morgan's to whom you were talking. What is his name? And his fiancée. Where is she from?"

"Hmmm." Christiana held up a finger, begging a moment, murmured something to the seamstress, and in mutual agreement watched as the woman adjusted the set of the shoulder approximately one quarter of an inch.

Mariel wanted to scream at them to finish and finish now but instead offered a prayer sending this trial to help all sinners.

Christiana settled on the small sofa tucked into the corner of the room. "His name is Edward Hadley."

Mariel considered. "Edward Hadley." It sounded proper, substantial, hardly suspect or lecherous.

"Yes, from Staffordshire. Hadley is arguably the best-liked man in London. Even without a title. I can think of no hostess who would not make him the first on her guest list."

"Best-liked?" It was that smile, Mariel decided.

Christiana shrugged. The gesture alone made Mariel's shoulders twitch. "Because he has the most infectious smile and charming manner of any man in London."

*I was right,* she thought with some chagrin. *He treats everyone that way.*

"And he is so wealthy that he has lost as much as a thousand guineas at play and done no more than shrug it off."

"Please," Mariel moaned, "do not say 'shrug,' for there is nothing more on this earth that I want to do."

The seamstress looked up, smiling around the pins in her mouth. "Only five more minutes, madam."

Mariel tried to smile graciously but feared it looked more like a sneer. "So he is a dandy and a gambler?" Good. Each adjective added to her picture of him even if it made his interest in her more of a puzzle.

"Yes, I suppose that neither would endear him to you. But you know, Mariel, the same argument could be made of gaming that we make regarding this venture."

Mariel wanted to raise her hand but did not, only marveled at how often she expressed herself that way. "You will never convince me that gaming is in any way noble or good for the country or mankind."

"Perhaps not, but what I meant was that it is fun. You must try it sometime."

Mariel mouthed the word "no." Christiana shrugged and then had the grace to look aghast in response to Mariel's glare.

"Do not shrug, Christiana!"

"Hadley." Christiana spoke hurriedly to make amends for her gaffe. "Let me see, what else can I recall of him?"

Mariel spoke over her. "What of his fiancée?"

"Estelle Macomb?"

"Was that the girl with him?"

"She is his cousin and he is her guardian." When Mariel raised her eyebrows in some surprise, Christiana nodded. "Yes, Hadley is marrying his ward."

"Is she wealthy?"

"There is some money, but Hadley would hardly risk censure for more of what he has in abundance."

"Some men would."

"Not Hadley." Christiana shook her head. "No, I think it must be a love match, which makes it all the more delectable."

"We are done, madam." The seamstress stood before her with the carefully pinned fabric in her hand, and Mariel stood on the dais in nothing more than her chemise. She looked at Christiana and then jumped down, waving her arms, spinning as though she were a circus performer.

She watched as Christiana covered her face in laughter at her outrageous antics.

"Christiana, that was far more like torture than fun. I shall be restless for hours. Now is the perfect time for me to go back to Hale House and take Anna to the park."

"But we have only begun, Mariel. We must consider hats and gloves and hair ornaments."

"If none of it involves holding still for hours, I am sure it will be lovely, even fun. But for now I feel the need to share today's adventure with Grandmère and play with Anna."

With a shrug, a gesture that made them both smile, Christiana accepted the delay.

Christiana went to confer over completion and delivery, leaving Mariel to dress with the assistant's help. As the woman shook the wrinkles from her now incredibly dowdy-looking gown, Mariel gave one final thought to her gentleman.

Edward Hadley.

She knew more of him now. More than a name. She knew him for a favorite of the ton, engaged, and a blatant flirt.

Chagrin, annoyance, and a little disappointment mingled with her hard-to-banish curiosity. Grandmère called their meetings chance, but she was not convinced.

# Four

Edward Hadley gave the coachman a signal and counted it more than a small blessing when the carriage pulled away from the curb with Estelle in it. She could discuss wedding plans with her mama quite efficiently without him there. The bribe of a new gown and hat to match was all it took to earn her cooperation and leave him free to consider this newer interest.

He climbed the few short steps and entered the lobby of his man of business. The clerks were busy at their slanted desks, but the door at the back of the room was closed, so with a nod to the head clerk he took a chair and waited, not objecting at all to a few moments of private contemplation.

He was more confused than concerned. He fingered the note in his pocket. It had started off his day with a jolt of surprise, which was, in fact, carefully tamped-down panic.

*Speculation regarding your activities in Kent and Dover has followed you to London. You will find someone of interest and equally interested in you at Bon Marché Drapers this morning.*

The note was unsigned, the wording and spelling unfamiliar. Even the penmanship was uncertain. Impossible to tell whether it had been penned by a man or a woman. None of that mattered in the face of being found out. He had hoped to go on as he had indefinitely. Once his odd diversion became common knowledge, he knew he would have to stop.

He had calmed himself enough to realize that perhaps his correspondent was not bent on revealing him. Blackmail seemed extreme, but perhaps this kind of discovery was not as ruinous as he had at first feared.

His own dear cousin, Estelle, had been exactly the excuse he needed to stop in at Bon Marché Drapers. For once her paralyzing indecision was an asset, as it gave him the time he needed to see who was the most likely spoilsport.

The promise of rain must have kept most patrons at home, for there was only one other pair of customers.

Lady Morgan Braedon was a charming confection, but her conversation had nothing to do with his private business, though it did give him a new inspiration.

He could hardly imagine Lady Morgan was the one he had been sent to meet. And if it were her husband who had caught on to his game, he would never use his new and treasured bride as a pawn. No, Braedon would be more likely to put it in the betting book at Whites so he could make a fortune from the embarrassment.

Edward was brought back to the moment by a raised voice, a woman's voice, no missing the fury in it, even through the closed office door. All heads turned to the door and then to the head clerk. When he did not leave his post, the staff returned to work again. Hadley settled more comfortably in his chair, prepared for an even longer wait.

What about the sister-in-law Lady Morgan had mentioned? Could she be the one who had sent the note? The idea struck him suddenly and was so obvious that he wanted to let out a wail himself.

If it were the sister-in-law, then he would be seeing her again. Judging by the time it took for her to arrange for her purchases, she had plans to attend many of the same social functions as he. They already littered his calendar like so many useless inkblots that could not be erased.

By the end of June they would all be a colossal bore. Late-spring ennui was becoming a too-familiar sensation. Last

Season he had reached the danger point when he begged Lockwood to dare him to shout his lack of interest from the dance floor. But even the usually encouraging Gerald Lockwood had been unwilling to set a wager on that one.

"Never do, old pal. Insulting all the hostesses by offending one. You might not want the invitations, but once they stopped coming, you'd miss 'em."

He supposed it was true, for after a winter at home the Season did have some appeal. New faces, new friendships, perhaps even a new mistress. That would put the boredom at bay for a while at least.

It could well have been the sister-in-law who had sent him the note. If he knew her name, then he might be able to tell if she had and, if so, how to play the game.

And he knew exactly who could identify her.

"So sorry to keep you waiting, Mr. Hadley."

Allen Matthew was so obviously embarrassed at Edward's ten spare minutes in the front room that he had come through the workroom himself instead of having the head clerk escort him back.

How had Matthew been able to calm the frantic woman so quickly? His private office was empty. Where had she disappeared to? Through the door into other office? The image of the woman gagged and stuffed into one of the chests that lined the wall made him laugh.

"Thank you, sir. I am so happy to see you in good spirits. But then, you always are."

"Mr. Matthew, I know we have some business matters to discuss, but if it will not delay your day's appointments, there is another subject I would like to pursue."

The man nodded gravely and gestured Edward to the comfortable leather chair near the fire.

"Do you know the Lambert family?"

"Would that be the same Miss Lambert who recently married Lord Morgan Braedon, the second son of the Marquis Straeford?"

"Yes, yes, exactly."

"I know of the Braedons, sir. And I am well acquainted with their man of business."

"This isn't about business, Matthew, but a small puzzle that I was given today."

"Ah, that is as well, sir, as Straeford's son, Viscount Crandall, has been appointed caretaker of the estate and all business is being done with him these days."

"What is the problem with that?"

"There is no technical problem. Only it is rare and one would have to be very certain that all agreements with the family would stand in court."

"The marquis is quite mad, Matthew. You may be as gentlemanly as you wish, but he burned down the big house and then tried to burn down the dower house. He's the one I would want no business with."

"I'll bear that in mind, sir."

"Yes, but as I said, this is not about business." He felt the need to remind both of them. "I simply want to find out who Lady Morgan Braedon's sister-in-law would be."

Matthew nodded. "Would that be a Braedon sister-in-law or a Lambert connection?"

"I have no idea. Lady Morgan mentioned that she would like me to meet her sister-in-law, and I was trying to determine who that might be."

Matthew nodded with a smile of perfect understanding.

Hadley was sure Matthew thought he was trying to avoid a meeting with a shrew. He would see it as yet another attempt to match him and his money with some deserving woman. Let him think what he would. It would be better than telling him about the note before he was sure of its import.

"I'm afraid, sir, that I do not know of any Lambert sisters-in-law. There may be some, but the family lives quietly, and news of them hardly makes the town papers."

Edward drummed the edge of the chair with his fingers and tried for patience. Matthew was a man for details, not all of them useful. This was not the first time he was grateful that he did not pay his man of business by the hour.

"The only Braedon sister-in-law would be the marquis's only surviving daughter." He seemed to draw the information from somewhere deep in his memory. "She married a vicar from Kent."

"Mrs. Whitlow?" Edward made the connection with a kind of amazement. It sounded like the same Mrs. Whitlow whom Harbisons had named. Was this some practical joke? No, no, Lockwood might concoct the scheme but would be too lazy to act on it. Besides, what kind of joke was it to put him in the way of a woman in whom he had expressed some interest and not be there when they met?

"Yes, that's her name. Mariel Braedon Whitlow."

"If she is the daughter of a marquis, how is it that she is not known as Lady Mariel?"

"She married much against her father's wishes, and he disowned her. I assume she chose not to retain the title but to use her married name instead." Matthew paused a moment and then added, "I read some time ago that her husband had died but did not know that the family had been reconciled.

"Mariel is a Welsh name. All the children from the marquis's second marriage have Welsh names—Lord Morgan, Lady Mariel, and Lord Rhys. It was a conceit of their mother's, I believe. She was the daughter of the fourth Duke of Hale."

"You are a wealth of information, Matthew."

Matthew's expression was all apology.

"No, no, man, that is a compliment. You have the knowledge or the means to find most anything I have ever asked of you. I appreciate it."

Matthew's expression eased. "Thank you, sir. I strive to meet your needs."

"This Mrs. Whitlow. How is it that I have never met her? Never heard of the scandal? She must have had a Season."

"Yes, I'm sure she did. Perhaps it was the year you were in Edinburgh?"

"Eighteen hundred two?" He nodded. "Yes, that could be if she was married for ten years." He thought about it a moment longer. "Charles Whitlow. I knew a Whitlow when I was at Oxford. Serious, and altogether too studious." And that was the last question he would ask about her, or else he would have to change today's byword to "curious."

"The third son of an earl." Matthew nodded. "Set up with a living that some near relatives had."

"The Harbisons."

Matthew nodded again and then waited, clearly uncertain what was expected of him. "Thank you, Matthew. You have already given me enough information to answer a purely social question."

Edward paused. Could it be that Mariel Whitlow had seen him often enough to find out his secret? Absurd. He had been circulating among the ton for years, and no one had found him out. A widow from Kent was hardly going to be the one to best him.

His apprehension faded away as he realized that the note had been nothing more—or less—than a clever effort to secure his attention. Rather flattering, in fact. Had the sly message come from someone on her side of the game or from her own hand? From their three brief meetings, he never would have thought her a coquette.

Later, he told himself. As hard as it was to let it go, he would think about it later. He had no desire to use up so much of his time with Matthew that he wound up in a chest alongside the shrill woman who had preceded him.

"I appreciate the information, Matthew, and trust that, as always, it will remain between us."

"The words said in this room will always remain here."

Not for the first time, Edward wondered what Allen Matthew talked about at home if not the myriad of stories that were told here. "I have a new candidate, Matthew."

"It has been a while, sir."

"It came to my attention this morning. It has to do with a dressmaker in Wales."

"There you are, Grandmère," Mariel said. "I will soon have eight new dresses and nowhere to show them off."

"That is easily remedied. Spreen says you have any number of envelopes awaiting your attention on the table in your boudoir."

"I do?" Mariel felt her throat tighten.

"Why are you so shocked? Of course you do. You are new to town. Here for the first time in ten years. Everyone will want to make your acquaintance."

She raised her hand to her throat to relieve the pressure. "But I am a widow."

"Stop that! You are still young, well-looking, and you are a Braedon. You will be welcome everywhere. Everywhere, that is, except at Almacks, and you would not want to go there anyway."

"This is not at all what I had in mind when I came to London."

"You would not be half as nervous if you had made more of your Season ten years ago."

"Exactly what do you mean by that? You know that I will tolerate no criticism of Charles, not even from you, Grandmère." She was feeling the flush steal up her face. She did not want to argue, but on this she would.

"It's you I am criticizing, not Charles. It was very convenient that you found the man you could give your heart to without having to bear the trials and tribulations of a Season with me."

"It was never you, Grandmère. It was the whole game of it. The gossip, the innuendo. I was used to a more serious life. A Season had no appeal at all."

"How unnatural of any girl of eighteen."

"Yes, but then, my life had hardly been normal. If it were not for the harp, I would have known no pleasures at Braemoor."

"And yet you now deny yourself even the pleasure of the harp?"

Mariel did no more than nod. She would not rise to an argument.

"Did you see anyone interesting today?"

"See anyone? Why, yes. I saw the man from the graveyard and the concert in Dover. Christiana tells me his name is Edward Hadley."

"You finally met him?" The old lady laughed in delight.

"No, I did not meet him. He left before I was finished with my business."

"You had a chance to make his acquaintance and did not step forward?" The delight disappeared, replaced by simmering annoyance.

"I was about to join them, and then I realized how odd it was that I should run into him yet again. Almost sinister. Four times in only a few weeks? Despite what you say, Grandmère, all these meetings cannot be accidental."

"And what sinister overtone did you create?"

"Oh, Grandmère," She could not help but smile even though she was offended. "You know I am not given to theatrics."

"Not usually."

"Seriously, I did wonder."

"Tell me what you thought of and I promise not to laugh."

"At least it will entertain you." The old lady nodded, so Mariel settled down to recount her misgivings. "At first I thought he might be a fortune hunter. You insist that I am well-enough-looking and I do have an acceptable income, but whoever heard of a man pursuing a widow with a child for her mediocre looks and small fortune? That was patently absurd."

"I'm glad you realize that."

"And Christiana tells me that Mr. Hadley is very wealthy in his own right."

"Any other explanation?"

Mariel had to forcibly remind herself that her grandmother longed for entertainment. Really, this was too embarrassing. "I thought perhaps it was something more insidious. Was he sent by my father to spy on me? Unlikely. To what end would he spy? Not only unlikely, but nonsense. The marquis is in Wales and no longer capable of such machinations."

"And James would never behave like that."

"I was not entirely sure, but he would hardly be seeking a secret reconciliation. In any case, surely he would send a representative directly or a letter."

"Or you could send him one."

"No, Grandmère, I wrote once and his reply was neither timely nor personal. I am hardly going to invite more rejection. Besides, I have enough changes in my life at the moment without inviting more."

"Ah, yes, coming to London, buying new clothes, facing rooms full of strangers. Very demanding."

Mariel's lips twitched. "Do not forget dealing with a stranger who follows me everywhere."

"Mariel, I sent that stranger a message telling him where you would be today."

It took a moment for the words to register. "You sent a message, Grandmère? How did you know who he was?"

Both the duchess and Mrs. Dayhull laughed. "My dear, you drew such a vivid word picture of him that I could have done a portrait. But it was the scar that was the biggest clue. I was there when he was injured."

"You were? What happened?" Mariel threw up her hands. "Wait. Wait." She said it to herself as much as to her audience. "That is not important." She walked around the chaise longue so that she could see both her grandmother and Mrs. Dayhull.

"You told him where I would be? But why?"

"Because you wanted to meet him, you ninny. Because he is the first man to attract your interest in two years. Because it is high time you move into the circles you were always meant to. Because I wanted to see you happy again." She picked at the shawl that covered her. "And perhaps because I was a trifle bored."

"But he is engaged! Surely you must know that my interest would end there."

"Engaged? What?" The dowager duchess looked at Mrs. Dayhull, who looked as surprised as she did.

"Your grace, I saw no announcement."

Mariel stood up with some impatience. "He was with a very pretty girl, a blonde, and she said that they were going to discuss wedding plans with her mother."

"Oh, my. More news I missed because of this." She looked about the room as though it were a prison. "Tomorrow I will dress and receive callers." Her disappointment was so obvious that Mariel hurried on to distract her.

"Grandmère, I am happy. Why is it so impossible for anyone to understand that?"

"You are not happy. Why is it so impossible for you to see it?"

Mariel raised her hands to cool her flushed cheeks. "I do not want to argue with you, Grandmère."

"What a shame, as I have been trying to start an argument for these last few minutes. It is exactly what I have my heart set on."

Mariel leaned over, took her grandmother's hand, and kissed it. "Arguing would upset both of us."

"Not me. I excel at it."

"Is it not enough, then, that it would upset me? You want to argue only because you are bored."

When she looked affronted, Mariel reminded her, "You just said it yourself. You are restless and bored."

"Humph."

Mariel watched as her grandmother looked away. She

did not let go of her hand. Almost a minute later she turned back to her granddaughter, both of them pretending that her frustration was gone.

"If we are not to argue, we will be philosophical. What do you mean when you say you're happy? What comes to mind?"

Such introspection was not like her grandmother, but Mariel answered honestly. "Being comfortable with your place in life and your surroundings. Having a child to love. Helping others."

"A wonderful definition, but not of happiness. Of contentment perhaps. Or if I were being unkind, a wonderful prescription for avoiding pain."

She still seemed inclined to argue, but Mariel ignored the slight. "And how would you define happiness?"

"Happiness is finding something that is more important to you than anything else. It can be a person. It can be an experience. But you know you are happy when you are so lost in the pleasure of the moment that time ceases to exist."

*When I played the harp. When Charles and I would lie together at night. When I held Anna for the first time.* Her eyes filled with tears, one or two making their way down her cheeks.

The duchess squeezed her hand more tightly than Mariel would have thought possible.

"Yes, my dear child, I know it hurts to remember happiness. And to realize that contentment is a poor second. But it is the first step out of the twilight to which you have confined yourself."

"I cannot believe that the happiness I once knew exists for me here." She drew a deep breath and the tears stopped falling.

"It can be found wherever you are, Mariel. London is as good a place as any. The first steps to discovering it are in your boudoir. Go and consider those invitations. If you like, you can bring them back here and I will advise you. There must be some that will prove entertaining."

# Five

"The Westbourne ball was the first ball I ever attended." Christiana spoke as the two walked arm in arm into the ballroom. They had spent almost an hour in the reception room after being announced, meeting, greeting, and being introduced.

They paused, at first puzzled by how few guests were actually dancing.

"Oh, they must be doing the *valso.*"

Mariel nodded and watched the couples. The room was a gentle swirl of color and grace. It was mesmerizing.

"None of the younger women will do it for fear that they will be denied admission to Almacks. They think approval by the patronesses there is their one true ticket to acceptance." Christiana leaned closer. "But I am married and you are a widow and we are perfectly free to try it. I must find Morgan."

Dancing the waltz with some barely met gentleman was not the way Mariel wanted to make her bow to London society. She turned her attention from the music and followed her sister-in-law, determined to find a group of dowagers with whom to pass the time.

"Are the decorations this well thought out every year?" Mariel looked up as she spoke. Garlands wound around the ballroom's three chandeliers. The countess had used white flowers, but sparingly, and woven them in with glossy greenery that dominated the arrangements. "Do you see the way she has made those arched and open gazebos that the young ladies are standing under?"

Christiana nodded.

"Dressed in white as they are, they look very like the flowers nestled in the greenery."

"Oh, yes, they do. Is that not romantic? Why, even that quiet girl in the corner looks pretty. If only she would smile."

*That was me ten years ago*, Mariel thought. *So very determined not to enjoy myself.* She was hardly sure much had changed. Finding a group of dowagers to talk with was the widow's version of the young girl who stood in the corner.

"Is Morgan in the card room?" she asked, for that is where they appeared to be headed.

Christiana nodded. "I would bet money on it." She turned back to look at Mariel, who smiled at the little joke. "He cannot resist it. He always insisted that playing was merely a means to make money when his father was so tightfisted. That is no longer an issue, and he still must see who is there and try a hand or two himself."

"And that does not worry you? I've always thought gambling a terrible vice."

Christiana laughed. "Oh, really, Mariel. You are sounding evangelical again. There is nothing vicelike about it as long as one does not play to excess or lose more than one can afford."

"But how many are able to control themselves?"

"Most everyone I know. Edward Hadley is a fine example. He has more money than he can spend, but he plays for reasonable stakes and never with anyone who cannot afford to lose."

"You once told me he lost a thousand guineas. Why, that is a fortune."

"Yes, and he did no more than smile, which gives you some idea of exactly how wealthy he is. Thirty thousand a year at least."

"That's amazing. Think of all the good one could do with that kind of money!"

"Mariel, charity is not what one normally thinks of when that kind of fortune is discussed." Christiana looked around as though she were afraid someone would overhear them.

Mariel accepted the rebuke even as she thought that more people should discuss it. "Does he win often?" That was a perfectly suitable question. *And why do I care about his fortune or how he uses it? The man is engaged.*

"He has the most magical luck." The music began again, a country dance this time, and Christiana made a face. "There is no rush now. I particularly want our first dance this Season to be a waltz." She took Mariel by the arm and led her to a spot that was somewhat private but still within sight of the card room.

"His luck is legendary, and even better, it seems to rub off on others. And not only in games of chance."

"Have you seen it yourself?"

"No, but Morgan has, more than once. Why, only last week Willy Gates was determined to have the high bid for a horse at Tattersalls, when everyone knew that Burnstead would go to the sky for it."

"What does that have to do with Mr. Hadley?"

"Gates was not even going to go to the auction." Christiana nodded to a couple but spoke only to Mariel. "Gates was all for giving up, but Hadley said that he should attend, as it was never wise to believe all the gossip one hears."

"And what happened?"

"There was some incident outside Richmond, and the road was inaccessible for hours. It kept Barnstead from the sale and Gates won his horse."

"So Willy Gates was in luck only because Mr. Hadley insisted he attend." Mariel shrugged, dismissing the story. "He did not give him the money to outbid Mr. Barnstead?"

"Oh, no, Hadley would never do that. Mariel, truly, there are any number of people who consider him their personal good-luck charm."

"It sounds nothing more than a story made up by a group

of very bored people. I expect that Barnstead is not one of his enthusiasts."

"Oh, but he is. For Hadley pointed out a horse superior to the one Barnstead had hoped to purchase. Gates bought that horse as well and then turned around and sold the first horse to Barnstead for twice what it cost him but far less than what he had been willing to pay."

"So Mr. Hadley is in everyone's good graces." *And I am the only one who wonders at his motives?* Would she ever have a chance to question him about their frequent meetings? And did it matter more, or less, now that she knew he was engaged. "I expect all that will change now that he has a fiancée."

"The fact that he is engaged changes very little. He still is one of the most interesting men in town. We may even see more of him now that he is attached. His interest will naturally shift from the young ladies to more sophisticated entertainments once his intentions are known."

Before she could ask exactly what Christiana meant by that, Morgan came from the card room together with Edward Hadley himself. She was introduced before she could do more than accept the inevitable.

"Mariel, have you met Edward Hadley? Hadley, this is my sister, Mariel Whitlow, lately of Kent." Morgan leaned close to Mariel, as though speaking in confidence when all of them could hear. "He particularly asked for an introduction."

"It seems almost anticlimactic, does it not?" Hadley smiled, his considerable charm aimed solely at her.

He looked wonderful in his black evening clothes. She was not interested, but Grandmère would want to know every detail. He wore the whitest of shirts, a most elegant butter-yellow waistcoat that made one long to touch it, and still no jewelry save a quizzing glass dangling from a black ribbon. He was freshly shaved and so clear-eyed that she could see the delicate pale gray circle around the deep blue of his eyes. His eyes were amazing.

He watched her devour him with her eyes and almost laughed aloud. Seduction? That was what the note had been about? As her smile softened and her eyes held his, any lingering doubt disappeared and he concentrated on making the most of this unexpected gift: a beautiful woman, a widow, in London, for the Season.

"We have seen each other three times, Mrs. Whitlow, and spoken all of two sentences. Or, to be more precise, I have spoken all of two sentences. Here we are, finally introduced, and you are struck dumb." He smiled, trusting that would make the small set-down an intimate tease.

Before she could speak, the orchestra began the next selection.

Perfect, he thought. "It appears that the Braedons have abandoned us."

She looked around as if only just noticing it herself.

Edward bowed and held out his hand. "Do you waltz?"

"I have never seen it before tonight."

"You, my lady, were made to waltz. I have seen the way you listen to music." He took her arm, and a moment before they reached the crowded room, he opened a door and led her onto the cool, night-darkened terrace.

The dark and empty terrace.

"Mr. Hadley, this is hardly the proper place—"

He did not let her finish the thought. "It is the perfect spot for some instruction. Of course, you will need hardly any. For the waltz is as natural as making love."

As he put his arm on her waist, he felt her stiffen. Was it from the gesture or what he had said? No matter. He took her hand and moved into the first steps, knowing that once they began the dance itself, she would be captivated.

In a moment he felt her body relax, become one with his as they moved in singular union. Though close enough to speak, neither said a word. It was, indeed, like making love.

Even though he wore gloves, the fabric of her dark blue gown felt as wonderful to the touch as it looked. It was so sensuously enticing that he moved his hand in small circles and smiled.

The sheen of the weave added a glow to her skin that made him realize that her mourning clothes had done her a real injustice. She was beautiful.

He held her completely with his eyes lest she lose herself in the music, as he knew she was inclined to do.

Could she see as deeply into his heart as he could into hers? Beyond uncertainty he saw longing, sadness, and desire. He moved a little closer and she stumbled. Stopped and then stepped back. The sensual longing he felt while he held her, the longing he saw in her eyes, gave way to chagrin if not outright offense.

"Thank you, Mr. Hadley. That was quite instructive."

He could not help it. He laughed out loud.

"Are you laughing at me?" She flushed and felt her temper rise.

He was sure there was nothing she wanted more than some disagreement that would give her an excuse to rush off. He took her hand.

"Everything you say charms me."

"You were laughing at me." This time it was a statement.

"Never at you, my dear. Only with you."

"I am not amused."

He laughed again. "Oh, you are irresistible. Almost. Please take one step closer and let me kiss all your indignation away."

"What are you thinking!" She pulled her hand from his but did not step away.

"That we will be lovers before the Season is over."

She looked so shocked, Edward realized that he may have miscalculated and spoken too soon.

"Not this Season. Not ever, Mr. Hadley. If you think I would dishonor my husband's memory, my daughter, with a tawdry affair with you—"

"Oh, surely not tawdry."

"Yes, and cheap and meaningless."

He had definitely spoken too soon. What a waste that such beauty should be wrapped around such a scrupulous heart.

She looked about as if expecting to see a troupe observing them. "Where is your cousin? Where is Miss Macomb?"

She added Estelle's name as though he needed a reminder. If there was something coy in that sentence, he missed it. It sounded more like an accusation.

"Estelle is at home tonight with the headache. Or more likely spending time alone with Gregori. I had no idea that you two had met."

"Who is Gregori?"

"An impoverished Italian count waiting for Napoleon's brother to be thrown out of his homeland." *And why do you care?*

"And you do not mind that she is with him?" She sounded genuinely confused.

"It hardly matters what I think. Estelle is a stubborn addlepate. Very hard to convince anyone who commands those two particular qualities that what they are doing is stupid or unwise." He waited, regretting that the mood was ruined and loath to do anything to damage it beyond repair. "The engagement will be in the paper before the Season ends. Everything will change, but not until then."

She stepped away from him. "The gossips may consider you the luckiest man in London, Mr. Hadley, but that hardly atones for your less admirable qualities."

"What less admirable qualities?" He was hardly perfect, but she had never even spoken to him before. How could she know that he belched when alone or that he was inclined to fall asleep whenever he watched one of Shakespeare's plays?

"I know more about you than you think, Mr. Hadley. Ten years as a minister's wife has given me more insight than most members of the ton. And more discretion."

"Do share your wisdom, madam." Not only scrupulous, but opinionated as well. And what did she know?

"This is neither the time or place."

"Name the place, then, and I will be there. Who better than a minister's wife to instruct me in my sins?" He moved closer, his hands clenched at his sides, his good humor eclipsed by a rare burst of anger. He wanted to take her by the shoulders, unsure whether he would shake her or kiss her. Something that would make her doubt her own superiority.

She reached for him but only to push him away.

"I am going to the card room, sir. Gambling is far safer than the game you are playing."

Mariel walked slowly up the stairs. The ground floor was in shadows as Hale House quieted for sleep. The porter was locking the front door, the butler snuffing the great hall candles. In a scant four hours it would be light and the house would come to life again. For now it was hers alone. She could be quiet with the thoughts that had been rioting through her head since she walked away from Edward Hadley.

For the twentieth time she reminded herself that his reasons for following did not matter anymore. He was engaged. His attempts at flirtation, seduction, were reprehensible.

She was worldly enough to know that engaged men were not always loyal and that they remained attractive despite their promise, but she was shocked to her heart to know that she was susceptible to such misguided attention.

*Oh, but that moment in his arms on the terrace.* His eyes, deep and dark, filled with approval, amusement, and yearning. His mouth, smiling in anticipation. And his hands, soothing her, exciting and inviting. Even that small scar above his eyebrow was testament to a vulnerability that was at odds with his conceit. It had been magic to feel that connection without words to know that he wanted her and she wanted him.

It was the waltz. No wonder the Almacks patronesses had banned it. If a woman with her life experience could be so compromised by it, then it was hardly the dance for a younger woman. Thank goodness she had stumbled and come to her senses.

It was only that she had been too long without a kind look. Mariel looked heavenward, her eyes raised in prayer. *Please let that be the only reason he has affected me so.*

"Is there something wrong, my lady?"

Spreen was on the steps beside Muriel before she realized she had stopped on the landing for a full minute.

"Oh, no, thank you, Spreen. Merely reliving the details of the Westbournes' ball."

She moved on up the stairs more purposefully. Despite her embarrassment with Hadley, she had learned something of immeasurable value tonight. Her heart was not buried with her husband. Her body even less so.

She could hardly thank Edward Hadley for that, but it had taken his shocking flirtation for her to finally come to terms with loss and longing.

There were still a few candles lit on the first floor and, indeed, a pool of light from one room, the music room. She walked down the hall to find out who might yet be awake and found Mrs. Dayhull staring at the violin that rested on the table near the pianoforte.

Mariel's gown brushed against the frame with a quiet swish of sound, and she looked up in some surprise. "Oh, Mrs. Whitlow! I didn't know that you had come home. You look beautiful. Was it lovely?"

Mariel gathered up her trailing scarf and draped it on the settee near the door. The thought of Mrs. Dayhull here in this empty house made Mariel look beyond her own discomfort for a description of some part of the evening worth sharing.

"It was amazing. Everything about it reminded me of a garden, the kind my sister, Maddie, used to delight in. Indeed, the countess had her flowers so arranged that the young girls themselves looked very like the fairies and sprites my sister always wished would appear."

Mrs. Dayhull's eyes filled, and she turned away. "It sounds perfect. You must tell her grace in the morning. I know how much she misses it."

Mariel closed her eyes with regret. "My apologies, Mrs. Dayhull. This must be so difficult for you."

"No, no. We have had a wonderful time together, she and I. I am the most fortunate of women to have all those years as her companion. It was always an adventure. And since your arrival, we are young again."

Mariel looked around the room, giving the woman time to compose herself. There was a fire still glowing and the remains of a tea tray and a book nearby. She walked toward the violin. "Were you thinking of playing?"

"No, only keeping the instruments company. I'm afraid my hands are too stiff to make the music sound as it should."

"When I came in, it looked as though you were longing to touch the bow and were very afraid that it would bite back. You know as well as I that the duke would be delighted if someone gave these instruments some attention."

Mrs. Dayhull glanced back at the violin and smiled the sad, small smile that Mariel knew meant memories.

"It is too late. The household is asleep."

Mariel nodded to the closed door. "In a house this size, no one will be disturbed."

"I am not at all sure I remember how, Mrs. Whitlow."

"Of course you do. One never truly forgets."

"Well, I suppose I could try," Mrs. Dayhull said timidly, and came closer, inspecting the instrument and its strings.

*That was easy,* Mariel thought.

"It has been a very quiet evening." She looked up and asked with some diffidence, "Will you stay for a few moments?"

Mariel's evening had been anything but quiet. Still, she would be the height of selfish to leave the poor woman when she was so obviously overset. "You play. I will listen."

"We could play together." She nodded toward the harp.

Mariel shook her head. "No, I cannot. It is too much like baring my soul."

Mrs. Dayhull nodded. "But you are safe here, Mrs. Whitlow. If I can play, surely you can."

It was Mariel's moment to turn away. Had her grandmother put her up to this? Nonsense, she was too much under the influence of Mr. Hadley's deception. Mrs. Dayhull could hardly sit here every night on the chance that she would stop by.

Mariel walked over to the harp, great and golden in its perfection. It called to her as it always had. Why should she deny herself this greatest consolation, her singular pleasure? At least this would harm no one.

With a sense of release Mariel sat in the elegant chair that her grandmother had designed especially for her.

She pulled the harp to her and without invitation or explanation began playing Mozart's *Sonata No. 12 for Harp and Violin*. The harp was slightly out of tune, but she ignored it, sure her fingers plucked as many wrong notes as true ones. *This is good-bye, Charles. How arrogant of me to demand that God's plans match my wants. It is beyond time to let you go.*

The violin joined the melody. Neither of them played perfectly. But the music came straight from their hearts, through their fingers, into their instruments, in a great cathartic melody that filled the room around them.

# Six

"The salon is not precisely crowded, Mrs. Dayhull, but you will admit that there are a sufficient number of callers to satisfy the most social of hearts."

Mariel spoke with satisfaction and Mrs. Dayhull nodded agreeably. "The duchess is enjoying it immensely.

"She is close enough to the fire to be warm, and that lovely dress you gave her adds just the right color to her cheeks."

"Do you think she minds that none of her visitors are young?"

"Not at all. They are the mothers and aunts of this year's young misses and are eager to share the triumph or disappointment without their young ladies in tow."

Mariel was as delighted as Grandmère. She and Christiana had spoken to a few of her grandmother's closest friends at the Westbournes' and those dears had done the rest. Indeed, the Countess of Westbourne herself was saying good-bye, promising a return visit to report on the latest Covent Garden production.

"I find it hard to believe that my few weeks in residence could be such a tonic. If I had not heard her cough, I would almost think that your letter to me was a ruse."

"Oh, but it was the complete truth, Mrs. Whitlow. No one could doubt the seriousness of her illness. It is only that she is so used to being part of the beau monde that I think her forced withdrawal from the ton was sending her into a decline."

Mariel shook her head. "I wonder that anyone can think of society as a restorative. I find it exhausting."

"You will grow more used to town hours. In time it will only seem right to sleep until noon."

Mariel stifled a yawn and nodded in polite agreement. She would never grow used to it. "I think I will adjourn to the library and spend some time with Anna. I had Miss Weber bring her down. I thought some of the ladies might wish to meet her. But"—she paused for emphasis—"I can see that was my mother's pride at work." She gestured to the group clustered around the fireplace. "It is their children who hold their interest. How could I have thought differently?"

"When you go to Astley's, you will find dozens eager to meet Anna. It is the perfect place to bring her to everyone's attention."

"If Grandmère should need me, you will know where I am."

Mrs. Dayhull nodded and settled in her corner. She did not seem to mind being left alone and looked content watching her employer's success.

Mariel slipped through the door into the next room, a corner room filled with the natural light of a brightening day.

The book salon was exactly what it sounded like. It served as a small library with very comfortable chairs and a great table under one wall of windows. The table was placed perfectly for studying atlases or books too large to hold on one's lap.

"Mama!" Anna slipped down from the stool she had been standing on and ran to Mariel. "Miss Weber and I have found the most amazing chess set. Can Miss Weber teach me how to play? Will you play with me?"

"Yes, of course. Such enthusiasm, Anna. If beautiful objects so inspire you, I shall have to see about purchasing a globe with mother-of-pearl seas and jade islands."

Anna nodded, obviously pleased at the prospect.

"Perhaps you can show me the chess set while Miss Weber takes some time for a quiet dinner?" She turned to the governess. "Come back here when you are finished eating, will you, but please do take your time."

With a quick smile and a rusty curtsy, Anna's governess left the room. Oh, her knees must be aching, Mariel thought. The damp of London could not be doing them any good. She would have to see about giving her some more time off. It was no burden for her to spend time with her own daughter.

"Look, Mama!"

Anna took her to the table that stood between the chairs in front of the fireplace. "I do know the names of the pieces. Look at the knights. Are they not cunning?"

Indeed, they were. The chess pieces were of ivory, one half the natural bone color, the other painted red, but still the grain of the ivory showed through. The pieces were long and finely turned and begged to be touched.

"Indeed, it is a work of art as much as it is a chess set."

"That is what Miss Weber said."

As they each chose a piece and exclaimed over the workmanship, there was tap at the door.

Spreen came in and Mariel could see someone waiting behind him. "Madam, the duchess said that I should bring Mr. Hadley to you here."

Edward Hadley stepped around Spreen and added, "And she announced it to a room full of people, so you cannot send me away without causing a great deal of embarrassment."

There was one small moment of pleased welcome. One small moment when she noticed the cut of his coat across his shoulders, the way his cheeks actually dimpled when he smiled. One small moment before her affront was firmly in place.

How could he have the nerve to call? Had she not made it clear that she would have no part of a liaison with an engaged man? With any man, she hastily reminded herself.

It was a purely internal rant, for Mariel was very aware of Anna standing nearby, all eyes and ears.

Her forced silence made her think a moment longer. There could be no doubt that he understood how she felt. Why was he here?

By the time Spreen had closed the door, Hadley crossed the room and was smiling at Anna.

"You must be Miss Anna Whitlow."

When Anna nodded and returned his smile. Mariel was not sure whether to be pleased at her daughter's composure or irritated at Hadley's ability to charm everyone he met.

He stooped down to sit on the stool near the globe, putting himself on the same level as Anna.

"Did you know that I knew your father?"

"You did?" The smile disappeared, replaced by a longing that twisted her mother's heart.

"Yes, I did. We went to school together. To Oxford. We were not the best of friends, mind you, as he was a far more conscientious student than I was, but we did share the same lodgings for the first two years and ate together nearly every day."

Anna nodded, clearly eager for more. So was Mariel. She had no idea Edward Hadley had known Charles.

"He loved strawberries."

Anna nodded with more enthusiasm.

"With cream."

She nodded again. "And he always said they were best right after the rain."

"When the sun has come out to warm them."

The two grinned at each other. He reached out a hand and smoothed her hair. "He was a kind man, and I can see that you are like him but blessed with your mama's beauty. What more could you want?"

Anna stepped back.

*Ah,* Mariel thought, *she has also inherited my inclination to caution, though in a child it would be called shyness.* Mariel walked over to them.

"Anna, darling, this is Mr. Hadley."

"How do you do, sir." She curtsied and he bowed.

"It is pure pleasure to meet you, but I must be honest and admit that I came to see your mama."

Anna grinned. "I knew that. I shall read a book while you talk to Mama, then you will think I am as studious as Papa."

They both watched as Anna took a book from a stack on the table and settled herself in a chair by the window. Mariel moved closer to the fire, which was far enough from where Anna sat to ensure their conversation would not be overheard.

She wanted to show him out regardless of her grandmother's welcome, but his kindness to Anna gave her pause. "You knew Charles? Surely you did not recall that bit of trivia about his fondness for strawberries from your Oxford days?"

"Everyone loves strawberries. I have to confess that it was only an educated guess. I am sorry for both you and your daughter that I do not recall more than his face and studious habits. Anna will have questions as she grows older."

Even without a smile he was all charm. He almost convinced her that she and Anna were all that he was interested in, all that he cared about. The street could explode in a cacophony of noise and he would not be distracted for a moment.

Mariel turned away from him, but only a little, so that she was looking at Anna rather than directly at him.

A child was not an adequate chaperon. What had Grandmère been thinking? Of course, she had not realized that Mariel had sent the child's governess to dinner.

It hardly mattered. Nothing untoward was going to happen. She had been cured of her interest and most of her curiosity regarding Edward Hadley.

"Mrs. Whitlow?"

She looked at him with a sigh and found him regarding her with an unusually serious face. "Yes, Mr. Hadley?"

She was pleased with the way that sounded. All Braedon, arrogance with an irritable patience that could prove short-lived.

"First, I will apologize if it will ease the tension between us." His cajoling look was as irritating as it was appealing.

"You want to apologize, Mr. Hadley?" How could he still be trying to win her over?

He nodded.

She gave him an ingratiating smile. "Only you are not sure what you must apologize for, is that it? Will it be for following me everywhere? For being so blatant in your attention? For being engaged?"

She had learned over the years in Cashton to hold her tongue, not rush to judgment, but he pushed her too far.

If sounding like a shrew were the only way to rid herself of this man who tempted her beyond reason, then she would outdo Katharina herself.

"Mrs. Whitlow, I am not engaged." He leaned forward in his seat and spoke slowly, emphasizing each word so that she could not mistake his meaning. "I am not engaged."

She did anyway. "You mean you have ended your engagement?"

"No." He spoke with quiet urgency, not angry so much as insistent on the right of his statement. "I mean I was never engaged, have never been engaged, and given the way I feel at this moment, never will be engaged."

She heard the words, understood them as English, but it was a long, long while before she comprehended their meaning. *He was not engaged. He never had been.* And longer still before she grasped their import.

"But you said you were." She thought back to the conversation she had overheard at the draper's, a confused memory that was weeks old. "I heard you say it."

He shook his head. "I can assure you that the words 'I am engaged' have never passed my lips."

"But your ward—"

"This is precisely why I called this morning. Do let me speak without interruption."

She nodded and sank into the closest chair. He sat in the chair facing hers.

"I ran into Braedon late last night and he asked if congratulations were in order. One thing led to another. I will not further disconcert you with the details, but I understand that you and Lady Morgan were confused about my relationship with my ward. The stupid girl will speak without thinking. Her idea of dropping tempting hints has caused more confusion than she will ever appreciate."

For Mariel, embarrassment replaced bewilderment. "You are speaking of the pretty girl with you at the draper's?"

"Yes, she is my ward and cousin, Estelle Macomb. The daughter of my mother's sister."

Mariel nodded, not even trying to sort out the relationship.

"As her guardian, I am handling the details of her engagement. Not an engagement to me. To someone else entirely."

She was not his fiancée, and judging by his irritation, not much in his favor at the moment.

"Once I was over my irritation with Estelle, it came to me that during our waltz you were laboring under some serious misinformation."

She thought back to the previous night. This conversation she could recall perfectly. "You said that *Estelle's* engagement was to be announced before the Season ended and that then everything would change."

She repeated the words that had so upset her. This time she heard them in an entirely different way. "Oh, dear. You did not mean"—she paused—"what I thought you meant."

"You thought that until our supposed engagement was announced I was free to make whatever connections I could wish?"

Mariel put her hands to her cheeks, wishing that she could actually run and hide. "Oh, dear, I am so embarrassed." *Mortified to death.*

"Please do not be. I can see that I phrased it in a way that must have misled, given your mistaken understanding." He bowed a little. "My apologies."

She stood, wanting only a few more details before she hid

for a week. "Dare I assume that her fiancé is the Italian count you spoke of, or do I have that wrong as well?"

"Count Gregori is her intended fiancé."

"The one who is living here until Italy is freed from Napoleon's influence?"

"The very one."

She could tell that he wanted her to smile. "In order to avoid any further confusion, may I ask if you use that tone of voice because you doubt he is a count or that Napoleon will ever be beaten?"

He laughed. "Oh, I have no doubt that we will thrash Boney soundly in time. The Peninsula will be won as long as Wellington goes on as he has at Ciudad Rodrigo. And I even believe that Gregori is a count, but that there will be land or money for him when Italy is free again, that is what I doubt."

"And you would consent to the marriage anyway?"

"Her mind is made up. Her random questions about Gretna Green were all the threat I needed."

"She wouldn't!"

"Oh, yes, she would. And if my approval means that I will be able to find a way to safeguard her fortune, then even if Gregori were a Bow Street Runner I would give my blessing."

He was the strangest man she had ever met, a mix of practical and cynical, blanketed with a charm that made the most insulting statement little more than a joke.

"My dear madam, are you quite convinced that my so-called engagement exists nowhere but as the fantasy of some desperate mama?"

"Yes, it is perfectly clear. Not that it was any of my business to begin with." She owed him at least that much penance.

"It could be, you know. For I will not apologize for my— what was that phrase you used—for my 'blatant attention.'"

He spoke so conversationally that she did not grasp his meaning at first. Then his bald statement from the previous night came back to her. *We will be lovers before the Season is over.*

Before she could react, before she could decide how to react to this less-direct enticement, he was asking another question. "Mrs. Whitlow, who might you have told about my supposed engagement?"

His question brought her back to the moment with a horrifying realization. "Gossip? I spread some totally false gossip?" She sank back into the chair, wishing for Mrs. Dayhull's vinaigrette, or perhaps actually fainting would be a better escape.

"It is not the first or the last time it has happened, Mrs. Whitlow. But I would like to know how far it has gone. I would hate to spoil Estelle's moment of glory."

She tried to think, tried to recall. "Only my grandmother and Mrs. Dayhull."

"Then that is all right. Your grandmother assures me that she learned long ago never to allude to such connections until she actually sees them in print. And Mrs. Dayhull follows her in all things."

Mariel nodded, wanting to welcome relief but still worried. "What about Morgan and Christiana Braedon?"

"I have no doubt they would have happily spread the word far and wide. Indeed, that was what Morgan's question was in preparation for. Since they have both been subject to some unwanted attention themselves, they are inclined to proceed with caution."

She leaned back in the chair, finally relaxing. "It appears that your notorious good luck has been contagious once again. Thank God."

"There are times when one must make one's own luck. No matter how divine the intervention, gossip spares no one. Estelle, Gregori, even my aunt, and certainly I appreciate your restraint."

Until the last, his charm had seemed the most natural thing in the world, but his small, satisfied smile made her realize that it was all a piece of a man the ton considered the most delightful in London.

She looked away from him and at the fireplace instead. The warmth of the fire was far easier to interpret than the warmth of his expression.

He put his arm on the back of her chair and leaned closer so that she was caught in his aura: virile, interested, and tempting. "I am touched by your concern. Can I take your interest as a sign of favor?"

"No." She had to look at him. He was close, too close, but she was prepared. His smile did not distract her this time.

"It was not concern but a simple expression of gratitude, Mr. Hadley. Not an invitation to anything more. No wonder London is rife with slander. One cannot even speak a simple sentence without fear of it."

He stood up, not at all chastened. "I may have been in town too long, but you have not been here long enough. Gossip will find you no matter how hard you may wish to avoid it."

"Is that a threat, Mr. Hadley?"

*"Touché,* Mrs. Whitlow. Now you mistake my meaning. A threat? By no means and never."

Oh, that smile was so winning, his eyes so filled with interest, she had to remind herself that if he was intent on seduction, it was not because she was the love of his life. It was because he was bored and looking for diversion.

With a perfunctory "Excuse me" she walked to Anna, which was as far from the force of his eyes and smile as the room would allow.

Would he take the hint and leave? Hardly a hint, it was as obvious a dismissal as opening the door and calling for a footman.

Anna seemed completely engrossed in her reading. But as soon as she saw that she had her mama's attention, she stood up and put the book on the table so they both could see it easily.

It was the *Britannia Illustrata.* Anna looked up at her mother, her eyes filled with wonder. "How was he able to find a tree tall enough to give him a view from the sky?"

Mariel looked at the plates one after the other, pen and ink engravings of great estates as seen from a bird's eye.

"Look, Mama, here is Fairlawn in Kent. We have been there, have we not?"

Mariel nodded. "And it looks exactly as I recall Remember the way the drive turns sharply into a grand boulevard as it approaches the house. The approach is far more impressive than the house."

"But how did he do it?"

"A Mongolfier balloon?" That was Hadley's suggestion.

He had spoken from across the room, and Anna walked away from the book, his smile as much an invitation to her as it was to women years older.

"What is a Magolfay balloon?"

"Mongolfier, my girl. Surely you are already working on your French. Try again. Mongolfier. Purse your lips on the *Mon* and swallow the g-o-l-f."

Anna giggled and made an excellent attempt at the word. By her third try she had it exactly.

*"Très bien, ma petite."*

Anna curtsied and then asked again, "But what is a Mongolfier balloon, Mr. Hadley?"

"A round sphere almost the size of this room that is filled with hydrogen and thus is able to rise into the sky. It carries a basket big enough for passengers, and you are indeed like a bird gliding over the countryside."

Anna's lips formed a soundless "Oh."

"There were no balloons when this book was written, Anna. It dates before the first ascension." How could she be jealous of her own daughter? Hadley had smiled at her with the same invitation. It had been her choice to ignore it. Perhaps it was not jealousy so much as embarrassment that Anna's honest interest should make her realize how false their behavior was. He was nothing more than a flirt, and she pretended his lures did not tempt her. *Liars, both of them.*

"The Mongolfier defies description, my girl. Perhaps while you are in London you will have a chance to see one."

Anna whirled to face her mother, her eyes beseeching.

Before Mariel could say more than it was not the sort of amusement meant for them, there was a light tap at the door and Miss Weber stepped into the room.

She stopped short when she saw a visitor.

Hadley turned to the newcomer and smiled. "Why, hello, Miss Weber." He walked closer to her, took her hand, and bowed over it in obvious delight.

"Mr. Hadley. How many years has it been?"

"Since Lockwood's sister came for her Season, I believe."

"And she recently sent me a letter announcing the birth of her third child."

Mariel watched the exchange with resignation. He knew everyone in England and had charmed them all.

He turned back to her and spoke the obvious. "You have a treasure here, Mrs. Whitlow."

Mariel could not resist a smile. "Yes, I know."

Not to be left out, Anna danced up to them. "She is going to teach me to play chess!" The child waved a hand at the set nearby.

"Yes, I saw this before. Impressive. One of Calvert's better efforts, and that is saying something since he is the best on Fleet Street." He lifted the delicate piece of ivory that was the king, tall and fine, like the miniature of a finial one might find on the top of a clock tower.

He looked at Mariel. "I expect that one plays better when inspired by such beauty." He put the piece down without looking away from her. "Do you play, Mrs. Whitlow?"

She pretended there was no double meaning in the question. "I fear I am not very good. I am much too direct." He could interpret that however he wanted.

"We shall have to match wits sometime."

"Oh, I have no doubt that you would win. You are clearly

far more experienced than I am." *At flirting, at chess, at making the most of a London Season.*

He bowed to her, stepped closer, and almost whispered, "An experience I would be happy to share."

She should be insulted, shouldn't she? This was more than flirtation. And in front of her daughter and a woman he knew since his own youth. The man had no manners and fewer inhibitions.

"It is very easy to learn the moves."

What was he suggesting? Then she realized that he was talking to Anna. "It is one thing to handle chess pieces, another thing entirely to learn how to handle an opponent."

"That bit of insight is much too advanced for Anna, Mr. Hadley." Miss Weber stepped forward, but Hadley gestured Anna to the seat.

"Come here, Anna, and let me show you how to move the pieces. It is so much easier than learning how to move people."

He stayed for another twenty minutes, as though Miss Weber's arrival had reset the clock on his call. Anna paid close attention and actually seemed to absorb his instruction. Miss Weber watched him with an indulgent smile, and Mariel stood apart from them, feeling ignored. She insisted that was exactly what she wanted.

When he left, all three ladies watched him go, one of them relieved, one half in love, and the third intrigued.

# Seven

"Mama, is this not amazing! Have you ever seen so many people in one place?"

"No, I have not. And yes, it is quite impressive." Mariel did her best not to pull Anna closer. The crowd was a mix of all of London, from one extreme to the other: the ton, so obvious in their carriages and on horseback mixed among the rest of London, on foot and badly dressed. But they were a jolly lot for the moment.

The balloon was still being filled, the envelope beginning to rise above the throng. It was a brilliant yellow, a man-made rival to the sun that was burning through the clouds above.

How long would it be before the balloon was fully expanded and what would entertain this mob of people until the Mongolfier was ready for an ascent?

This had been a bad idea. Why had she allowed Anna to nag her into it? Mariel looked behind her to see if the two footmen who had accompanied them were as distracted as her daughter, but at her very glance both came up to her.

"Why such a crowd? I thought these ascents were commonplace." She tried to sound curious and not nervous.

Jonas nodded, but it was his brother Ezra who answered. "It's the first one this spring, Mrs. Whitlow. Rain has delayed 'em all month. People have been longing for some entertainment since Easter. And this one is free."

"Can't keep it a secret, ma'am. It would be impossible to hide." Jonas nodded to the balloon that was growing slowly and steadily in size as the inflammable air filled the silk.

"Why, look, Mama, there is someone selling meat pies. Can I have one?"

Mariel allowed Anna to pull her toward the vendor. As they walked, she turned back to the footmen. "Would either of you care for a meat pie?"

They looked doubtful.

"Not from that seller, ma'am." Ezra nodded to a place by the wide-open gate. "That one over there is known to us and is most reliable. You know you are getting exactly what she says when you buy from her. Why, last month the kitchen maid took sick from a pie and she's not been the same since."

Mariel nodded and hoped he would give no more details. "Then would you please find a seller you trust and bring one back for Anna, even if you do not care for one yourself."

Mariel felt Anna press closer, as though the news of a less than reliable peddler made the whole outing suspect. *This is supposed to be fun,* Mariel reminded herself, *not an exercise that will bring on nightmares.* It was difficult to say something cheering when she was wishing for a hand to hold herself.

A man approached. He was well dressed and carried a cane, but his grin was more a leer than a greeting. He had opened his mouth to speak, even removed his hat to bow, when he saw Anna. Then his interest was gone, and within a moment he was too.

Ezra came back with a handful of pies, and the four of them moved away to find a suitable picnic spot. As the sunshine grew, the day was warming and the breeze that had been so light before was noticeably brisk. Mariel gestured to the trees at the edge of the field. The small group walked closer, moving away from the crowd. "This looks like the perfect spot."

"Not here, ma'am," the footman whispered. With a jerk of his chin he gestured for her to look up.

The trees were filled with small boys. Any number sat on the most stout of the branches, having claimed what looked like a familiar spot from which to watch the show.

"Oh, Mama, I wish I could be up there."

One of the boys looked down at her and grinned. " 'Ere's a hand, miss." He leaned down on his branch, spit on his hand, and stuck it out for Anna to grab.

Mariel was about to protest, when Anna answered, "Thank you, but I am not dressed for climbing today."

The invitation, though friendly, was the final blow to Mariel's waning confidence. "We will go back to the carriage and eat our food in comfort. I am sure we can see the ascension from there."

"No, Mama, that will not work. You said so yourself before."

"I could find a place for you on that raised viewing platform, ma'am."

Ezra spoke with some doubt, and Mariel could see why. Not only was the platform a good many feet above the rabble, it was already filled with men and women. They were a well-dressed group, but that was the only thing that distinguished them from the people below. Mariel thought a face or two among the men looked familiar. Was one of them Lord Griffon? The women who accompanied the gentlemen were completely unknown to her. And she could guess why.

"No, thank you, Ezra. We will go back to the carriage and come another time. We would be wiser to come with a larger group." *One that includes an escort of at least three or four gentlemen.*

"Ohhhh, Mama."

Anna did not wail, not exactly, but her disappointment was evident.

At least the footmen did not objet. Ezra and Jonas walked ahead of them, clearing the path that was even more crowded than it had been before. Curricles and more staid carriages lined the walkway and parked on the grass. Mariel moved along without raising her head, not eager to see or be seen.

"Mama! Look. There is Mr. Hadley."

"Of course he is here. He follows me everywhere." She only mumbled the words quite under her breath, but clamped her mouth shut anyway.

Anna waved vigorously and Hadley waved back.

*This is exactly what I needed to put the complete ruin on this venture.*

He was not alone. Mariel recognized his cousin. The gentleman she was hanging on to must be her fiancé. There was an older woman wearing a deep maroon dress, a garish bonnet, and too much face paint. Two young bucks were at the side of the barouche, astride restless horses, chatting with the group.

Hadley broke off the minute Anna began waving and jumped down from the open carriage.

"We have been looking for you, Miss Whitlow." He spoke to Anna and then bowed to Mariel.

Mariel returned a hurried curtsy, but before she could ask why he was looking for them, he had turned back to Anna. He offered her his hand, and she slipped hers into his without hesitation.

"Have you been practicing chess?"

"Yes, sir." Anna nodded vigorously. "And watching my opponents as well. Mama raises her hand to her throat when she is surprised by a move."

"Very good." He spoke as though he were impressed with her powers of observation. As though learning to read people and use that knowledge to your own advantage were as important as learning Christian charity and the Ten Commandments.

Still holding Anna's hand, he turned to give her his full attention. "I was quite sure I would find you here."

"You were?"

"But certainly." He winked at Anna. "I knew you would be here because you follow me everywhere."

"What?" She wanted to grab him by the lapels of his perfectly tailored coat and shake him. "It is *you* who follow *me* everywhere."

"Do you think so?" His expression was devilish, as though he would not deny it.

"It's the truth."

"What? I followed you to Dover after following you to the cemetery?"

She was totally inept when it came to flirtation, for that was all this was. If she could come up with a teasing rejoinder, the subject would be dropped, but all she could do was think of ways to defend herself from his silly accusation.

He must have seen her discomfiture. "We can argue about it later." Hadley patted her arm as he took it in his. "Come, Mrs. Whitlow. Come and meet my family."

*His family? That woman was his mother? She was much too young.*

Mariel was swept along as by a wave. The footman considered his word an order, and Anna was not to be denied the superior vantage point that Hadley's carriage offered.

It was the usual babble of names and greetings. The older woman was his aunt Macomb, his mother's youngest sister. She was his hostess this Season while Estelle had her come-out. That explained Mrs. Macomb's age. She was not under forty, but still too young to have given birth to a man at least thirty.

And it was not face paint at all. "What an awful way to meet you, Mrs. Whitlow. My face all red from some rash. I would eat too many strawberries, you know. Estelle insisted that this bonnet would distract attention, but I think it only attracts it."

Mrs. Macomb had the right of it, and Mariel searched for a diplomatic response. "It has a wonderful brim that will protect you from the sun."

"Protection or not, I am throwing it away the moment I return home. I hate it. But I could not miss this ascension. The Duke of Redmond is one of the aeronauts today."

That further explained the crowd milling about, growing more restless, but now a safe distance away.

Hadley began to direct his growing entourage to seats. Adding two people, even one as small as Anna to the already full barouche, made it almost as crowded as the ground below.

At Hadley's urging, Estelle and her count made the driver step down and the two of them settled on his seat. Mrs.

Macomb patted the seat beside her, and Anna climbed up with some help from their host.

The only remaining seat was next to Hadley.

Even as Mariel tried to come up with some excuse to change places with Anna, they were all distracted by the cry "Stop, thief!"

Mrs. Macomb turned from them to help Anna kneel up on the seat so she could watch the hubbub, leaving Mariel and Hadley in some privacy.

"You do know of the labor troubles elsewhere? Crowds can so easily turn unfriendly these days." Hadley's tone was conversational, but he was fiddling with his quizzing glass and not quite smiling. "What were you thinking to come here alone?"

"You sound positively straitlaced, Mr. Hadley." Mariel was embarrassed at her naïveté but refused to let him see it. "Attending an ascension was your idea."

"When I suggested Anna see one?" He did not wait for an answer. "I would have made it an invitation if I thought there was any chance you would agree to come with me."

"So when you decided that Anna and I would not accept your invitation, you determined to follow us instead." She could flirt after all. Bringing up the subject again made her feel daring and a little dangerous. Mariel gave him a look that dared him to deny it.

"Indeed, you think I organized this entire charade to follow you, ma'am?" He threw out his arm to encompass his aunt, cousin, the count, and the entire crowd beyond, and then shook his head. "I think not."

He put his arm up along the back of the carriage, not touching her but making their conversation all the more intimate. "On the other hand, you knew that I was fond of balloon ascensions and may well have come, inappropriately escorted, in hope that I would see you and invite you to join me."

She could not mask her exasperation. "You are absurd."

"My congratulations." He mistook her pique for more teasing. "Your plan worked."

His expression was edged with temptation. His eyes alive with it. Even here, surrounded by a crowd, he made her feel that the two of them were alone and complete.

"There is no convincing you, is there, Mr. Hadley? I am no more following you than you are following me." She turned to face him more fully, smiling in that patronizing way she used when Anna said something too silly to be believed. "Our meetings are only a series of coincidences. Mere chance."

"Not chance, madam. It was luck, the best of luck."

His amusement was as much an intimate invitation as the way they sat, close together, she in the circle of his arm still stretched along the back of the carriage seat.

"You must be honest with me, Mrs. Whitlow. It was not all luck, was it? What about the note you sent me?"

"What note? I never sent you a note."

"The one telling me to come to Bon Marché Drapers."

*The one her grandmother had sent.*

He looked so surprised at her blush that she told the truth. "My grandmother sent it to you."

"The Dowager Duchess of Hale sent me that intriguing little billet doux?"

She considered his description and almost asked to see it, but he went on before she could speak.

"Mariel"—his voice was filled with teasing disapproval— "how cowardly of you to draw your grandmother into this. Why would she send me a note about you?"

"She wanted us to meet."

He angled his head and looked at her as if trying to decide whether to believe her. Thank heaven he did not think to ask why Grandmère wanted them to meet.

"I did not send it, Mr. Hadley. You can think what you like, but I would never even think of sending such a note."

"I live for the day you do."

"You will wait in vain." She tried to sound disapproving, but the gesture he made as though a stab to his heart almost had her smiling. "That gesture is much better suited to the theatrics you ascribe to your cousin."

"You have never seen an Italian gentleman in distress."

They both looked over their shoulders, behind them, and up at Estelle and her count. As if on cue, Gregori made the same gesture himself.

"Do let yourself laugh, my dear. For some reason, your serious face is a greater temptation than your laughing one."

*Really, he was too charming.*

He leaned closer. "Even if you had just eaten a lemon, your lips would be hard to resist."

*So are yours*. Instead of completing the invitation with those words, she turned her head, broke the spell, and realized that it would be so like him to actually kiss her in public with a thousand witnesses.

When the silence between them grew uncomfortable, she glanced back at him. He looked smug, as though tempting her to impropriety were all the success he had hoped for.

He folded his arms and bent his head, all innocent curiosity. "Why would your grandmother wish for us to meet?"

*Oh, drat*. She fumbled for a simple explanation. "Because we hadn't actually been introduced."

"And how did she know that?"

He spoke as though he knew that he had been the subject of intense conversation. What could she say without admitting exactly that? Oh, please heaven, she prayed, Grandmama had not used the term "mysterious gentleman" in her note, had she? Mariel bit her lip again, determined to say no more until she had reasoned out a less embarrassing explanation or talked to her grandmother about the wording of this note gone wrong.

She gestured to Anna, who was hanging over the back of the carriage, listening while Mrs. Macomb talked to a couple on horseback. "I really should be the one to sit with Anna. She is becoming quite restless."

"No, you should stay as you are, next to me." He handed her the lap robe that Estelle had dismissed. "I am entirely too old to sit next to my aunt, especially when there is a beautiful woman present. I would be the laughingstock of the ton."

"Look, Mama."

Not only Mama, but the entire group within hearing of Anna's shout of excitement turned to look where she was pointing. The balloon was full but not quite taut, and towered over them. It was not menacing, but decidedly ready for release.

"One would mistake it for the sun if it were not for the Redmond crest." Hadley raised a hand to shade his eyes from the reflected glare.

"The sun? That is exactly what I thought before."

"I expect that is the precise comparison the duke wished, but it is delightful to actually be in agreement with you for once."

His smile coaxed one from her, and she studied his face as he did hers. The balloon was not nearly as intriguing as he was. How had he come by the scar near his eyebrow?

A gasp from the crowd and a shriek from Estelle drew their attention to the balloon. One of the ropes had come loose and the taut, filled balloon was at an odd angle, so steeply pitched that it looked as though it would upset the basket beneath.

Mariel gasped, grabbed Hadley's arm, and turned her face into his coat. When she realized what she had done and that he had brought his other arm up to pull her close, she pushed away and sat bolt upright, putting her hands over her eyes.

"Everyone is safe." Hadley patted her shoulder. "Someone has caught the rope and secured it again. I'm certain that it was quite deliberate. They did it to entertain us a bit."

"Entertain? They think this is fun? Whose idea of being entertained includes possible death?"

Hadley considered her question. "The Romans watching the gladiators? The French revolutionaries who cheered at the guillotine? Man comes from a long line of bloodthirsty thrill seekers."

If he had been laughing at her, she might well have hit him with her reticule. But he had taken her question quite seriously.

"Then man has a very warped idea of what fun is."

"Oh, yes, he does. I have observed that myself more than once."

She regarded him with some interest. He looked up to the sky and at the crowd surrounding them, and then turned to give Mariel his full attention once again.

"Everyone here, rich or poor, is hoping for something that will raise their life from the mundane. Estelle balked at coming, insisting that these ascensions were much too predictable. When Gregori pleaded, saying he had never seen one, Estelle agreed to come along but said that she hoped something exciting would happen or she would die of boredom."

"For me a safe ascension will be quite adequate entertainment."

"How would *you* define fun, Mrs. Whitlow?" He emphasized the "you" as though her perspective would be unique from all others.

Was he really interested in what she thought? In something as intellectual as how she would define fun? He did look sincerely curious, and she was flattered.

She gave the question some thought and he waited. That alone surprised her. Charles would never have waited while she marshaled her thoughts, or even asked for them in the first place.

"How would I define fun?"

He nodded and she answered.

"True fun does not hurt anyone," she said cautiously, and he nodded encouragement. "Neither their physical person nor their sensibilities."

He considered it. "Boxing? It is quite entertaining."

"Disgusting and never fun."

"We may have to disagree on that one particular. We can attribute our differing viewpoints to our respective genders, can we not? But on the whole I agree with you. True fun is not hurtful."

"Which is why I do not find gossip fun." She said it even

though it was embarrassing to recall her own recent misunderstanding of Estelle's engagement. "Gossip is too often painful."

"And sometimes even destructive."

She nodded and went on with more confidence. "True fun never becomes boring."

"Give me an example."

"Easily. I sometimes tire of playing the harp, but only because I am never as good at it as I would like. It is always a challenge, sometimes delightful, sometimes frustrating, but never boring."

"You play the harp?" he asked with some interest. "My mother played the harp. It is one of the few things about her that I recall. She died when I was seven."

Mariel had the sudden picture of a small, dark-haired boy, his engaging grin as lost as he was. Then another thought occurred to her. "You truly do understand how Anna feels, then. Even better than I can."

"No one can understand a child as well as her mother. But in that loss, I do share some knowledge."

His eyes softened as she nodded. And there it was again. That complete moment of communion. She wished she could blame it on the moment. But this was hardly a romantic setting. And besides, she had seen it, felt it, before, when a dozen gravestones had separated them. When his look had invited her to share the absurdity of life with him. And no one would ever call a cemetery a romantic contrivance.

The intimate regard they shared was so bewitching that at this moment, like the other, she forgot time and place, ignored everything but the whispering of their hearts. He was the one who looked away.

"Those, then, are your criteria for happiness, Mrs. Whitlow? It must hurt no one and never grow boring?"

"I am not quite finished. It should always make one feel better."

"Is that not the same as causing no hurt?" He answered that

himself after the briefest of pauses. "No, of course not. I have a friend who drowns his sorrows in brandy in hope of easing the pain. In the end it does not make him feel better."

Hadley gestured toward the balloon. Mariel had been so engrossed in their discussion, in him, that she had forgotten it.

The balloon began its slow, silent ascent. The crowd cheered, and Hadley reached over to take her arm as they stood to watch.

"Why are we standing?" she whispered, her mouth very close to his ear, as the enthusiasm of the crowd would make her words hard to hear.

"We are standing because we envy them their bravery. We are standing because we so want to be with them, but this is as close as we dare come."

She could feel his gaze on her but could not tear her eyes from the ascent: the feeling of power tangible even on the ground, the figures onboard, some busy, one saluting the earthbound with a glass of champagne.

The bright golden globe rose above them, sailed toward them for a moment, and then moved off to the west slowly, elegantly.

She shook her head and let her smile become a grin. Anna still had her back to the group. Mariel knew she would watch the glorious yellow globe until it was completely out of sight.

"And was that fun, Mariel Whitlow?" he whispered to her this time.

She shook her head, unwilling to define the feeling.

"Think about it." His arm slipped from her elbow to take her hand. "That moment when the balloon casts off the bounds of earth. In that moment there is no fear for their safety, only awe at the majesty and the hope of the moment."

"You mistake my silence, sir. The silly three-letter word 'fun' hardly does this justice."

"Ah, but, my dear, that is an entirely different discussion."

"Then yes, Edward Hadley, it was fun. It truly was."

# Eight

Mariel sank down onto the settee as the last of the callers left the room.

Christiana remained standing, apparently still full of energy. "The Duke of Redmond, Mariel. How lovely."

"He came to see Grandmère and stayed only so as not to appear rude."

"He may have *said* he came to see her, but he stayed quite twenty minutes and would not leave your side."

"Christiana, his grace is very kind, but his interest in aeronautics is all-consuming."

"So you are not interested?"

"No, I am not. And he came to see Grandmère, not me."

"We will see whom he asks for the next time."

"It will not be me. He must find someone more sympathetic than I am. How can he spend his fortune on something so useless, when the very people who come to watch him are in such need."

Christiana looked shocked at her bluntness. "What did he say to that?"

"Only that he supports hundreds of people by employing them, and each man must make time for entertainment."

"Oh, well said."

"It is not enough." Mariel sighed. "He has a fortune at his command. He could use it for the benefit of all instead of his own personal gratification."

"He'll never come back again."

Mariel laughed and patted her sister-in-law's hand. "I did

not preach him that part. It is only what I think. He will come back. Grandmère is his godmother after all. And I shall be happy to stand in for her as I did today. And I promise to listen with nothing less than an encouraging smile."

"All right, then. Good." Christiana sat down on the settee next to her.

"Do you and Morgan think I make too much of our responsibility to the poor?"

"We do understand that it has been your life these last years. We both wish you knew as much about having a good time as you do about responsibility."

"I do know how to have fun."

"Oh, really." Christiana looked skeptical.

"The balloon ascension was marvelous and the concert in Dover was heavenly."

Christiana nodded encouragingly.

"The time I spend with Anna is fun."

"To be sure, but there is always the element of parental supervision that diminishes the pleasure."

Mariel laughed. "Oh, that is so true. I suppose I must still be learning, then. Fun has not been the focus of my life. I have had other responsibilities."

"Think of all you know who are tightlipped and grudging."

Mariel pictured the prune-faced woman who ran the orphanage on the outskirts of Cashton.

"And think of the people you actually enjoy being with."

Mariel smiled. *Edward Hadley.* "The Harbisons. They are amazingly adept at providing amusement for everyone in the neighborhood. One never doubts of having a pleasant evening at the manor."

"My point is proved. Fun must take precedence, for you have been too long without it. It is what being here for the Season is all about."

Mariel could see Christiana was quite prepared to stay the whole afternoon. For her part, she had been quite serious about a rest.

"Are you not exhausted, Christiana? It has been three weeks of nonstop balls and parties, afternoons in Hyde Park, and shopping whenever our social schedule permits."

"And the theater."

"Oh, and the opera." Mariel leaned back on the sofa cushions and tried to hum the most memorable of the arias from *Così fan tutte*. "Signora Rouselli has a truly remarkable voice. It was worth every bit of the expense and effort to bring her here."

"And so romantic. Smuggling her from Italy as though she were contraband. Quite delicious actually. I wonder who was responsible for it?"

"I should love to thank whoever it was. What a gift to give us." Signora Rouselli's dramatic arrival had been the talk of the ton for days. "Does Morgan have any idea who is responsible?"

"Morgan thinks it was Hadley." Christiana spoke as though she had yet to be convinced.

"Edward Hadley?"

"It's what everyone thinks when something amazing happens."

"How ridiculous."

"That is what Hadley says. But he was out of town for the last weeks. Surely you noticed?"

Mariel nodded. Of course she had noticed his absence. She admitted to a wee bit of relief that he had not been avoiding her. "What was his explanation for his absence?"

"Family business." Christiana nodded knowingly. "A commonplace enough excuse until one realizes that Count Gregori is Italian and about to become part of his family."

"And what does Signora Rouselli say?"

"Oh, no one I know has actually questioned her. She has that imperious look that promises a set-down."

"Do not tell me that the ton is intimidated?" Mariel did not even try to hide her amusement. "Do they think that they invented that look? Have they never heard of the Medici?"

"They are interested for the moment, but it will not last much longer. Everyone will wait until she claims a lover, then we will know who is behind her escape."

Mariel nodded and insisted to herself she would not care if it was Edward Hadley.

"I promise to leave soon, really. Then you can have your rest. But I have some news. It's quite amazing and no, I am not increasing."

Mariel nodded, her interest quite caught as Christiana stood up again and turned to face her as though making a grand pronouncement. "My modiste is moving to London."

"Your modiste from Wales? The one whom you wanted to come to Bath?"

"Exactly. Morgan says that he heard from his steward that she is coming to London instead. She received some sort of bonus from a grateful client and has the funds for an independent move."

"How wonderful for you." Mariel considered the explanation. "But, Christiana, what client would be so grateful that she would give her that much money? It would take hundreds, would it not?"

"I should think so. But perhaps it is a patron of a more personal nature."

"A lover? One who wants her to move to London?"

"Perhaps." Christiana shrugged, acknowledging it as not very likely.

"I know! Edward Hadley gave her the money."

Taking it as the joke she intended, Christiana shook her head on a giggle. "That would be carrying his generosity too far. It's luck he freely dispenses, not money. Besides, how would he even know of my modiste?"

"Because you told him that day you saw him at Bon Marché Drapers." Mariel just then recalled it herself. "He even suggested that you fund the move."

"Why, that's right." Christiana waved her hand with a dismissive shake of her head. "Why would he do it? He had no reason to want my favorite modiste in town."

Mariel considered the question and the Edward Hadley that she knew so little about. "Could he have done it just for fun?"

"Checkmate, Hadley."

How had that happened? Edward examined the board while Lockwood preened. "Well done, Lockwood. It appears that I need more practice."

"Beat you with the Fool's Mate." Lockwood laughed as though he could not contain his elation and then spoke with reluctant honesty. "Never would have tried that gambit except you are so distracted."

"Was I? Distracted?" Yes, indeed, "distracted" was his mantra for tonight. Instead of concentrating on the game, he had been attempting to figure the odds on running into Mariel Whitlow again, given that there were at least a dozen different invitations for this evening alone. He had decided that some things could not be left to fate when Lockwood had called an end to the game.

"See, there you go again."

Edward nodded and with a rueful shake of his head got up to pour them both a drink.

"Do tell me what has you in such a quandary, Hadley. Your life is so delightfully complicated."

Before he could come up with a suitable red herring, Lockwood presented one himself. "Where were you these last few weeks?" Lockwood held up his quizzing glass and used it to study his friend more closely. "And that 'family business' line is twaddle. It won't wash with me."

"I escorted my aunt to Bath so that she could take the waters and cure that persistent rash."

"She looked well enough this evening."

Hadley raised his glass. "The waters worked."

Lockwood raised his glass in response, then narrowed his eyes. "But did you stay in Bath?"

"For God's sake, this really is exasperating. I know exactly what you are hinting, and I will tell you this. I was not in Italy and have nothing at all to do with bringing that opera singer over here. Not a thing." He spoke with special emphasis on the last three words.

"You protest too much."

"Even using Redmond's Montgolfier balloon I could not have traveled from Bath to Italy and back in so short a time."

Lockwood gave a half-nod of agreement but seemed loath to let go of such a good story.

"Lockwood, I hate opera. I have never been. I never plan to attend. I would not know this woman if she came to the door right now."

Lockwood looked at the door expectantly. He then stood up, walked over, pulled it open with a dramatic flourish, and bowed to whoever would enter. When no one came through the door, he shut it and turned back to a laughing Hadley.

"Do you believe me?"

"I dunno, Hadley. She could have missed her cue."

"Never. She is a professional. She is gracing someone else's salon and quite obviously not mine."

Lockwood put his glass on the table and considered his chronometer.

"Yes, go home, old fellow. I have work to do."

"I thought Matthew did all your work for you?"

"Letters. I need to write some personal letters that must be sent off first thing in the morning."

"Very well, there is a game at the Quarter Moon tonight. Might see who thinks they're lucky. Join me later?"

Without waiting for an answer, he was out the door, calling for his hat, and then sent the butler back to remind Edward of the Harbisons' ball on the morrow.

Hadley put his head back and closed his eyes. The quiet was a blessed relief. From some distance he could hear the sound of carriage wheels on cobblestones, but in this room there were no sounds save the occasional swoosh of coals as the fire faded.

This peace was his for no more than an hour. His aunt and Estelle would be back from the theater. Gregori was settling firmly into his good graces by his willingness to escort the ladies almost everywhere they wanted to go and leaving him free to pursue his other interests. Gregori and Estelle seemed like-minded when it came to the importance of the Season. It would make for a good marriage in that respect at least.

Gregori's offices were especially appreciated tonight when even his best friend was eager to find out whether he was Signora Rouselli's rescuer.

If he set to work now, he could be away by the time they returned. Whether to a card game or bed he had yet to decide.

He walked over to the desk in the corner of the room and sat down. Paper and pen were waiting. He had only to think how to word the message.

He wanted to see her. He wanted to spend time with her. He wanted to understand how her mind work, how her heart kept time, and what it felt like to kiss her. It had been weeks since the balloon ascension, and he missed her. Had she missed him?

As distracted as he was by his foray to Bath and then to Wales, he found Mariel Whitlow at the center of his thoughts more often than not. The country around the Glamorgan was spectacular. He wondered what she would think of it, she who had spent the last ten years in the quiet gentility of Kent.

He had heard a shepherd playing some sort of homemade instrument and he wondered if she could play a tune like that on the harp. He had seen a woman wearing a gown in that deep and shining blue that so suited her and recalled their waltz with a haze of pleasure even if that evening had ended badly.

He replaced that memory with the way her body felt pressed against his. He owed Redmond his thanks for that little incident before the ascension, the one that had frightened her so that she had thrown herself into his arms. But nearly as marvelous was the rapture on her face as she watched the balloon sail away.

What he would give to have her look at him that way. Anticipation was well and good. He needed to act to make that happen.

He picked up the pen, tested the ink, and began:

> *Speculation regarding your activities in Kent and Dover has followed you to London.*
> *You will find someone of interest and equally interested in you in the card room at the Harbison's ball this evening.*

"You have already worn that blue gown three times, Mariel."

"I know, Grandmère, but I do love it so. Besides, who notices what I wear."

"Everyone who cares about clothes, and that is everyone but the most complete nodcock."

"No one ever said anything in Kent."

"The roosting ground of the world's finest nodcocks."

That made them both laugh.

"All right. I will wear the dark rose satin. It is comfortable enough even if the décolletage is a trifle extreme."

"No, save the rose gown for the Ponsonbys' rout. The Regent is almost sure to attend that, and you'll want to look your best."

*Not for that philandering, selfish fool.* Since that was perilously close to treason and he was a favorite of her grandmother's, Mariel kept the thought to herself.

"Wear the blue again, but use that turquoise necklace your mother left you. It will change the look of the gown completely. And I will lend you that beautiful Spanish shawl that Rhys sent me."

She nodded, thoroughly distracted by the last sentence. "My brother Rhys is in Spain?"

"Yes. He's been there for some time."

"Has he taken a commission? Is he fighting?" She raised a hand to her throat to ease the knot lodged there.

"No, no. He's gone for some astronomer's adventure."

"To Spain. In the middle of a war?"

"He has a friend who suggested that he come last year to view the comet, and since he was in the middle of an argument with James, he used the letter as an excuse to leave the country."

"Oh, well, that explains it." James could quite thoroughly alienate anyone and with very little effort. "If I wear the blue gown and shawl it will remind me to pray for Rhys's safety."

"Hopefully you will be too busy dancing to do that."

"Grandmère, there is one more thing I must ask." Mariel pulled the note from her pocket. "Will you please stop sending these anonymous notes to people."

The duchess took the paper from her, held it as far away as she could, squinted her eyes, read it, and then barked with laughter. It devolved into the familiar but no less wrenching coughing fit. As usual, the duchess completely ignored the interruption once it was over.

"I no more wrote this than you did. You know that's not my handwriting."

"I thought you might have had Mrs. Dayhull write it for you."

Mrs. Dayhull walked over to the bed, looked at the note, and shook her head with disapproval. "An impossible hand. Not very graceful at all."

"Hadley's."

Mrs. Dayhull nodded at the duchess's single-word explanation, and Mariel straightened in surprise. She snatched the paper back and looked at it with new eyes.

"How do you know?"

"Because that is the exact wording I used when I wrote to him." She looked as though she wanted to laugh again but thought better of the aftereffects. She settled for slapping her hand on the bedcovers. "What a devil."

"Yes, he most certainly is."

# Nine

"This is what is meant by a crush, is it not?" No sooner had Mariel spoken than a couple, somewhat the worse for champagne, pushed her into her brother's arms.

"Yes. And perhaps a trifle overdone at that." Morgan took a step back and led her closer to the great tubs of blooming dogwood that helped create the forest ambiance, a theme that the Westbournes had made de rigueur this Season. "The Harbisons have a reputation for lavish entertaining, and they never would want to fail expectations. They must be delighted."

Mariel nodded. "Indeed, they can never manage more than fifty at Cashton. Mr. Harbison continually threatens to build a folly for 'larger' parties."

They had spent the last ten minutes chatting while Christiana was in the withdrawing room, helping a friend whose curls had suffered from the damp air.

"Will there be many women in the card room tonight?" Mariel hoped it sounded like casual conversation rather than a subject that had plagued her for the last ten hours.

"More than usual, I suspect. You know that Mrs. Harbison is as fond of cards as is her husband." He looked at her as though he had only then decided to pay attention to their conversation. "When did your interest in cards revive? Do you want to play? It will be whist only, you know. Are you looking for a partner?"

"No, I think I already have one." She twisted her reticule and felt the note inside.

"You have a partner? I hope it is Edward Hadley."

"It is!" she said with some surprise. "How did you know?"

"Lucky guess. You were with him at the ascension, and the only other man who has been calling is Redmond, and he has never found the card room in his life."

"I hate gossip."

"It's hardly gossip, Mariel. You are much too sensitive." He spoke with gentle exasperation. "In Cashton, did you not look out the window and say to your maid, 'Oh, there is Mrs. So-and-So on her way to the market?' Or 'I wonder why the Harbisons' maid is at the apothecary?' "

"Yes, but they are people I know and care about."

"London may be larger than Cashton, but the ton knows and cares about one another in the same way as the people of a small town. Some are malicious, I will grant you that, and there are others who will always embellish a story, but they are easily named."

She could mentally list five women like that but knew very little of the men.

"I know you deplore gossip, have seen the way it can complicate a life, your own and others, but noticing that you are in Hadley's company or that Redmond calls is nothing more than neighborly interest."

"But it can so easily grow into something less mundane."

"Yes, it can, and those of us who have been caught in its web are careful what we spin, but that is all we can do. Be careful. If you want no gossip, you go nowhere and see no one." He thought a moment. "Of course, that would create its own gossip, would it not?"

She nodded and smiled as he intended. "You are right. I am allowing my sensibilities to overcome my good sense."

"Well put."

She almost asked if he had read Miss Austen's book of that title but realized that she was far more interested in the possibilities of the card room.

"Tell me, why I am lucky to have Hadley as a partner?"

"Because he is the best card player in London—excepting me, of course. But I do think he is even better than I am at whist. Does he know how good you are?"

She shook her head.

"When I think of the endless hands Father made us all play so he was not bored . . ." His voice trailed off.

"Yes, and Maddie never once realized that when you were going to lose you would drop a card on the floor and then insist that there had been a misdeal."

"It took you and Father a week to catch on yourselves."

"Only because you did it too often."

"My favorite was when I would throw the hand down and declare the rest of the tricks mine."

"That worked only once."

"And Father taught me the hard way not to cheat."

Neither could so much as smile at the recollection of the marquis's beatings.

Morgan looked around the room as if measuring her chances by what was in the air. "This is a good place to test your skills. The players will be relaxed by the food and drink, and the stakes will be reasonable."

"How do you know that?"

"Look at who is here and who is not. There is a marathon game ongoing at the Quarter Moon. Been on for more than twenty-four hours. I suspect that is where the serious gamers are."

"Hadley is not one of them?"

"No, those kinds of games never interest him. He likes the challenge of serious play. It explains why he is such a good whist player. It's more about skill than money to him."

This did not make her feel more relaxed.

"Would you like me to escort you to the card room? Play will not start for a while. You can see how it is set up, choose the best table, and take a few minutes to imagine play. That will ease your nerves."

This was advice from a man who had made a living at the

tables for the years before his marriage. It was good advice, or would be if it were her skill at the game that was making her uncomfortable.

"No, no, you do not need to escort me, but I will take your advice."

"Do you need money for play, Mariel?"

He asked the question with a beneficent smile. It was very generous of him. "No, no. I came prepared." She was twisting her reticule, and he reached out and stayed its spinning.

"Stop looking so nervous." He raised his quizzing glass. "Or better yet, stay nervous. Let them think you are over your head in this. Will they be surprised."

Morgan waved her off as she began to thread her way through the crowd. She paused and greeted several other guests but moved purposefully toward the stairs, bits of conversation coming to her.

From one group: "Did you hear that the Queen may host a drawing room this Season? It will be the first for ladies in an age."

"Since the King's birthday two years ago."

And from another group: "The Harbisons rented this house for *four* years."

"Until the three girls all had their come-outs."

"What will we do without them? They are as much a part of London as the fog."

Mariel could have told them that Mrs. Harbison was going to sponsor a niece next Season. But she kept the thought to herself as she considered what Morgan had said. In some ways it *was* like Cashton, she realized.

The card room was on the first floor of the tall, double-fronted town house. She stood at the bottom of the stairs, fingering her reticule and the paper inside, telling herself she could still refuse the summons.

"Are you coward or brazen?"

The words came from behind her, and she looked back with a sharp turn of her head to see who was talking to her.

Two young women stood in the hall a few feet away, one friend quieting the other as they laughed at some little plot. They were not talking to her, but they could have been.

*Coward or brazen?* Not that playing cards with Hadley would label her as such in any eyes but her own. *Stop being so missish,* she lectured herself. You are hardly choosing a life of debauchery by playing a few hands of whist. She hurried up the stairs.

She would think of it as entertainment for Grandmère. Details from the card room would be a change from the bits about the Queen's drawing room and the staggering crowd here tonight.

She was at the top of the steps when yet another conversation reached her.

"Oh, come, there is no reason for you to deny it. Jeremy's gout was dreadful until you came to call. Of a sudden it has subsided enough for him to accompany me tonight."

The voice came from inside the card room, which was the first doorway down the hall from the top of the stairs. Mariel walked closer, disappointed that some of the players were already present.

"I am not a physician. Not even a surgeon."

She recognized Hadley's voice immediately but not the woman's.

"No, you are definitely not a surgeon."

The woman's breathy voice was Mariel's first sign that this was not some casual party conversation but the beginnings of a seduction. Even as she realized this, she came within sight of them. She was still in the hall, and they were a foot or so inside the card room. The woman's back blocked Mariel from more than a glimpse of Hadley's shoulders.

"No, you are not a medical man. What you are is lucky."

The woman moved closer to him. Mariel was sure that her bosom was pressed against his chest.

"Hadley, I would not mind at all if you rubbed some of that luck on me."

He tried to step back then and turned his head, obviously looking for escape. In that gesture of a desperate man, Mariel's hideous embarrassment turned to relief, even mischief. Oh, she had been in London too long if she found amusement in his discomfiture, if shock was so easily dismissed.

When he saw her, she merely raised her eyebrows and allowed a half-smile to show.

He cleared his throat and put his hands on the woman's shoulders, but only to turn her to face Mariel.

"Aha, here is my partner for whist. If his gout is so much improved, I am sure your husband would love to escort you into supper."

The woman looked over her shoulder and blew a kiss at Hadley, turned, and gave Mariel a much more malevolent look as she slowly made her way to the stairs. Mariel was almost sure she whispered "He's mine next" as she moved past her.

Mariel could not help but notice the woman's gown, cut so low that her areolas made pink half-circles at the lace edging of her décolletage. She felt positively modest in the rose gown she had finally decided to wear. She did not recognize the woman but knew without doubt that Christiana would describe her with one word: slut.

Hadley came to her then, took her hand, kissed it, and gave her an almost royal bow. "Thank you, madam, for the rescue."

"She was hardly stronger than you, sir. You could have easily discouraged her."

"I did not say I was not enjoying the attention, but it was moving far too fast. I have other plans for this evening."

Her nerves came back so quickly, they could not have gone far. With them came irritation. "Do you mean that as a joke? Or are you putting me in the same class as that woman?"

"No, no, never!" He took her hand as if she would run away unless he restrained her. "I misspoke. It is only that I was mortified to be in need of assistance and trying to sound nonchalant. Should it not be the man who rescues the lady?"

He did look embarrassed, and she took pity.

"I warn you, Mr. Hadley, it is impossible for me to tell the difference between your cynicism and your idea of humor."

"I meant to tease you, not insult you. A woman like that is very difficult. Men, or at least this man, like the idea that he is the one pursuing."

He did not pull her close, he did not even press her hand any more firmly, but the expression in his eyes touched her as surely as a kiss.

"And are you pursuing me?" When she heard her own words, she wanted to sink through the floor. They might have worked if she had sounded arch, but she knew there was nothing coy at all about the straightforward question.

"As you wish, Mrs. Whitlow."

He was smiling, the smile its own invitation, and she knew she would never be able to match his way with words. She pulled her hand from his, well aware of how often she had to do that.

"What I want is a card partner. Nothing more." She waited a moment, then spoke the two words with clear emphasis: "Nothing more, Mr. Hadley."

He was still smiling. Had he even heard what she said?

"Listen to me, and listen carefully. I have no desire to be pursued, seduced, or made love to." She drew a breath and would have spoken on, but Hadley raised his hand.

"Any more and I will insist that you are protesting too much. Indeed, I do believe you already have."

"How can I convince you?"

"I will be convinced when you have convinced yourself."

He turned from her and walked into the card room.

So he thought she was willing, but afraid. She stood where she was, frozen by the realization that he might be right.

"Come choose a table, Mrs. Whitlow."

She came into the room and walked past him. There were five tables, each with four chairs, the cards in place, and a table set up for refreshment. Except for them, the room was empty. She surveyed the arrangements and spoke without turning to look at him.

"Mr. Hadley, I came tonight because I received your note."

"What note?"

She whirled back, shocked at her mistake, and he laughed.

"Oh, I love the way you do that. That gorgeous red silk swirls in such a way that you look like a smoldering fire bursting into flame."

"You did send that note, did you not?"

"Of course I did."

"Would you stop teasing me!"

"Never." He was in front of her. Very close. So close that his one word was a whisper. He leaned even closer. "I sent the note." She was pressed against the back of the chair behind her. "For I will not leave everything to chance."

He smelled of sandalwood and freshly ironed linen. His eyes had the smallest of lines at their corners. In time they would age him; now they only emphasized his genuine interest in her. She closed her eyes.

"Hadley, you must turn the chair around to help her sit in it."

They moved apart, Mariel more quickly than Hadley. The speaker was their hostess herself.

"Letty Harbison, everyone knows that you are the reigning etiquette expert. I bow to your knowledge." He did just that and looked up from the sketchy bow. "And your blind eye?"

She smiled benignly. "Of course. I am only happy to see my dear Mariel enjoying herself."

From anyone else it would have sounded like the beginning of the next *on-dit,* but Mariel knew Letty Harbison for the soul of kindness and discretion. Letty insisted one could not have three daughters and two nieces close by and be anything less than aware of mankind's inclination to impulsive stupidity.

Hadley bowed again. "Thank you."

Letty nodded a casual dismissal. "We will start play as

soon as a fourth arrives. I do believe Harbison is trying to coax your brother to make up a table."

Mariel relaxed, grateful for the change of subject. "He will not. Whist is too tame a game for him."

"Harbison must find that out for himself." Her vague annoyance indicated it was a lesson he had to learn frequently. Letty Harbison sat in the chair Edward held for her and then settled Mariel before finding his own seat opposite her.

"Mariel, how is it that I have not seen you in Hyde Park these afternoons?"

"I usually spend a few hours with Anna before her dinner and bed."

"Your governess came with you from Kent, did she not?" Letty asked.

"Yes," Mariel answered. She should have known that motherhood would be an inadequate excuse to anyone so involved in the Season.

Letty turned to look at Hadley. She did not have to say a word to encourage the invitation.

"May I ask for your company, Mrs. Whitlow? Tomorrow, at five o'clock. I shall bring my curricle, or would you prefer something more tame?"

Letty turned to Mariel, and Mariel responded as though she were the same sort of puppet that Hadley appeared to be. "That would be lovely. And the curricle would be fun, would it not?"

The private catch-word made the invitation their own despite the heavy hand of Letty Harbison's matchmaking.

Pleased with herself, Mrs. Harbison picked up the cards and shuffled. "Have you played with Mariel before, Hadley? "No."

Letty smiled. "I promise you will have your hands full. Ah, here is Mr. Harbison. Let's begin, shall we?"

# Ten

The group of players left the room with much back-slapping among the gentlemen, laughter among the ladies, and urging to "find the supper room." A servant did step into the room to see if it was empty, but the table of players nearest the door was intent on their game, clearly in a close contest. Mariel and Hadley were left alone at their table.

"That last hand was incredible." Her smile became a very unladylike grin and then dissolved into a jubilant laugh. "It required all my concentration. I could see the win was there, but, oh, it was a challenge to discover the key." She pressed her lips together and made an effort to control her elation. "It was the most fun I have had in an age."

Hadley was sitting back in his chair, playing with a few of the cards now scattered across the tabletop. He was smiling too.

"So, I see before me a woman of secrets." He dropped the cards and gave her his full attention. "Where did you learn to play whist?"

The awe in his voice was quite flattering.

"My father taught me."

"While you were still in the cradle? You play better than most men who make a career of it."

"I learned to play when I was twelve, when my mother was sick and my father wanted to stay home with her." She drew a deep breath. "While she was so ill he was not inclined to entertain or be entertained, and he was bored. Wanting distraction, he decided to teach the oldest of us to play, Morgan, our sister Maddie, and me."

"And you have been playing ever since?" It was a rhetorical question. "I imagine you actually supported the vicar and built a home for orphans and a shelter for indigent widows with the proceeds."

"No." The word came on another laugh. "We did play with the Harbisons at least once a fortnight, but Charles would never play for money."

"A shame, that." He pushed the cards to the center of the table. "Well done, partner. Saving that trump for the last round." He shook his head. "What a coup! Did we win every hand?"

"Every one that counted." She raised her hand to her mouth to hold back another giggle.

"Which only served to make Harbison bet more."

"Until Letty kicked him."

"Is that why he winced?" Hadley's laughter was silent but lit his whole face.

"Oh, yes, I have seen her do it before. He will never admit defeat until she forces him to it."

"Aha, the sign of good marriage. She tolerates his excesses and he allows her managing ways."

Mariel was not at all sure that was how she would define a good marriage but was not to be drawn into that discussion. Not tonight, at any rate. "I do feel rather bad that Mr. Harbison was our opponent. He is our host after all."

"He should not have kept raising the stakes, hoping our luck would fade."

"Mr. Hadley! It was skill, not luck."

"You speak as if the word 'luck' is an insult. If he has played with you before, then he should have known better than to tempt fate."

That was true. Perhaps Mr. Harbison had thought Charles was the master, when in truth it had been she who had carried him. "In all honesty, I played better than I ever have before, especially when you consider it has been more than two years since I held cards."

"Because of your partner, no doubt."

She laughed again, so relieved that the evening had gone well, she thought her laughter might become hysterical.

"Would you care to guess how much we won?"

She raised her shoulders, uncertain, and guessed. "A few guineas?"

"Closer to two hundred."

She gasped and he nodded. "You said yourself that Harbison kept raising the stakes."

"But that is shocking and wholly inappropriate for this kind of evening." She could see he was not convinced. "It was a game among friends."

"A friend who likes to play high and loses with good grace. Leave it, my dear, and enjoy the winnings."

"Very well, but only because it would offend Mr. Harbison's sense of honor if I refused." That presented a whole new set of problems. "That much money is a responsibility, is it not?"

"Not necessarily, Mariel. You could buy some more gowns or a new piece of jewelry."

She raised a hand to touch the necklace she wore. "These diamonds are my grandmother's. I have no desire for such expensive pieces myself. Not when there is so much need."

"Very noble."

He bowed his head in acknowledgment of her sentiment, but the glint in his eye made his tease clear.

She flipped a card at him. "Not noble at all. When I see so much need around me, I feel more guilt than generosity of spirit."

"Why should you feel guilt when no one else in the ton even notices?"

"I wonder that myself. But I do know that for all my moralizing, I have yet to act on the need."

"Then this windfall can be the beginning."

At that moment a footman came into the room bearing a leather bag and a tray holding two glasses of champagne. He bowed slightly. "From Mr. and Mrs. Harbison." He set it all down between them and left.

Mariel eyed the pale gold liquid. "She thinks all the world should be in twos, does she not."

"God bless her." Hadley took a glass and gestured for Mariel to do the same. "Her timing is perfect." He raised his glass. "To a more generous spirit."

She took a sip and he went on.

"And to closer alliances."

She sipped again and set the glass down. She did not need the bubbles to make her feel heady. She eyed the leather pouch, still convinced the winnings were more of a headache than a boon. "What *shall* we do with the money?"

Hadley opened the bag, shook out some coins, counted out five, and dropped them onto the tray that had held the glasses.

"But how do you know who will take them?"

He shrugged.

"You mean you would let anyone claim it?"

"Why not?"

"Because we will not know who receives it and how it is spent."

One by one Hadley took the coins from the tray. "You mean that either one of us could waste it on some useless frippery, but a footman should not have the same choice?"

*Of course not,* she thought, but did not say the words out loud.

He nodded. "Even you know how foolish your words would sound."

"Yes. I am sitting here thinking. Of course he should not be allowed to choose. He might not choose what I would." She picked up a coin and examined it for a moment, as though she had never really looked at it before. "How presumptuous of me."

"And a footman is a man to whom you entrust your personal

safety, your hard-bought hats and books. Even your daughter's well-being."

Mariel thought of Jonas and Ezra and wondered if Mrs. Harbison's footmen were as reliable. She took the coins and put them on the tray.

"Thank you, Mariel." He inclined his head

"No, sir. It is I who should thank you for the insight. I had never thought of it in that way before."

Her smile was thoughtful and he was reminded of their first meeting. It was the smile, he thought. The sweet acknowledgment that they understood each other: that time and this. He could grow quite addicted to that smile.

He reached over, took the coin she was toying with, and used it as the first in the small stack of five he began.

"Would you please put all that money away." She looked over her shoulder as though she expected some maven of the proprieties to swoop down on them.

"There are still almost two hundred guineas left." He began to place them, as quietly as he could, back into the leather pouch. "And as strongly as I believe that our generosity usually comes with too many strings attached, I am more than willing to bow to your much wider experience of the truly needy."

She folded her hands in front of her, and looked too much like a vicar's wife. This despite the wine-red dress that was anything but demure.

He leaned across the table, upsetting two of the stacks of coins he had not yet stuffed back into the bag. "Let us make this our next alliance. We shall devise a plan between us. One that we both approve of. It will certainly entertain us, not bore us, no matter how long it takes to decide. Giving a bequest of any kind always makes me feel better. And if we can find a cause that will hurt no one, then we have met your criteria for having fun, have we not?"

"Yes." Her expression was pained. "Do I always sound that pedantic?"

He looked up from his renewed counting. "Never. Do I?"

She shook her head with some energy. "It is only that I am not at all used to intelligent conversations at these gatherings."

"Then we are fortunate to have found each other, since I feel the same and by the end of the Season wish mightily for something more than the latest *on-dit.*"

"But you seem so at ease in any situation, so in command: at the balloon ascension, even that day in the cemetery."

"Practice. As many years among the ton as you spent in Kent." *And not always in command.* If she did not recall that stupid incident with Jeremy's wife not three hours earlier, then he was hardly going to remind her. "By the end of the Season I am desperate for a few weeks fishing in Scotland or some time staring at the Channel, someplace totally out of fashion. By the end of the Season, silence is preferable to pointless banter."

Where had that admission come from? he wondered. That sweet smile of understanding must have already bewitched him if it was drawing such confessions from him.

He raised the bag and let it fall to the table, knowing that the chink and clunk of the coins would upset her. She reached over, and when he would have taken her hand, she pulled it away.

"How shall we decide what to do with all this money?"

He smiled at her attempt to sound practical. "We could split it between us and each give our share away. Then, like the parable from Mark, the one where the master gives out the talents to his servants, we could compare who uses the money for what end."

Mariel wrinkled her nose. "I cannot help but think that this much money could truly make a difference to someone's life. Someone like the cello player we heard in Dover."

*Good God, if she only knew how true that was.* "Does he need money?"

"Not anymore, at least I think not. But at one time he was able to continue his music only because of the generosity of a patron. One who was nameless, or at least that is what Signor Ponto insisted."

"By gad." He slapped the table with his hand. "Someone has stolen our idea!"

"Or we are about to steal his."

"Yes, let's make it our own, shall we?"

Her face was alight with excitement. She really did think giving away near two hundred guineas would be fun. Who would ever have thought he would find someone so inclined? "We are agreed that we will find deserving people with whom we can share this small fortune. That we will do it secretly and it will be our adventure alone."

She nodded. "But, Mr. Hadley, how can we give it to them without them knowing who we are?"

Always a tricky problem. "I can hire someone to deliver the funds."

She looked so crestfallen that she did not have to say a word for him to know this approach was unacceptable.

"You think we should deliver it in person?" he asked.

"Yes!" She gripped the edge of the table and spoke with some urgency. "Is not half the fun seeing their faces when they realize their good fortune?"

"All right." He drank some more of the champagne and blamed it for his next harebrained idea. "We will do it in disguise."

"In disguise?" She looked doubtful but did not reject the idea.

"Yes. I will dress up as a lady in mourning, become known as the Angel in Black." He waited, wondering if she would respond as he hoped.

"Oh, dear, that will never work. You could no more pass for a lady than I could dress in your clothes and pass as her manservant."

"Done." Oh, that was much too easy. "We will do it together, each dressed as our opposite."

He came over to where she sat and held out his hand. She

stood up and he took it in a handshake. Then Hadley leaned forward and pressed his lips to hers. Not a kiss so much as a sealing of their secret. Even in that briefest of touches he felt her heart skip and his own match it.

When he let her go, she glanced over her shoulder at the players lost in their own world. "What do you think you are doing?" She spoke with more shock than anger.

"If you have to ask, then I did not do it very well."

She shook her head and tossed back a comment. He took her arm and they moved quietly past the table where the gamers were still at their own version of the contest. As they proceeded down the stairs, he did not give her a moment to rethink her rash commitment or take offense at his chaste kiss. "When I call tomorrow at five o'clock, we can begin our discussion of who is to benefit from our good fortune."

The crowd had thinned considerably, and Morgan found them almost immediately. "It must have been a successful evening. You were gone for hours."

"Really? Well, you do know how much I enjoy cards, Morgan. And Mr. Hadley is an excellent partner."

Hadley was relieved that Mariel did not elaborate any further.

They were spared more questioning when Christiana came up to take her husband's arm. "Please, Morgan, will you ask for our carriage to join the queue? It has been a wonderful ball, but only to you will I admit that I am beyond fatigue."

With a good-night to Hadley, Morgan left to find the porter and with a word Christiana made a tactful exit to "collect their wraps."

Mariel turned to him. "I am having second thoughts, sir. This idea of dressing up is foolish. What was I thinking? It is asking for discovery. Your first idea is the best one. We will have someone deliver the money and forgo the pleasure of seeing their reaction."

"Coward."

"I am not. My talents at masquerade and acting are not well honed. They are nonexistent, as a matter of fact."

"How can you say that? You did very well with Morgan a moment ago when he asked how we did."

"That was discretion, not acting. Dressing as for a masquerade would be anything but discreet."

"Very well." He hurried to find a compromise lest she attempt to cry off altogether. "I will allow that it is good sense and not cowardice that has you reneging. But I still plan to mask myself as the Angel in Black." He gave an extravagant sigh followed by a theatrical gesture of inspiration. "Aha, I have the perfect solution. I will go in disguise and you can appear as if by accident. Following me is something you already excel at."

# Eleven

Mariel dashed up the stairs, amazed that she could feel so awake at three in the morning. A fire still glowed in the music room, and several candles were lit, but other than that the room was empty. Of course no one would be there. The household would be awake in less than four hours and Anna soon after, but for now the house was hers alone.

The harp awaited her. She sat down and at first did no more than pull it close.

Alone and away from the intoxicating influence of his company, her mind was a riot of thought. Uncertainty rapidly overtook excitement.

She began playing the lullabies that she had learned early on and then entertained Anna with not so many years before. The notes came easily, familiar and comforting, leaving her mind free for thought.

He had offered a toast to "closer alliances." She had not pressed him then, it was their venture he had been talking about, a chance to act on a long-held wish. Of course she would drink to that.

But the kiss: that idiotic, almost not but impossible to deny kiss. With that, ambiguity had niggled its way into her complacency. The toast took on a new dimension, more personal, intimate, suggestive.

What did he want? What did she want? Were they laying the foundation for heartache? Adventure? A love affair?

Stilling her fingers, Mariel rested her forehead on the gilt-edged frame. She thought she had handled the kiss well enough. She did not overreact despite the fact that the lightest touch of his lips was enough to undo her. She was even able to flirt, if only a little. Why did that seem such a huge accomplishment?

Everyone else in her world lived in the moment, blissfully accepting whatever pleasure came their way. Why was it not true for her? Why did even the thought of an affair frighten her more than thrill her?

Mariel began playing again, a Mozart piece that required some concentration. But still the question plagued her, nudging up against her deliberation, until she stopped the piece with a discordant thrum on the strings.

She wanted the pleasure, the companionship, the sharing, the intimacy. She wanted all of it. But along with it came a host of other elements, not nearly as appealing. Secrecy, for one.

She would not advertise their affair. At the moment she could barely admit her own interest to herself. The need for secrecy would mean lying to those closest to her. Grandmère, Christiana, and even her daughter.

Those falsehoods would jeopardize the whole. She knew it would.

Integrity was as important to her as gossip was repugnant. Surely the compromise of that belief would lead to insecurity, misunderstanding, and finally abandonment.

Raising a hand to her throat, she rubbed at the tightness there. *You are being absurd,* she thought. *Ten minutes ago you were wondering if he wanted an affair and now it is already over.* She laughed a little at herself and her rigid morality. But the question persisted. Did the risk outweigh the prize?

Did anyone else wonder? Not that she had ever observed. The ton would make a joke of her scruples.

Hadley would laugh, more kindly than the beau monde, but with equal disbelief. She had heard enough of his exploits to know that he took each opportunity and embraced it for all it was worth. When did he give up a new interest? When the newness was gone? When a prettier face came along? When a bigger challenge presented itself?

She was new and a challenge.

No more than a handshake and the hint of a kiss and still she knew that spending time with him meant risking her heart. She knew a dozen women who would urge her to seize the moment and deal with the future when it was upon her. She had never once in her life done that and was not sure she could start now.

Mariel set the harp upright, took a moment to cover it, and went up to her bedroom. Her maid roused herself from her half- sleep to help her undress.

Did lovers lie together and talk of their day as husbands and wives did? Did they lie in bed and share more than their bodies?

If they were next to each other at this moment alone, could she tell Hadley that the prospect of giving money away was the first thing that had happened in two months that was wholly exciting? Would he hug her? Kiss her? Reassure her?

No, no. He would pretend offense that it was not he who excited her. He would say it with a laugh, not the booming laugh he was so known for, but the quiet, intimate one that she had heard for the first time that night.

She would insist that he did excite her, only with that excitement came a range of emotions that made pleasure suspect.

Then she was sure he would come to her, look into her eyes as though he could read her mind. He had done that more than once already. He would pull her to him and show her how to build a world in which there was nothing but the moment and him.


Hadley stood a few steps inside the door of the Quarter Moon. The room was smoke-filled and littered with glasses and half-eaten meals. He could see that there was only one table of players remaining in the marathon game. They had attracted quite a crowd. The table was surrounded three deep by observers, watching with whispered comments and a nudge here and there.

Edward turned to the man closest to him. "How many left?"

He was a complete stranger, but he answered with all the camaraderie Edward could have wished. "Started with twenty. Down to two. Clever idea to call a marathon. Lots of watchers who all drink. They ain't worried about anything but who they're betting on."

"Who are the two?" Hadley realized that he was the most sober person in the room, except perhaps for the two players, and fatigue must certainly have rendered them near senseless.

"Two left. Chartwell and Lockwood."

"Lockwood? Lockwood made it to the end?" With every intent of cheering his friend on, Edward began to weave his way through the crowd. Finally he was close enough to see the players. Indeed, there was Lockwood, looking hollow-eyed but determined.

His opponent, Chartwell, was a navy captain who had made quite a reputation for himself in the card rooms of various clubs and dives these last three years. He looked tired but far more alert than Lockwood. Hadley could imagine that life at sea had trained him to long days and sleepless nights.

Edward edged closer.

It was uninspired play for paltry sums, but that hardly mattered. This game was about endurance. Neither player wanted the other to lose because they were short on funds.

Several of the observers made room for him, and soon he was standing behind Lockwood. A murmur ran through the crowd, and both players paused a moment to look around. Lockwood let out a whoop of triumph when he saw Hadley nearby.

"I have luck on my side, Chartwell. There can be no doubt who will win."

Chartwell did no more than raise his chin in acknowledgment of the challenge.

Edward folded his arms across his chest and observed the play. Not the cards, but the players themselves. He knew Lockwood well enough to recognize fatigue in the way his body was turned in on itself, his shoulders hunched, and his knees drawn together. He would not be good for much longer. Chartwell was more difficult to read. Even as he had the thought, Lockwood's opponent raised a hand to his head and rubbed his forehead with his fingers.

In that one gesture Hadley realized that Chartwell looked familiar. He studied the man's sun-darkened skin, blond hair, and dark gray eyes. He stared so hard that Chartwell looked away from his cards and directly at him.

The regard could last only a moment, but Hadley could not mistake the challenge. A promise of retribution. Why? For taking his friend's side? Surely he did not believe that nonsense about luck. Hadley was distracted from his consideration by the chair that someone pushed his way, urging the crowd aside as the bearer scraped it along the floor.

Hadley swore silently. Since he had thrown his support to Lockwood, he could not leave until this was over. It was almost daylight. Surely they could not last another twelve hours? The way Lockwood looked, he would not last another twelve minutes. Then someone set a pot of coffee at Lockwood's elbow.

Damnation. With coffee for fuel, Lockwood could well go on into next week. He tried to visualize Mariel Whitlow's expression if she found out why he was unavoidably detained.

If she was disappointed, it would be in the delay of the plans for their shared charity. She cared nothing for the parade of clothes and carriages, the bits of gossip, the chance to see who declared themselves couples, friends, if not potential lovers. For Mariel Whitlow their ride through Hyde Park served a purpose the ton would never guess. He had never met anyone less interested in the London social whirl.

His reasons for the five o'clock meeting were far more conventional. If the kiss had not given her a hint of what his hopes were, then he would, in time, be more direct.

He settled himself comfortably and closed his eyes. When someone protested, it was Lockwood who came to his defense.

"Rules are that *I* have to stay awake. Not anyone else."

When it came to cards, Edward decided that he had won the prize tonight. Not only could his partner play the game, but she was a feast for the eyes. The wine-red dress with the deep décolletage had set off her looks to perfection, and the diamonds had rested so invitingly on her bare skin that it was all he could do to pay attention to the cards dealt him.

In the end he had to be satisfied with the most meager of kisses, when he wanted nothing more than to taste every inch of her.

He felt his head nod at an odd angle and he opened his eyes, straightening a little, trying to shake off the fatigue. He watched Lockwood lose a hand he should have won and knew the end was not far off.

While Lockwood concentrated on shuffling the cards, Edward watched a young lad work his way through the crowd. Dressed in the scruffy clothes of a cabin boy—one could not say he wore a uniform—he resembled someone who had spent time in the navy.

The boy stopped at Chartwell's elbow and waited.

"What is it, Angus?"

"A message for you, sir." When Chartwell did not answer, the boy continued. "From the Admiralty."

"The first was enough, boy. You have no need to announce my business to everyone here."

The boy flushed scarlet.

Chartwell played the hand, won it, and took the note that young Angus had laid on the table.

Reading it was all for show, Hadley was sure. It was a summons, one that would end the game with Lockwood the victor.

And so it was. Five minutes later Chartwell's chair was empty and Lockwood was euphoric.

"I won! I won! And all because of you. Come, Hadley, help me celebrate!"

No sooner were the words spoken than Lockwood dropped like a stone to the floor.

Edward revived him with a sluice of water, and with some help from his inebriated friends, Edward managed to get Lockwood into his carriage and back to his rooms at the Falcon, all in less than an hour.

As Edward urged his friend up the stairs to his first-floor room, Chartwell himself came down, resplendent in a dress uniform. The gilt epaulet announced him a post captain, one who could command any situation. He moved briskly, as though he had enjoyed a full night's sleep.

Lockwood begged for a moment's rest as he stumbled up the stairs. Edward allowed the pause and looked at Chartwell as he came abreast of them on the stairs.

"Hadley." He nodded curtly. "Tell Lockwood that I expect a rematch." He did not wait for an answer but hurried on down.

*Arrogant bastard.* Even as he had the thought, Edward realized who Chartwell reminded him of.

He turned and called out, "Captain!"

At the door, Chartwell turned and stepped back to the stairs. He stood there but did not speak.

"Sir, do you know the Braedons of Sussex, the Marquis Straeford's family?"

Chartwell looked surprised, even shocked by the question. He narrowed his eyes and his expression hardened until Edward feared that he had insulted the man.

"My name is Chartwell." With that he turned on his heel and was out of the door before Edward could himself react.

Chartwell's answer was its own revelation, for Edward had not asked what his name was, merely if he knew the Braedons. With a grimace of embarrassment at his gaffe, Edward urged Lockwood up the last few steps.

If Chartwell was a baseborn relation, it was entirely possible that he did not wish to acknowledge the connection.

He might not wish it, but he had the look of a Braedon. The different surname did not keep him from showing the same arrogant conceit that was a hallmark of the marquis and his heir, Crandall. A trait obviously passed by blood and not upbringing.

Lockwood tripped on the top step, distracting Edward from his musings. His friend appeared ready to accept the floor as bed. Edward went off to rouse Lockwood's manservant and left him with the task of shifting him from floor to bed. Edward finally ordered his carriage home.

It was full daylight before he was in bed and more than ready for sleep. He urged his valet to draw the curtains tightly shut and to tell the housekeeper to keep the household quiet until he had at least six hours' rest.

It was one thing to command quiet. It was another to command sleep. He listened to the rain that had begun again as he had arrived at his door. Not the usual gentle drip so familiar in London, one that the windows and curtains would muffle, but a steady, driving downpour that would please the flowers but dampen the enthusiasm of the beau monde.

No one drove in Hyde Park in closed carriages. The whole point was to see and be seen. If the rain precluded their five o'clock rendezvous, there must be something else he and Mariel could do that would give them some time alone together.

He almost left the bed to riffle through the post he had brought up from the entry hall table. Certainly there was some invitation that would give them a few moments to talk. Then he decided to leave it until later in case the rain should stop.

He settled against the thin pillow he preferred and crossed his arms under his head.

She would certainly agree to almost anything reasonable, especially if he threatened to leave the money in some hackney for the next passenger to discover. Not a bad idea, he thought. He hoped he would remember it when he awoke.

If he teased her with that, she would believe him and toss back some withering criticism a moment before she realized the joke.

Mariel Whitlow needed teasing more than any other woman he had ever met. She had, apparently, spent a lifetime without it. Her reaction to it was all the proof he needed. The way she would take offense and take him to task. He loved it when the only thing soft about her was the sensuous fabrics she favored.

She was learning though. Her reaction to his kiss had been a surprise. At first she had responded with modest outrage. "What do you think you are doing?" That had been predictable.

His answer could have been no less than what she expected. "If you have to ask, then I did not do it very well."

But it was his turn to be surprised into silence when she had answered with "Then perhaps you should practice more."

"Oh, how I want to." He did not have the words then, but he breathed them aloud now.

With any luck at all, he would have his chance to "practice more." Finding a means to distribute the money they had won was a brilliant excuse to spend some time away from the unblinking eyes of the ton.

How long before she realized that choosing a beneficiary and arranging the anonymous delivery of the money would take some secrecy? That they would need time and a place where they would not be seen by the people they kept their secret from? Which, at the moment, appeared to be the entire world.

Playing at decorum was what the ton excelled at. The young girls looking for husbands were obliged to do more than play at it, but almost everyone was less constrained. Men, single or married, grand dames, widows, and most of the married women he knew were free to cheat at the game of propriety, with as much or as little discretion as they dared.

Mrs. Fitzherbert had insisted on marriage even though everyone knew that the Prince of Wales could not truly marry a Catholic. But she had insisted on the farce and the Prince had acquiesced. One had to guess whether it was lust or love that had driven him to such an absurdity.

Edward had always preferred to conduct his affairs as privately as possible and had found his lovers like-minded. Mariel would be so inclined as well, he was sure. What he was less certain about was whether she would even consider him as a lover.

It would make their life so much simpler. Look how complicated this scheme was. He had started by devising a way to spend innocent time together: playing cards. That had the happy result of winning money, lots of money. Grabbing hold of that heaven-sent opportunity, he had to form a plan to distribute the money. To do that he had to find a way to speak with her privately but in a way that would not harm her reputation.

If they were lovers, none of that would be necessary.

He settled for sleep, deciding that "imagination" would be his mantra. If she was beside him tonight, they could debate who should receive the money, how it should be delivered, and when. They could talk about it without interruption.

For as long as it held their interest.

For his part, that would be only as long as it took to distract her as much as her very presence distracted him. He could imagine her hair in a long sweep of dark curls, her eyes intensely aware of everything, her body pressed against his. At long last, he dropped off and into an erotic dream that had him smiling in his sleep.

# Twelve

". . . and be sure that Anna wears her oldest half-boots."
Mariel ended her list of preparations. Miss Weber nodded and
Mariel reminded them, "Try not to be too long, I should not
like to keep Mr. Hadley waiting. Especially since taking you
along with us was my idea."

"Yes, ma'am."

Mariel knew it was excitement that had her prattling on
like a ninny. With a self-conscious nod at Miss Weber she left
the room.

"Please, Miss Weber, not the shoes that hurt my feet," Anna
said.

Mariel started to turn around, but realized that she herself
would be late if she delayed her toilette any longer. She left
Miss Weber to see to the comfort of her daughter.

Christiana was in her room, studying the two dresses
spread on the bed.

Mariel was glad enough to see Christiana and told her so
in a harried rush. "But where is Wheatley?" she added. "I am
pressed for time as it is."

Glancing up from her careful consideration of the walking
dresses, Christiana explained the maid's absence. "I sent
Wheatley to tell Grandmère that you would stop in to see
her before you left. I will be your maid."

Mariel nodded, relieved to have someone to whom she
could vent her feelings. Wheatley was a Hale House servant
and Mariel was not inclined to confide in her as she might

have to Polly back at home. "You would think this is a wedding. It is nothing more than a simple family outing."

"What happened last night to make you so agitated this morning?" Christiana spoke with some amusement.

"Last night? Nothing happened."

It was a lie, but she was determined no one but she and Edward should know the true reason for today's outing. Besides, if one person knew of their charity, then everyone would, and that would be too self-serving to be true giving.

"Hadley did not object when you suggested taking Anna and Miss Weber?"

"His note was everything that was charming, as always."

She should not have smiled so when she said that because, of course, Christiana asked, "What did he say?"

Mariel busied herself with the gowns. "Only what one would expect." This was not the truth either. She glanced at the drawer of her dressing table, where the note lay cushioned by her handkerchiefs as though it deserved the comfort of a well-earned rest. She had read it at least thirty times.

> *I see you weaken already, my dear. Did you not insist that you would never send a note? It gives me hope for the future.*
>
> *Of course Anna and Miss Weber are welcome to join us since the rain has changed our plans. They will provide an excellent distraction while we discuss The Plan. I shall call for you all at four.*

When had she said that she would never write him a note? She thought back over their few meetings. *At the balloon ascension.* Oh, but her note today had not been suggestive. It had been direct and to the point, without a hint of romantic intrigue. She glanced again at her drawer. Not like his note. She could hear his teasing voice in the words. *It gives me hope for the future.*

"Mariel, if you keep staring off in such a thoughtful way, I will be convinced that the note was anything but conventional."

"Is Hadley ever conventional?" Mariel did not need an answer to that and turned her full attention to her toilette. "It would be wiser to wear the deep green, would it not? Rain spots will not show. Besides, I am beginning to think this pink much too young for me."

Christiana picked up the pink gown. "This is a wonderful color for you. And it is not a real pink at all. It is called 'new love' and is far more red than pink." She held it up to the window. "See how the color deepens in the light?"

" 'New love'? Definitely the green, then."

Even without Wheatley in the room, they made short work of dressing.

"Hadley invited you to the park at the ball last night?"

"Yes, only it was at Mrs. Harbison's suggestion. He could hardly not offer the invitation without appearing churlish."

Christiana patted her on the shoulder as she finished the last of the buttons. Mariel sat at her dressing table and watched Christiana from the mirror as she held the pink gown against her. She walked a few steps to the glass to see the effect.

"He is never churlish, Mariel, but Hadley can always find a way out if he does not want to do something. Do you know Mrs. MacDonald? She played at the musicale Grandmère gave during my Season? The one you performed at. She was Miss Perry then."

"Miss Perry? Yes, I do believe so. She was quite accomplished at the pianoforte."

Christiana turned from the mirror, tossed the gown on the bed, and came up behind her. "Your hair looks lovely, Mariel. Any more and it will be overdone."

Mariel put the brush down and turned toward her sister-in-law.

"Besides," Christiana continued, "it does not matter what your hair looks like. You are positively glowing. This outing must be about more than a visit to Leicester Square." Christiana shook her head. "Do not try to think of an explanation. I am not asking for one."

Mariel turned back to the mirror. She did look happy and excited, the blush on her cheeks entirely natural. "It's nothing really, Christiana, only something that Edward and I discussed yesterday."

It sounded vague, too vague. Why had she said anything when Christiana had specifically told her not to? She stood up. "What were you saying about Mr. Hadley and Miss Perry?"

Christiana leaned against the bedpost, accepting the change of subject without further comment. "This was years ago, you know."

She nodded. Did she expect her to be jealous?

"Well, here is the story. Miss Perry was quite determined to count Hadley on her list of beaus. A day or so before the concert we were together in a group and Miss Perry asked him if he was attending the musicale."

"And Hadley told her no?" He must have, for it had been her only visit to town in ten years and the guests had been a very select group. Surely she would have remembered if he was there.

"Hadley said he planned to decline the invitation. Then Miss Perry gave him that simper she thought so coy and asked if he would not come to hear her."

Even told secondhand, the direct question made Mariel grimace. "He did not give her too bruising a set-down, did he?"

"Only a small one, and veiled in compliment. He pretended to misunderstand. He told her that he could hear her much better in a room empty of a pianoforte and the people who would torture it."

"Oh, how could he! How is it that people do not take offense when he makes such outrageous statements?"

"I do believe it is because he says exactly what the rest are thinking and so wishing they had the nerve to say." Christiana went back to the long mirror and stood there a moment, checking her appearance. "He will be exactly on time. Do you want to keep him waiting?"

Mariel shrugged and picked up the long pelisse that matched her dress. She shook the wrinkles from it and began to examine the hat that went with the ensemble.

Christiana walked to the door. "Shall I collect Anna and Miss Weber and meet you in Grandmère's suite?"

"Oh, thank you. I do need only a few moments more. Then I will come and say good-bye and we shall not keep him waiting above ten minutes."

Christiana opened the door and then turned around again for one more comment before quitting the room. "Even though he was not at the musicale, he did send Miss Perry an extravagant bouquet afterward and made it quite plain that he was charmed by her, if not by her music."

Alone in her room, Mariel sat on the edge of her bed. The excitement faded. She stared at the small nosegay of spring flowers that had come with the second note and wondered if it was excitement or nerves that had her so full of life.

Excitement surely. Expectation. Impatience for the meeting.

There was no reason to be nervous. He was a gentleman and she was a lady and the two of them were doing no more than meeting to plan an enterprise that was right and good.

There was no reason to be uncertain. The flowers announced something less than passion, perhaps more than friendship, but certainly a willingness to proceed as she wished.

There was no reason to keep him waiting. It was a coquettish thing to do. Surely they were beyond that. Any man who was as thoughtful as he deserved honesty and as little affectation as the ton allowed.

She stood up, but before she went down to promise her grandmother that she would return with the latest *on-dits*, Mariel raised the bouquet and breathed in the fragrance of the sweet spring offering.

\* \* \*

"Miss Weber, the dowager duchess says that Mrs. Linwood's work won notice after she was introduced to the Queen sometime before 1790." Mariel looked down at her daughter. "Anna, that was long before you were born. She has been popular for quite a while."

She turned to Edward, who was pretending interest in whatever tidbit she fed him. "Patience" was his mantra today. Their plans had been upset and he would be patient until they found time alone together.

"And you, Mr. Hadley? You are bored."

Miss Weber and Anna turned to see if they could read the ennui that Mariel had guessed at.

"I most certainly am not. How could I be when I am in the company of three beautiful women?"

Anna shuffled her feet, Miss Weber smiled, and Mariel Whitlow took his arm. It was some consolation.

At her urging they moved to stand in front of Mrs. Linwood's needle-pointed "Woodsman in a Storm," which appeared very like some themes of the painter Gainsborough.

"Look closely." Mariel raised a hand to direct their gaze. "Is it not amazing how she can convey the feel of the woods and the storm with nothing more than colored thread. I was never able to master the most basic of stitches, and Mrs. Linwood went far beyond that to develop a stitch of her own."

Hadley stepped close and then moved back, asking her sotto voce, "See that glitter at his feet? Do you think it is coins someone has left for him?"

Mariel actually looked before she realized he was teasing her. "I do believe it is meant to be a puddle of water."

"Ahh, how disappointing." He stared at the picture and then directed her attention to the deep shadow at the edge of the work. "But do look closely, in the background. Are there not two people there. I do believe"—he narrowed his eyes and leaned closer to the work—"yes, I am convinced those are people, obviously in disguise."

"As trees?" she asked in a dry voice.

He took her arm and they followed Anna and Miss Weber, who had moved on to the next exhibit. "An unfortunate choice of costume, for are they not then compelled to stay in one place?"

Before Mariel could respond, Anna turned back to call to them to "hurry and look at this one."

Edward considered the artist's version of David with his sling and shook his head with some regret. "Anna, my dear, I must take you to the Royal Academy, then you will see real art."

Anna looked at him with some affront.

"Could it be my appreciation fails because I have never even attempted needlework? Perhaps I should."

The little girl giggled.

"What? You do not think I could do it?"

"You're a man. Men never sew."

"But of course they do. Some of the finest tailors are men. This very jacket was made by a man named Weston. And men sew leather all the time."

Anna was not completely convinced. She looked at her mother for confirmation. Mariel nodded. Anna regarded him again.

"No, Mr. Hadley. You like to make people laugh, but if you were to start sewing, they would laugh in a mean way."

Hadley looked at Mariel. "How does she know this?"

"From one of the lessons of Hannah More, I suspect."

Miss Weber nodded. "We read one yesterday about the difference between being amusing and being the object of amusement."

He nodded. How young they were taught the vagaries of the ton, though he suspected Hannah More thought it more of a Christian education. No matter, it would serve both.

The next illustration was at the end of a corridor lined with black velvet. When they reached it, he let the three of them move forward and examine the piece, an illustration of Lady Jane Grey in the tower.

Edward watched them study it. *Patience. Patience. Patience.*

He decided that his ladies were far more intriguing than Mrs. Linwood's art.

Anna was patently thrilled to be included in the outing and was doing her best to behave like her mama. She had imitated her mother's expressions in the carriage on the brief ride to Leicester Square and at this moment had her head bent at the same angle. The way she was biting her lip was all her own though.

Miss Weber was not as obviously pleased but seemed genuinely interested in the needle painting. How old was she? In her sixth decade surely. Should she not be resting in some cottage. Then he realized that life in Cashton with only one charge must count as rest to a woman who was more used to teaching a house full of children. Mariel's generosity at work, no doubt. As was the invitation today.

And then there was Mariel, the reason the rest of them were here at all. She might think that her role was to entertain them so that their odd little group was comfortable together, but the truth was that each member of this small following wanted only to see her smile.

He studied her as intently as she was studying the needlework in front of her.

She stood out, singular among the people around her. And the effect came from more than the light cast by the mass of candles at the end of the dark entryway.

It radiated from somewhere deep inside. She was a different woman from the one he had seen in the graveyard or even asked to dance at the Westbournes' ball. She was more than an observer of life. She was living it and it filled her with animation. He wanted to bask in that glow, have it fall fully on him. Patience triumphed heavily over the temptation to kiss her here and now.

She turned and he hoped his expression was not as unguarded as his thoughts.

"Oh, Mr. Hadley, you have been so patient. Shall we adjourn to the tearoom? If the tea and cake do not hold your interest, I am certain that we can discover any number of subjects that will entertain you."

Edward bowed in agreement, but he could see Miss Weber hesitate.

She turned to her employer. "Mrs. Whitlow? May I take Anna back to that cavern opening to study the sea view again? She was quite intrigued by it."

"Yes, of course, but do avoid the one of the bird starved to death in its cage. It is dreary enough today without adding that sort of melancholy."

The governess nodded and the two turned back to the main hallway. Mariel watched them work their way through the crowd. "I knew that both of them would enjoy this, but I am grateful for few a moments alone."

He laughed, largely at himself. Anyone else would have thought that the most obvious of flirtations. He knew it was not.

"Mr. Hadley, our small project—" She hesitated and then looked around as if the curious were everywhere, when in fact they were alone in the hall. "—Our small project is as close as I have come to a lifetime wish to do more good works. For years I have waited for the right moment."

He took her arm and they began to move slowly down the hall.

"How foolish of me. Did Mrs. Linwood wait for the right moment to pursue her calling? No, she did not. She overcame obstacles, criticism, and disinterest to create something that hundreds have enjoyed."

She stopped walking, let go of his arm, and turned to face him fully, as though about to confess a failing.

"Oh, I suppose I had no real opportunity before I married and then little support from Charles. But if I had been more strong-minded, I could have won him over."

"*More* strong-minded? Mariel," he said, laughing. "I doubt that is possible."

Whether it was his laugh or the growing number of people

in the entry hall, she suddenly dropped the subject. "It is only that this is a beginning for me, and I owe that to you."

She took his arm and they moved on.

Here he was, grateful for time alone with her, a few moments to watch her eyes and tease her into a smile, to feel the warmth of her hand on his arm.

She saw those same few moments as the chance to change her life for the good of others.

If he kept seeing her, who would convert whom?

"Say what you will, Mariel. I venture that Mrs. Linwood cannot play the harp a quarter as well as you do."

"Absurd flattery, sir. You have never heard me play the harp." She gave him a patronizing look: raised eyebrows and the tiniest of smiles.

That took the charm from his compliment, but it did give him an opening.

"Is that an invitation to a private recital?"

"I don't know." She considered him for a minute, then smiled. "Probably not."

Before he could respond with more than a grin, they were at the entrance of the tearoom, and what they saw stopped them short. Half the beau monde must have decided on this as the alternate entertainment on a rainy day. Who could know that patience would be such a sorely tested virtue?

"That puts paid to our hoped-for discussion." He glanced at her. "Do not look so disappointed, for everyone watching will name their own reason for it."

There was one table for four remaining, and Hadley claimed it. He sat down next to her rather than across, and then was made to stand twice to greet friends before he and Mariel could exchange a word.

After a brief greeting and an introduction to Mariel his friends continued out the door. Edward sat again even though he saw someone else trying to catch his attention.

"Since we obviously must delay our other discussion, let

us look about for some *on-dit* that will entertain your grandmother."

They both stood to share a word with Miss Harbison. After
his own brief hello, Edward scanned the room for some familiar faces since he really was not interested in "the darling
bonnet" she had found that morning.

He did not have to look far to find something more intriguing. This year's diamond and her mother were sitting at
a table with the Duke of Redmond, who was enthusiastically
describing something—balloons, no doubt. Miss Wiggins
was listening with wide-eyed interest, her restlessly tapping
foot her only sign of boredom.

Edward was drawn into the usual exchange of pleasantries,
when Willy Gates came up, obviously angling for an introduction to Miss Harbison. With bows and curtsies made and
the whole room watching this new duo, Edward let Mariel su-
pervise and scanned the rest of the tables.

Closer to the back door, at a table that he would have refused, he caught sight of his cousin and Gregori. They were
with his aunt, and he cringed. He should go over and say
hello, but he did not want to leave Mariel unaccompanied.

"Mrs. Whitlow. Hadley."

He turned to find Redmond bowing to them. Apparently
his party had left.

"Would you care to join us, your grace?" Mariel asked.

*Please do,* Edward thought sourly, *for we are not meant to
have even a moment alone.*

Redmond accepted the invitation, and no sooner had he sat
than a waiter was at his elbow. As soon as they placed their
orders, Edward accepted his fate, excused himself, and went
over to greet his aunt.

From that moment on he lost even the illusion of control
over the situation. Mariel never left her seat, but soon she and
Redmond were greeted by the Westbournes, and Redmond
invited them to sit. That left Hadley without a seat at his own

table, which would thoroughly confuse not only the waiters but also the gossip hunters of the day.

While Hadley listened to his aunt go on about her favorite of the needle paintings, he watched Redmond excuse himself and leave the room. The Westbournes looked confused, and Edward stayed where he was, coward enough to let Mariel construct an explanation.

"Tell me, my dear, how many times has Redmond left his card this last month?" The countess spoke with casual interest.

"Only twice." *Oh, curse her honesty.*

"Twice more than he has called on any other eligible lady."

"Oh, no, my lady, he was here with Miss Wiggins. Surely you saw her leave as you came in."

The countess shook her head.

"You know how eager he is to have an audience for his discussion of hot air balloons, and he seeks me out only because I am interested enough to listen."

"You are probably right about that, Mariel." The countess gave up with a laugh. "He is a widower with an heir and has a very comfortable relationship with Lady Godmersham."

"One wonders why he does not talk to Lady Godmersham about his balloons." *Please never let anyone speak of her as part of a "comfortable relationship."*

"I imagine because they have been together for three years and she is tired of it."

*Charles's work never bored me.* But she was learning, Mariel decided, for she did stop herself from speaking that thought out loud.

"Whom did you come with, if not his grace?"

"Mr. Hadley invited Anna and me. You know that he and Mr. Whitlow were at school together? Anna is always interested in his stories of her father." Oh, dear, that sounded like a contrived excuse to be together, even to her ears.

"I see Hadley talking to his cousin and her Italian count.

We will go over and say hello and leave the table for you and your party."

He must have seen the couple stand, because Edward was back at the table before Mariel had been alone for more than a minute, if you could consider yourself alone in a room so filled with interested eyes and ears.

"We will never be able to discuss our plans here. It's worse than Hyde Park. At least there we would have had the privacy of your carriage."

He nodded and then turned to see Miss Weber and Anna standing at the door. As he rose to collect them, Mariel looked up at him. "Perhaps a private concert is the answer."

# Thirteen

"It was a challenge, I tell you." Edward began his explanation the moment Spreen had closed the door. "I spent a few minutes at the rout, an hour at the ball, stopped in at the theater and made sure my laugh was heard throughout the farce, and then had my coachman drop me at the end of the block.

"I did you the unheard-of favor of walking, in the shadows, risking life and limb and possible discovery. And I arrive here well before midnight." Mariel rose from the chair and came closer. Her smile grew with each new element of his tale. With his finale, "Everyone has seen me and no one knows where I am," she laughed.

The sound made every bit of the effort worthwhile. She moved toward him.

Self-lecture had occupied him as he made his way through the ton to this rendezvous. "Temptation" was his new byword. He would tease her and tempt her until she begged for his embrace. It would call for rarely used restraint, but Mariel Whitlow was worth the effort. A woman untouched by the ton's practiced schemes, she was a treasure. A woman with a mind and a heart that she had only begun to share with him. In the end their liaison would be as fine as a brandy that had aged for twenty years.

He hoped he did not have to wait that long.

As she came closer, he dared to hope that he would not have to wait at all.

"You definitely deserve a reward for all those machinations." She touched his arm and moved past him, to the nearest table, filled with glasses and a decanter. Looking over her shoulder, her expression changed from inquiry to amusement. "You were hoping for something more than brandy?"

"I most certainly was." She had learned how to tease quickly enough. He ignored the disappointment and decided her agile mind gave him hope instead. "That walk took me past four houses. I did count each one. "Being on foot was the difference between discovery and discretion."

"Virtue, sir. Virtue is its own reward."

"I was hoping for the harp, at least."

They were in a true library this time, not the small book-lined room they had met in once before. The darkness of the shelves and their cache of leather-bound books was alleviated by pale green walls that reflected the light of a dozen candles set in sconces. There was not an instrument in sight.

"Oh, dear, but I thought that was only a means to the end."

*Yes, darling it is,* he thought. Though he was sure the two of them would define "the end" in an entirely different way. He wanted to take her in his arms and give her his answer with a kiss.

He came to her and took her hand. Looking deeply into her eyes, he did no more than raise her hand to his lips. "I should very much like to hear you play."

"All right," she answered slowly, her eyes still enthralled by his. She blinked and looked away and then added, "You told me that your mother played the harp."

"Indeed, she did," he said, delighted at the effort it took her to pursue the mundane. "But that is not why I wish to hear you. It merely explains how it is that I can be so unmusical and yet treasure the sound of Mozart on a Naderman harp."

She did not ask him why he wished to hear her play, and a chance for something more intimate slipped by.

"You look like nothing less than the belle of the ton tonight."

Her blue dress was familiar, but the turquoise parure changed the look of the fabric from blue to aqua and made her skin glow. The Spanish shawl gave her the illusion of mystery and drama. And his patience was fueled by the thought that it was all for him.

"I wanted Grandmere to think that I was going to the Kerseys' ball."

*Oh, not for him after all.*

"The way we have schemed tonight"—Mariel shook her head—"one would think this is a clandestine meeting."

"Mariel, this *is* a clandestine meeting." He took the glass she handed him and raised it in a salute before taking a sip.

Her brief confusion gave way to understanding. "Oh, yes, perhaps so, but not for the reason that the ton would assume if they found out."

"It could be."

She merely shook her head, but she was smiling.

There was a table in the center of the room lit with candles. Mariel moved toward it. The light cast her in shadow, and he watched her move. He played with the adjectives that came to mind with unrepentant indulgence. Graceful, elegant, supple, sensuous. When she turned yet again to look at him over her shoulder, he had to add tempting, alluring, seductive.

Mariel gestured him to the chair across from her at the oblong table. "Shall we start?"

Edward eyed the too-businesslike arrangement and the paper and pens on the table. "You do not really intend to write anything down, do you?"

"You think it unwise?"

"Most definitely. Besides, we should be able to hold our plans in our heads." He tapped his brow with two fingers. "Hmm, yes, I think there is room up there."

She turned away from the table. "It is only that I am so used to writing everything down. Charles insisted that it helped to avoid confusion."

"I thrive on confusion." He pursed his lips and added, "And I am not Charles."

She looked at him for such a long, silent while that he felt compelled to ask, "Do you wish I were Charles, Mariel? Do you wish he were here instead of me." He had come closer and whispered the words, mortally afraid of her answer.

"What a horrible question, Edward." She turned from him. "Of course I wish he had not died. That we could have watched Anna grow and spend a lifetime together. But that was not God's will. And now I know that if my life had gone on like that, I would never have met you. Or at least never known you as I do."

She moved closer to him. "Loving Charles made me a different, I hope better, person, but I cannot wish to never grow more. Already I am a different person for knowing you."

"Better?" Why did he persist in asking these questions?

"Yes." She looked over her shoulder, and her expression was all he could have wished—soft, even loving, as though she thought his questions came from a lack of confidence rather than wanting. "Yes, Edward. I am a much better person for our friendship. Thank you."

" 'Friendship' is not the word I would have you use." She made it sound so virtuous. And his thoughts were anything but.

"Fascinated?" She was the one who stepped closer and reached out to touch his arm. "Intrigued? Interested?"

"Much more promising." He murmured the words before he pulled her into his arms and his lips touched hers. *Temptation. Temptation. Temptation.* He repeated the mantra and let it rule this kiss, this first kiss. He traced her inner lip with the tip of his tongue and did not press for more. He wanted everything she could give but would not ask for it all yet.

He let himself be satisfied by the way her lips clung to his as he ended the embrace.

"More than friendship." She smiled a little shyly. "Much more."

He was sure, almost positive, that Charles would no longer come between them.

He bowed her to her seat and then sat next to her rather than in the chair opposite. He raised the shawl that had slipped and settled it on her shoulders again, letting his bare hands rest a moment on her satiny skin.

"Have you devised some plans on how to use the money?"

She sounded so businesslike that he wondered at her control. He reached over and pulled on one of the curls that had slipped its pin. When she reached up a hand to secure it, he stayed her. "Leave it. It's much, um, friendlier, like that."

She bent her head and looked reproving. "If you keep on like this, we will never devise a plan."

"Oh, dear," He used one of her favorite phrases and feigned distress. "Then we would have to meet again." He paused.

"I have no doubt that we can contrive that whether we have a plan or not."

"I will take that as a promise." Before she could rescind the idea, he answered her earlier question. "I have several ideas but should like to hear yours first."

"One from me, then one from you." She folded her hands in her lap, all business, and totally unaware of how that one stray curl made a lie of her propriety. "You first, Mr. Hadley."

"Give the money to Mrs. Malburrey so she can finally buy a new hat. The one she is wearing is at least five years old."

"Are you serious?"

"Only a little. And your first idea?"

"Give the money to the Archbishop of Canterbury for the enrichment of the church."

"Are you serious?"

"As serious as you are." She grinned at him.

"I think we should put it in a hackney and see what the person who finds it does with it."

To his surprise, she considered this. "How would you find out who took the money or what they did with it? Would you take the driver into our confidence and have him report back?"

"No, pay the driver to take an hour off and become the

drivers ourselves. You said before that half the fun is seeing the reaction of the people who receive the gift."

There was some internal debate before she went on. "Find a needy widow with children and hope that the money will give her security and comfort."

She was not smiling.

"This is more than a game to you, is it not?"

"Much more." She nodded as she spoke.

"Helping a widow is a very good idea, and I can understand why it would appeal to you. It does not have to be only the money we have won, you know. I could contribute enough to make her secure for life."

Mariel relaxed her hands and reached over to touch his wrist. "I know you would. How much do you think it would take?"

They talked about it for a few moments without resolution.

"It is impossible to know without talking to the woman herself."

"And equally impossible to know if she will be careful with the money or be a spendthrift."

"But we established when we left the five guineas at the Harbisons that we do not control the use of the money, only the giving."

"Very well." Edward sat back. "We will find someone and trust that the money we have will be all that is needed to make a difference in her life."

"It will certainly do that, but how do we find her?"

"My man of business. Tomorrow or as soon as we can manage, I will take you to meet him. You can tell your grandmother that you are considering switching your affairs to someone new and I am taking you to meet Mr. Matthew. He is above reproach and will be the perfect place to start our search."

"Your man of business will know someone widowed and in need?"

"He is a man after your own heart, Mariel. He takes his

clients from all walks and demands only payment that they can afford." It was not quite the truth, but the small lie would protect his own interests awhile longer.

They sat in silence. He was not ready to leave. Not yet.

"Would you like to come to the music room?"

He stood up in answer and offered her his arm, as thoroughly tempted as he wanted her to be.

The music room was three doors down from the library and had not been readied for their use, though a small fire kept the room warm. She really had meant her invitation as nothing more than an excuse to discuss their charity.

Mariel moved around the room, lighting the candles nearest the harp and on the pianoforte. "I have had Spreen keep a fire in here even when the room is not in use. It is far better for the instruments to be kept at a constant temperature rather than suffer extremes."

She gestured him to a seat that was in her line of sight and then settled in the elegant little chair near the harp. With a nod and a very personal smile she began the first strains of a piece that seemed simple. He listened.

Playful. That was it. That was how he would describe the music, and her expression. She finished the last of the tripping notes and did not wait for his reaction but began another piece.

The first notes transported him instantly to his childhood. He could see the music room at Hadley Hall, light pouring in through the long arched window, creating a halo around his mother as she played, an aura of warmth and welcome.

In this memory the whole household was gathered. It must have been Christmas or Michaelmas, one of those big holidays when the rules were eased and everyone seemed part of the family. It had been as his father had said at her funeral: While she played they had all been her servants.

His mother would end her concert and there was that moment of silence that meant appreciation, and then applause. Father would step forward and speak the familiar words.

"That was a magnificent gift, my dear. What can we give you?"

She would answer as she always did. "You have given me everything I could want. I ask only that you give kindness with no expectations."

His father tried, but it was the one gift he never was able to give completely. At least not to his son. He would give him money and add, "Do not spend it all in one place." Or a horse, and before the gift was a minute old he would say, "Beat Lockwood in your next race."

Even in his last will and testament he had felt compelled to add: "Invest wisely, have a care for the family name, and marry well." As if he had been raised to behave differently. As if his father had ever set any other example.

In the years without him Edward had come to realize that his father had loved him but had never trusted him. He wondered with sudden insight if his delay in marriage was a small, silent rebellion.

"I have made you sad."

Called back to the moment by her voice, Edward admitted ruefully, "That was one of my mother's favorites."

"Oh, dear, I am so sorry."

"No, do not apologize. It was lovely to hear it again. The sadness comes from the truth that what I recall can be no more than memories."

She didn't answer with more than a nod of approval, and she began again. What could he say that did her playing justice? "Accomplished" was nigh an insult. "Beautiful" too trite. She studied the strings for the most part, with occasional glances his way. It was those momentary looks that he was watching for.

With those glimpses she drew him into her singular world, the one where music opened her mind and heart. It was not bliss that he saw on her face. It was hardly euphoria. Neither would have included him. It was pure happiness. Each glance told him that her happiness was made greater by the sharing of it—with him. Like calling someone to share a glorious sunrise.

The music transformed the world that held them into something seductive and enthralling.

He stood up and moved to where she sat. She stopped playing, or perhaps she had plucked the last note and he drew her up from the chair.

"That was an invitation in music."

She shook her head a very little and he raised his hand to touch her lips.

"If you deny it, Mariel, then your mind is lying to your heart." He turned her so that she faced him fully and the harp was no longer between them. He took her face in his hands and with the gentlest of moves leaned closer. "Let me—"

Those two words were all the invitation she needed. The harp had worked its magic on her as well, and she gave herself to him as fully as she had given herself to the harp.

He could feel the echo of the music as she kissed him. His hands moved from her face to pull her more fully into his arms, and she raised her own hands to draw him as close. There was more passion than love in this kiss, an edge of wanting long denied. He gentled the pressure, did not ask for all that she would be willing to give, knowing that the music had woven a spell around her as thoroughly as it had entrapped him. A spell that he never wanted her to regret.

She ended the kiss with a shaky sigh and laid her head on his shoulder. "Oh, Edward, I can lie to myself so much more easily than I can lie to the ton."

He kissed her forehead and then her hair.

"I told myself that this meeting tonight was about charity, about doing good. I pretended it had nothing to do with the fun we have together, with the pull of happiness I feel whenever I see you. With the pure pleasure of your company."

"With this." He pressed his mouth to hers again and showed her what he knew she was not ready to put into words.

When they separated again, he bent down and picked up the

shawl that had fallen to the floor. He draped it over her shoulders and used it as an excuse to pull her into his arms yet again. This time he held her, rocked her, as though giving comfort.

"I have to leave, Mariel."

She nodded against his chest but made no move to end the embrace.

"Tomorrow is almost upon us. I shall be with you in less than twelve hours—sooner if you wish. Matthew will see us at any time. And after we have met with him, we can talk of what invitations we have accepted and where there is a waltz we can dance to."

"On a terrace, like the first time?" she asked, still nestled close.

He nodded. "But only if you promise that virtue will not be my only reward."

# Fourteen

Mariel made herself comfortable on the settee and considered the six invitations culled from the assortment on the table in her boudoir. She had thought it might be difficult to choose which gathering they would both enjoy the most, but it looked like this was the rare evening when little was offered.

"It is an odd collection, Christiana. There are two routs, something called 'an intimate dance party,' a musicale at the Harbisons, and two more cards from people I have never met."

Christiana did not respond but remained where she was, looking out the window onto the mews and the stable.

Mariel could see that she was distracted. "Christiana? Is something wrong?"

"Not a thing." She turned around and shook her head so sharply that Mariel knew it was not the truth.

Whatever it was, Mariel recognized the moment when Christiana decided not to speak of it. Instead, she came away from the window. "A dance party? The invitation is from the Bentleys, is it not?"

Mariel glanced at the elegant cream-colored paper. "Yes."

"They host one every May." Her face was alight with interest. "Everyone knows that the last Thursday is reserved for the Bentleys, just as the Westbournes are known to give the first true ball after Easter." She came over to Mariel and took the invitation from her outstretched hand.

"But, Christiana, what is 'an intimate dance party'?" Surely they would waltz. It did sound like something she and Edward might enjoy.

"I have never been to one, so I cannot tell you precisely. I wonder how many years it will be before Morgan and I are invited?"

"Why would you not be?"

"We are too newly married." Christiana put the invitation down and looked at Mariel. "It is not a party for those making their debut."

"Or the newly married?" Mariel looked at the invitation with some suspicion. "It does not sound quite proper."

"Oh, but it is. The story goes that the Bentleys tired of being surrounded by the young and untried, so they decided to host a party to include all the single men and women they know, bachelors, widows, widowers, and any number of married couples as well, so as to ease the appearance that they are matchmaking."

"It does not sound different from the usual rout except for the average age of the guests."

"Morgan says it is. He and James have attended several times in the past."

"I suppose Mr. Hadley has been invited." *A dozen times at least.*

"Since the beginning, I am sure, for he and Bentley are good friends."

"If Mr. Bentley has a wife and there are other couples included, then I do not understand why Morgan would be dropped because you two are married."

"Not all the pairing occurs among unmarried couples." She spoke with some exasperation. "Mariel, you must know that not everyone is as happy with marriage as we are and you and Charles were. The Bentleys give their guests an opportunity to meet people in similar situations without the constraint of a flock of young women demanding attention."

This was a meeting place for potential lovers? Mariel considered the ramification. "I don't know, Christiana, it sounds tasteless at best."

"Morgan insists not." Christiana shrugged. "You must attend and report back to me. Anyone who is not chaperoning some young lady for the Season will be there."

Would Edward want to go? Of course he would. She glanced at the other cards. She would enjoy the musicale, but he would not. They could go to either of the routs, but they promised to be thin of interesting company if everyone was at the Bentleys.

*Be honest,* she chided herself. *It hardly matters where you go as long as you are together.* She set the Bentleys' invitation aside. She would trust him to tell her if it would be too risqué to suit her.

Christiana was standing at the window again.

"Is something happening outside?" Mariel stood up and was about to join her at the window, when Christiana turned away and let the curtain fall back in place.

"Have you decided what to wear for your appointment with Hadley's man of business?"

"Yes, I thought the silver-gray walking dress."

"Perfect. Mr. Matthew will think you are all business and Hadley will not be able to take his eyes from you."

Mariel smiled a little, as that was exactly what she wished.

"If you have a few minutes, Mariel, there is something that I need to talk with you about."

Christiana came to sit on the settee next to her as Mariel watched her. She was not smiling. That was not good. She looked almost timid. That was worse.

"Morgan and I talked about this, and even though he is your brother we decided that I should be the one to speak with you."

Christiana continued before Mariel had a chance to mentally list no more than three possible catastrophes.

"Your brother James and his wife are coming to town."

With a slow nod Mariel absorbed this bit of news with some relief. She had not insulted the Regent aloud, no one had found out about last night's rendezvous with Edward, and her grandmother was still as healthy as her age would permit.

*James and his wife are coming to town.*

She bent her head for a moment, staring at her hands folded tightly in her lap. "I suppose you and Morgan want me to meet with him?"

Christiana nodded. "We were hoping that you could put the past behind you and give him a chance to make amends for his own ill-usage of you."

She relaxed her hands and wished ending years of bad feeling were as easy. "You were still in the schoolroom when my father disowned me, were you not?"

Christiana nodded.

Mariel looked up in time to see the gesture and nodded back. "I imagine your mother would remember. It was the talk of the ton for weeks. Rowlandson even did a cartoon of me being shoved out the front door wearing only a nightgown."

"Oh, my."

"That was not how it happened, but I suppose it made a more effective image." Mariel tried for a matter-of-fact tone. "Charles longed for the marquis's approval, but he and his family were well aware of how difficult Father could be."

"Morgan says that he tried to control everyone and everything."

"Yes, which is precisely the reason Charles turned down the living he offered."

"That was when he disowned you?"

"Not quite then. He did not precisely forbid the marriage, but he refused to discuss a settlement. He did allow the banns. And we thought he might relent. But he refused to attend the wedding even though the archbishop was the celebrant. Two months later he put an announcement in the paper and then sent a letter along with a trunk."

"In the London paper? He sent you your clothes?"

"And my favorite books, even my toys from childhood. They were ripped to shreds, crushed or cut, but all ruined beyond repair."

"Mariel, how awful." Christiana's eyes were wide with shock.

"I have not seen the marquis, or James or Rhys, in ten years. Morgan was always a rebel." She paused and they both smiled. "Morgan ignored our father's demands and was a regular visitor in Cashton. He made the rejection bearable."

They sat silent until Mariel spoke her thoughts aloud. "So much has changed. Braemoor is gone, the marquis himself is in exile, and James is married."

"You will like Marguerite." Christiana shook her head. "That is hardly the point, is it? Only, I can think of nothing to say. How could anyone treat his daughter that way? Morgan has said his father was never the same after your mother died, but you would think that if he truly loved her, it would have changed him for the better."

"I do believe he loved her—as much as he was able. But he never recovered from his grief, and then Maddie died not long after. In my more generous moments I think he was afraid that I would die and leave him too."

"So he sent you away before it would happen?"

"Yes." She paused, her heart aching at the memory. "I had Charles and we were very happy and managed to build a good life for ourselves and Anna. It has been more difficult since he died. Until recently I have felt quite adrift. Now that I am here I feel more anchored. There is Grandmère and you and Morgan." *And Edward.* She paused. "I cannot imagine it."

"The meeting?"

"Yes, I truly have no wish to meet him."

"But why not? It is James and not the marquis."

"But James stood with Father. He never once tried to see me as Morgan did." Mariel looked up, feeling defiant and vulnerable at the same time.

"He wrote to you when he finally did find out about Charles's death."

"It was nothing more than a formal expression of sympathy. A secretary could have written it for all the sensibility it conveyed."

"But he did write, Mariel. And you did not."

"You mean he is the one who feels slighted?"

"I have no certainty of that. James has spent a lifetime guarding his feelings. That has changed some since he married Marguerite. This invitation comes through us, but it is expressly his wish."

"Why here? Why London during the Season, when it is impossible to be private, to avoid gossip?"

"For that very reason. It will be a very public declaration of family unity."

"I can hardly say no without creating even worse gossip, can I? Do you think James did that on purpose?"

"No, I think meeting here in London was Marguerite's idea. She will do almost anything to bring him happiness. To bring the family together. She thinks family everything. You see, hers was lost in the revolution. She has found a new one in the Braedons, and there is nothing more important than making it whole again."

"And she thinks she can orchestrate that?" Mariel shook her head, amazed at the woman's overconfidence. "She sounds a handful."

"Wait until you meet her." Christiana thought a moment and added, "It would mean the world to Grandmère. You know how many times she tried to effect a reconciliation."

Mariel stood up and nodded. "Yes, yes." Now she was the restless one. She paced the room twice and then turned to face her sister-in-law. "I cannot decide when all my sensibilities are roused."

"But you will consider it?"

"Yes. Yes, I will."

"You are not saying this to end the discussion?"

She was. Instead of answering that question she asked one of her own. "Has he changed much?"

"Immeasurably. He is happy. Morgan says he cannot ever recall seeing him so content, so easily amused."

"And it is because of her?"

"Oh, yes. Marguerite has shown him how to make the most of every moment and find pleasure in every day."

Edward came to mind. "She knows how to have fun."

"Exactly."

After Christiana left, Mariel hurried to her grandmother's room, hoping for a show of support from her, even if it was only agreement that the best time to attempt a reconciliation would be in the summer, away from town and curious eyes.

"Nonsense, Mariel. If you refuse his invitation, you will only exacerbate a situation that has gone on years too long. No one will see you at the town house. You can be as private there as you would in Cashton, even more so. You flatter yourself if you think that every eye is on you here as it is in Kent. There are at least a dozen others of more interest."

Mrs. Dayhull nodded. Either she was dozing or agreed completely with the dowager duchess.

"There is more than that, Grandmère, you know there is. If I do meet him, then I shall have to decide if I should tell him what Mama told me about his brother. About William."

"It's been more than twenty years since William was sent to Braemoor."

"And sent away almost as fast," Mariel added bitterly.

"Yes, I am sure you can understand what that felt like."

"And he was only ten. Mama tried, she said she did, but the marquis would not even consider acknowledging him."

"Mariel, if the boy was alive and cared anything for the Braedon name, he would have made himself known. It's a poor excuse for avoiding James."

She accepted what amounted to a reprimand, kissed her grandmother, and went back to her room to change and wait for Spreen to announce Edward's arrival.

\* \* \*

It was a relief to see him even though her head was pounding. She was cured of trying to find an ally, so when he asked what was wrong, she blamed the sun for her headache.

"It is bright," he said agreeably. "We have seen it little enough this last week."

She accepted his hand into the carriage. The way he pressed her fingers before he let them go eased the sense of isolation, and with that the pain in her head eased some as well. It was such a comfort that she wanted nothing more than to put her head on his shoulder and cry.

Instead, she sat ramrod straight and watched London pass by.

"Mariel." He spoke very quietly, as though a louder voice would aggravate her.

She turned to look at him, and to her dismay the tears began, seemingly of their own accord.

When he would have pulled her close, she held up her hand, sure that his touch would cause the emotion to bubble over into sobs.

He watched her, his face filled with concern, and then asked, "At least tell me if it's something I've done."

She gave a watery laugh. "No, no, at this moment you are my one consolation."

"Ahhh," he said on a pleased sigh, and now he did pull her close.

Instead of worsening, the tears stopped. He held her as he had last night, gently, but there was more comfort than passion in this embrace. Mariel eased from his hold and turned a little so she was facing him fully.

"You must know about the estrangement between me and my family."

"Only as a story. I was away from London that year." He took her hand. "Tell me."

She did, as concisely as she could. It still hurt to recount the infamy. "And now my brother is coming to town and he wants me to call on him."

Hadley nodded, raised her hand, and pressed a gentle kiss to it. "All the old wounds are made new, are they not?"

She nodded and was silent, her sensibilities roused by his understanding and his touch. She spoke when she could be sure that her voice was steady. "Yes, but none of them sees that. Even Grandmère was angry with me for hesitating."

"And why do you?"

She drew her hand from his, feeling as though he were a traitor. She knew she looked offended, was certain of it when he reached over and put a finger at each corner of her mouth. He pressed up a little, as if that would be all that it would take to make her smile.

"Do not sulk, my dear girl. I would rather have a yelling row than have you turn silent on me."

"I've never had a yelling argument in my life!"

"No?" he asked in some surprise. "They are the best way I know of to find the heart of a problem. If you do no more than debate it in your own head, then you never do understand the opposing view." He stopped and with a resigned shrug asked, "We might as well start, as we mean to go on. Have you considered that James is as afraid as you are?"

"Never." His lack of support annoyed her. "And I can see that you are on their side too."

"No, not necessarily."

"Oh, stop being so understanding. You are the one who said you like to argue."

"But what is there to argue about? Your brother has made a gesture that will end an estrangement. What can you do but agree to try?"

"Oh, so there has to be something *worth* arguing about. And who named you the arbiter of that?"

"Apparently, no one. But it is rather a challenge to argue about nothing. So difficult to take a stand on something that is so, ahem, ephemeral."

"Not for me."

"So I see. And you said that you have never argued before."

"I said I never had a *yelling* argument before."

"I stand corrected."

He fell silent. Was he the one sulking? She looked at him and never in a dozen years could you call his expression sulky. It was caught somewhere between patient and patronizing. He was waiting for her, was he?

"If James is serious about a reconciliation, then he can come to me at Hale House. That is the way it is done. He is the one who asked."

"No meeting him halfway, is there?"

"What do you mean by that? That would imply that the rift was my fault, and you know as well as I do that it was not." She said the last three words with some vehemence.

"Agreeing to meet him at the Braedon town house will show that there is some hope of renewing family ties."

She did not answer right away, and he asked the next question with some suspicion in his voice. "Or is it that you want him to suffer as you have?"

It was such a surprising insight that her anger evaporated. Was she that vindictive? "Yes, that is it. As mean and smallminded as it is, that is precisely it." Guilt renewed her headache. "I want him to know what it feels like to come up against someone unwilling to compromise, someone who holds your heart in her hand and has no idea of the value of it. Someone who can hurt you and walk away without a backward glance."

"Oh, darling girl, he knows that. You may have had different mothers, but the marquis was his father as well as yours. He remembers you well enough to know that you could not treat him that way. I understand it too, or you would not be crying at the prospect. It is only that you are afraid."

"I am not."

"Yes. You are. You're afraid to trust him."

He could be right. The grip around her heart felt suspiciously like it. "My heart has suffered enough in these last years and is only beginning to heal."

"Then that should give you strength."

"I would be a fool to invite another blow."

"Yes, you would. But what does it say that everyone but you feels this meeting will make the healing complete rather than the reverse?"

She shook her head.

"You and James have a chance to undo your father's injustice. Rise to the occasion, Mariel. Or you will be more your father's daughter than James is his son."

She was silent for a long time, knowing that he was right, accepting that they all were. "There is something else that makes me afraid, Edward." She reached over and touched his hand; he turned his and took firm hold of hers. "Edward, this is something no one knows but my father, Grandmère, and I. I have not even told Christiana or Morgan. If I trust you with this—"

Before she could finish, he interrupted. "You do not even have to ask. It will go no farther than this carriage."

She looked away from him for a moment and then at her hands. "When my father's first wife ran away to France, she was pregnant, pregnant by my father. She died giving birth to a son, another Braedon, a true Braedon. He was kept in France with her lover until he died. The boy was ten."

"And your father had no idea of his existence?" He spoke the question as though it were not at all unusual to have a child kept from you, but she was grateful for his calm.

"He never knew until the boy was brought to Braemoor and virtually left on the doorstep." She gripped his hand even harder. "My father would have none of him and sent him away. He has not been heard from since. That was twenty years ago. I was not yet ten myself and have no recollection of it."

"Your mother told you?"

"On her deathbed and made me promise never to speak of it unless William should present himself to us."

"That was his name?"

Mariel let go of his hand and raised hers to her throat. "Yes. All I know of this brother is that his name is William

Braedon." She was angry and added, "How am I to know him if he should appear?"

"Do you know where your father sent him?"

"I have no idea. To the colonies? I do not even know where in France he came from. If Father sent him back there, he could well be dead. The guillotine was so indiscriminate."

"If he lived and you have never heard from him, then he has made another life for himself."

"Grandmère agrees. She says it has been twenty years, and if he is still alive, then he does not wish to be known to us." She rubbed at the lump in her throat. "I do not know whether I should tell James or not. That is, if I meet him." She looked at him and wished he had the answer. He was lost in thought himself, and she waited patiently for his insight.

"I think you must tell him." He spoke with some consideration, hesitancy even. "But not right away. You can wait until you are comfortable with each other again and then speak of it."

She nodded, waiting for more.

"Mariel, it may be that he already knows."

"I never thought of that." She spoke with some relief and actually felt it. Could it be that this secret was not hers alone. "It could be so, Edward. He would have no more reason to tell me than I would to speak to him before now."

"But you must ask. If he has never heard of his brother, he may want to talk to his father about it, and he should have the opportunity to do that. Yes, I think you must tell him of it while the marquis lives, but not necessarily tomorrow."

"Will it not appear that I am keeping secrets?"

"Only choosing your moment."

When she did speak, it was with quiet resolve. "You are right. I will meet with James. I must meet with him. It will be whenever and wherever he requests. And no matter how the meeting goes, I will find a way to tell him of his brother."

"Thank you, Mariel." With a finger under her chin he tipped her face up. "Your trust in me means as much as your affection.

I am right in this, but then, so are you. There is always risk. But it is worth the effort, and you are not without support."

He kissed her a little and felt her smile beneath his lips. "Mariel, darling, the best part of the argument is making up."

"Is that what that kiss was for?"

"Well, it was a very small disagreement."

# Fifteen

They continued the ride in silence, a companionable one. Mariel sat with her head on his shoulder, her eyes closed. He hoped she could not feel the uncertainty that had his heart thumping.

No sooner had she mentioned her lost half brother than the image of Chartwell popped into his head. The arrogant, imposing naval captain who looked amazingly like Straeford's heir.

Could Captain Chartwell be Viscount Crandall's long-lost brother? It was possible, he was sure of it. The man was the right age. But then, that was a period of time, between his two marriages, when the old marquis's habits were sure to have been less than restrained. God only knew how many baseborn children might claim him as their father, some surely in their thirties, as was Chartwell.

He shifted a little, and Mariel raised her head and made to move away. He kissed her forehead, and she smiled, settling back and closing her eyes. She looked bruised and tired but not as hurt as she had when he had first seen her.

His heart swelled with love. Yes, it was love. Her trust in him today fixed it in his mind and heart and convinced him that she felt the same.

He would not pretend that he wanted some casual affair that would be over in a week or even a month. It would take him much longer to explore her body, her mind, her heart. And to share his.

What to do about Chartwell? This was hardly the time to

tell her. She was overset as it was and burdened enough with her mother's story.

He would tell Crandall himself, go directly to the head of the family. That was the right and proper way to handle this.

Crandall was the one to decide if there should be an investigation, whether to tell the others.

The carriage stopped and Mariel straightened.

"Are you feeling better, Mariel? Would you prefer to delay this meeting with Matthew?"

Her eyes were not red, but her smile was a weak one and he was loath to tax her any more than was necessary.

"Oh, no, Edward. I am well enough and I have been looking forward to it all day."

"I must tell Matthew. I cannot think of anyone who has ever expressed that much enthusiasm for a meeting with him before."

She laughed, and he was sure the headache was gone. "Then do not tell him that it is the project as much as his expertise that has me so intrigued."

The porter opened the door for them. This time there was no waiting. The senior clerk relieved them of cloaks, walking stick, and parasol and showed them to Matthew's office immediately.

While the more junior workers did not actually watch them pass, Edward was aware of more than one covert glance. He hoped Mariel did not notice their interest. And was further glad that none of them had access to Whites' betting book. Perhaps he should have called Matthew to Berkley Square. Too late now.

Matthew gave them his usual effusive welcome. Introductions were made, seats offered and taken. Matthew looked from one to the other, asked how he could help them.

"Mrs. Whitlow and I played whist together not long ago. Due to her brilliant play and my support, we came away from the game with near two hundred guineas to our credit."

"Congratulations." Matthew spoke without expression.

"Thank you. We have agreed that we should like to give the money away."

"I see."

Edward was sure that he did.

Mariel spoke then. "We would like to find a widow with children to whom the money would be a help, a significant help. Mr. Hadley suggested that you would be in a position to name the person and assist us with the presentation."

"I see," Matthew said again. He looked at him, and Edward nodded. "I can think of two or three people who would benefit. One of them quite desperate actually."

He saw Mariel bite her lip and wondered if she was regretting their decision not to augment the small fortune.

"Will you tell us her story?"

When Matthew hesitated, Mariel added, "Anonymously, of course."

Matthew stood up, put his hands behind his back, and began. "She was widowed with a stepdaughter and three children of her own. The oldest girl's godmother has offered to pay for her come-out, but that is the least of her worries."

"She is of the beau monde?" Mariel asked, and then added, "How can our money help her? We mean the widow to be relieved of significant debt or find comfortable lodging."

"Her husband left her with debt of all kinds, including significant gaming debt. In time she will have access to funds that will enable her to meet the demands of creditors. But there is one debt that she is being strongly pressured to meet. The gentleman is willing to forgive it in exchange for certain favors which my client would infinitely prefer not to extend."

Edward watched as Mariel raised her hand to her throat, not at all mistaking his meaning. For his part, he could imagine the woman's desperation if she was forced to tell Matthew.

"I was going to lend her the money," Matthew continued, "but she was not at all comfortable about borrowing from me. She insists that she will never borrow money. Besides," he added with an easing of his formality, "it seems appropriate that winnings should be used to save her from a gamester."

"Though you understand, Matthew, that if we give her the money, she can spend it as she chooses?"

"Yes," Mariel added, "she may still want to borrow the money from you."

"I understand, and since I have already offered the loan, that is entirely possible. But unlikely."

Edward looked at Mariel, who bit her lip, obviously still full of questions but not comfortable asking them in Matthew's presence.

Before Matthew could sit down, Edward nodded to him. "Could you give us a moment or two to discuss this?"

"Surely, but this is only the first one that comes to mind. It would be easy enough for me to think of others if this does not suit."

He left the room and Mariel looked at Edward. "If it does not suit? How could he think it would not?"

"Do you know who Mr. Matthew is talking about?" Edward asked.

"No. How could I?" Mariel looked taken aback. "Do you?"

"I think so." He nodded slowly. "Lady Lucy Brevier."

"I have never heard of her."

"She is in mourning this Season of course, though I do believe she is living here in London. I imagine once the estate is settled and she leaves, she will not have the resources to return, unless she does perhaps come for her stepdaughter's Season. But that will not be for at least a year."

Mariel reached over to touch his sleeve. "Mr. Matthew said that she will eventually have some money."

"Yes, he did." Edward considered that idea. "Do you think we should allow her to borrow the money from Matthew and ask him to find someone more needy?"

"Edward, what do you think it must feel like to borrow money from a man one barely knows in order to pay another who is pressuring for sex as payment?"

He grimaced at his own callousness. "Yes, yes, of course, you are right." He covered her hand on his arm. "I remember her from her first Season. "What must she think of men. Her husband was the worst kind of spendthrift. What he did not lose gaming, he spent on women and horses. I imagine Lucy Brevier is used to practicing economy and discouraging creditors."

"Except for this one." She spoke with real disgust. "Do you know who he is?"

"I can guess but will not. For if it is who I think, then he is not the end you would name him."

"How could he not be?"

"Men do strange things in the throes of love."

"Edward, it is not love if he is threatening her."

"Not our kind of love, but each has his own way of showing it. Only a while ago you were speaking of your mother and father. There was a love neither one of us can understand."

Her expression had changed from earnest to bemused.

"Our kind of love, Edward?"

"I can't define it. Can you? But what is between us is dear and precious and growing. Does that not sound like love to you?"

"Yes. It is only that I am hardly able to admit it to myself, much less say it out loud."

"You did before. When you said that your heart had healed. Or was that presumptuous of me?"

She reached across the small space between them and took his hand. "Not presumptuous at all. You are the reason I am smiling again."

He pulled on the hand that held his and she came closer. As their lips met, there was a knock on the door.

Mariel made to move away, but Edward whispered, "Ignore it. He will go away." Then his mouth claimed hers and he did his best to make her forget the door, the office, and all else. He could spend months learning the feel of her. Her lips were only the beginning. But seated feet apart in chairs did not invite more.

When he made to end the kiss, she kissed him. A quick, light kiss that was as welcome as port after a perfect meal.

There was another tap at the door. This time neither of them was startled. Edward stood up and went to the door. It was Matthew's clerk, who explained that "Mr. Matthew wanted me to ask if you would care for some refreshment?"

For his part, Edward was feeling very refreshed and he said no. The door was closed before he realized that perhaps Mariel would like something. He would have asked, but she spoke before he could.

"If we give Lady Brevier the money, we must do it anonymously. I cannot think she would appreciate anyone knowing of her need."

"Yes. Is that a disappointment you can bear?"

"Of course. I am not so selfish as to put my own gratification before someone else's apprehension."

The next knock on the door was Matthew himself. They gave him their decision and spent the next few minutes arranging the details of the transaction.

"How will she know it is not a gift from you?" Mariel asked, and then added hastily, "Not that I would mind at all."

"Because I am a man of business and we are a notoriously unsentimental lot. I would never give my clients money. I have already explained that to Lady Brevier. If I made a habit of that, indeed if I did it even once, I would be a philanthropist and not a businessman." He glanced at Edward, who did his best to remain expressionless. "Do not misunderstand me. There is an honored and valued place for philanthropy in our world but not here in business."

They left Mr. Matthew in perfect accord. Edward escorted Mariel back through the front room. There was a carriage, not his, at the door, and as they watched, Mr. Harbison and his wife descended from it.

"The circle is complete, is it not?" Edward whispered to Mariel in some amusement, and then added, "Don't look panicked. We are here on a perfectly respectable errand."

Edward waved the porter away and opened the door to welcome their former opponents.

It was all confusion as each explained their errands. Edward wondered if their "need to sign some papers" was as much a lie as his It hardly mattered. They were more than acquaintances, and he had every expectation that nothing remarkable would be made of their respective meetings with Mr. Matthew.

His smug comfort was eroded by Letty Harbison.

"You both must stop giving money away so casually."

He could feel Mariel stiffen, and his own polite interest was more than a little forced. He pressed Mariel's arm held in the crook of his and opted for silence.

"It was you who left the coins on the tray," Letty continued. "The night of our ball? In the card room? After you won so impressively. It was you, was it not?"

Edward nodded, his anxiety eased a little.

"You caused the footman no end of distress. He took the money."

"Of course he took the money, Letty. They left it for him. See, I told you they did." This was Harbison, clearly harking back to a much-discussed topic.

Letty Harbison looked at her husband. "Now we know, but it did throw all of us into confusion when he brought the money to the steward."

"He took the money to the house steward?" It was Mariel's turn to enter the discussion. The entire room was listening.

Letty Harbison nodded. "He did hold on to it overnight, but then admitted that guilt would keep him from spending money not earned. That, and he did not want to be accused of stealing."

Edward rolled his eyes. "What do you teach your people down there in Kent, Harbison? Honesty and loyalty in a servant. A rare commodity. Is it in the water or is it your good example?"

Harbison brushed off the compliment. "We told him to share the money with the staff, and they all went off happier."

"What I want to know, Hadley, is how often you do this?" Letty Harbison asked with an arch smile.

"It was an impulse." Mariel spoke, saving him from a lie. She reached out and touched Letty Harbison's arm. "We were so amazed at our good luck and wanted to share some of it."

"Not luck at all," Harbison conceded. "Skill. Not sure I ever want to play with the two of you again."

"Of course we do." Letty winked at them. "Only for smaller stakes next time."

Amid promises of "a proper card party soon" the two couples split apart, the Harbisons to their meeting with Matthew while Edward and Mariel headed to their carriage with real relief.

"That was a near thing." Edward swiped at his forehead with his hand, not surprised to find some sweat there.

Mariel began to laugh, her quiet mirth giving way to unrestrained laughter. "I wish you could have seen your expression. You were trying hard to look so unconcerned, but your smile was positively frozen."

"I'm glad you were so entertained." He tried to relax, but it was difficult when one feared a lifetime of secrets was about to be exposed.

"Who would have thought that the footman would turn the money in?" She settled her skirts around her, apparently without concern for the near miss.

"Do you realize how close we came to being found out?"

"Why, yes, I do. But we were not." She looked at him. "It was rather fun, was it not?"

Not from his perspective. He had more at stake. But he pushed his worry aside and let himself be distracted by her obvious high spirits. "Have you decided where you would like to meet this evening?"

That question seemed to sober her, not at all what he had intended.

"There were very few invitations. There was one from the Bentleys, though." Her sentence was more of a question.

"Bentleys, of course," He slapped his forehead with three fingers. "Perfect. If I had remembered that invitation, I would have spared you the trouble of the research."

"You have been before?"

"Since before Mrs. Bentley."

"But Christiana said that it was a party the two of them concocted."

"You must promise that you will not be scandalized, and I will tell you the truth."

She nodded, but there was uncertainty in her eyes. He decided he would tell her anyway.

"Before he was married, Bentley would host a party for only single men and women."

"That does not sound so shocking." She paused. "Unless they were not all of the ton."

"I assure you they were not. Everyone from Harriette Wilson and the rest of the high flyers to the loveliest actresses on stage. The Prince of Wales even came after he broke with Mrs. Fitzherbert."

"The fact that the Prince was there does nothing to convince me of its respectability."

"Nor should it. It is odd though. It was less ribald then than it is these days. Have no idea why."

"Christiana said that Mrs. Bentley was a steadying influence."

He laughed. "To my mind 'a steadying influence' means that she drained his life of fun. Hardly. She is as wild as he is. But Bentley does spend more time with the ton than he used to."

"Perhaps that is what confused Christiana. I assume before, it was all gaming hells and places I should not know about."

"Just so."

With a deceptively bland expression, she added, "Christiana tells me that you and Bentley are the best of friends."

He knew a trap when he heard one. "We were, but ten years of marriage on his part and Father's death for my part have separated us. I no longer go to the places that you should not know about. Gaming hells? That is something else. There are some frequented by women. Would you like to go?"

"No, thank you."

"But we will go to Bentleys'. It is exactly the sort of gathering we are looking for. Filled with the cream of the ton and no one under twenty-five."

"You think I will enjoy it. I am trusting you on this, you know."

"I think you will, yes, I do. Indeed, I do believe your more Methodist expressions have disappeared almost completely."

"Oh, dear, I am not at all sure that I like the idea that I am that easily influenced."

"It is only your evangelical observations that are dissipated. Your natural conservatism is still as sincere a part of you as your hatred of gossip." He thought back to the kiss in Matthew's office and wondered if that was entirely true. "As for gossip, the Bentleys' will be rife with it. It is the perfect place for us. We will barely be noticed."

"Somehow I doubt that. No one ever ignores you. You walk into a room and the hostess considers her party a success. If we walk in together, we will be remarked on."

"You truly do not want to go?" He tried to conceal his disappointment even though it felt as though someone had taken a treat he had anticipated and tossed it onto the floor.

"No, I said I would trust you, and I will." Despite the statement, she spoke with false enthusiasm. "Edward, will I be embarrassed?"

"Of course you will." He laughed and took her hand. "Everyone is slightly more risqué than usual, drinks more champagne than they should be and flirts with complete abandon. Do wear the red dress you wore the night we played whist. Without the diamonds."

"No jewelry? But the décolletage is so deep. It will draw attention to . . ." She let her voice trail off, trusting he would understand her meaning.

"Precisely. One is allowed, at the Bentleys, to be a little

outré. Or very outré in private if you are so fortunate as to make that sort of connection."

She still looked hesitant.

"You said that you would trust me. Do, then. I tell you that you will enjoy it; you will laugh more than you have in a month. It is quite a charming collection of people."

# Sixteen

She did not wear the red gown, with or without diamonds. He would be disappointed, but the green gown she chose was almost as impressive. It looked modest enough to the casual observer, which he was not. On closer inspection, it was obvious that the gauze overlay covered an amazingly sheer green silk that gave the illusion, alas only the illusion, of transparency. *Indulgence,* he thought. "Indulgence" would be his byword tonight.

When he complimented her on the gown, she looked slightly self-conscious. "It was Christiana's idea to purchase this. I had every expectation that it would stay in the wardrobe forever."

"Tell me, what are her favorite flowers? I am sending her a room full."

Mariel laughed. It was exactly the tone he hoped to set for the evening.

They had arrived in the same carriage, but it attracted no notice. It was raining again, and the men and women separated as soon as they were inside, the ladies hurrying to the withdrawing rooms to rid themselves of cloaks and exchange compliments.

When he saw Mariel again in the ballroom, she was agog. "I believe you."

He watched the Westbournes come into the room. The countess was quite giddy, and he could have sworn that the earl had just pinched her.

"Has everyone left their inhibitions at the door?" Mariel

asked. When he only nodded, she continued. "Oh, dear, I thought my dress would invite comment, but there are some that are quite shocking."

"Oh, do point them out to me, please." Despite the tease, he did not take his eyes from her. He lost himself in the smile that reached her eyes. It was as intoxicating as champagne.

Before she could answer, the small chamber quartet began to play the first dance. A waltz. She held out her hand, still mesmerizing him with her smile, and he realized that he should have mentioned something before.

He took her hand and held it with both of his. "Mariel, by tradition, this first dance sends a message. Not everyone will dance. And if you do, you announce that you are already attached."

She did not reply but looked at the dance floor. He followed her gaze. Two married couples, the Westbournes were one, made their bow to each other. Only two. Would Mariel notice that most of the married couples were not among the dancers? Would she care?

The other five couples were not married, to each other or anyone else. He hoped she did notice that.

"Where are the Duke of Redmond and Lady Godmersham?" she asked, making a brief survey of the small crowd.

"Not arrived yet. Which may mean something or nothing."

"Why did we have to be here for the first waltz?"

She sounded petulant, and he looked at her and did not hide his disappointment. "Mariel."

She moved closer to him and raised her fingers to his mouth to silence him. "Edward, it is you and only you, but will this not lead to gossip?"

"No more than your fingers resting on my lips." He pulled her into his arms and onto the floor without a bow of invitation. The room itself added to the intimacy. The Bentleys' town house lacked a ballroom, so they converted their main salon to the purpose. Even with the carpet and most of the furniture removed, it was a cozy space in which to host a group. No one seemed to mind the excuse to stand closer and speak more softly.

The dance floor was a little more crowded now, but Mariel and Edward ignored the others. The first two hours swirled by, the food and champagne adding to the sense of indulgence. He was determined not to ask if she was enjoying herself, but did watch to see if he could judge.

It was easy enough, as he never left her side. They would drift up to groups and talk of the usual things, staying longer with the people who were discussing politics—the shock of the Prime Minister's assassination, just a few weeks before, had left them all unsettled, or the war—Wellington was making rapid advances in the Peninsula since taking Badajoz and the new modiste recently arrived from Wales.

The hours passed, an evening of frankness and flirtation that moved from lighthearted to intense and then back to something too comfortable for a couple who were not yet lovers.

One of the more sybaritic waltzes was ending, when the butler opened the ballroom door and announced, "Lady Lucy Brevier."

The entire room silenced and turned as one to the door. Mariel and Edward were leaving the dance floor. They stopped in place and Mariel looked at him, her eyes wide with surprise. He patted her arm. "Try not to look so alarmed. Matthew has not given us away."

Lady Brevier walked into the center of the room, carrying a small leather bag. A fierce expression triumphed over a face lined with exhaustion. She was dressed in black, the deepest of mourning, a wool that reflected not a spark of light. No one assumed that she was a guest come late to the party.

She passed them without a glance, and he felt Mariel relax a little. He saw where she was going and whispered, "I suspect we are to witness the use of our largesse after all."

Lady Brevier did not cross the room completely as he thought she would, but stopped almost in the center of the dance floor. Couples stepped to the edge until it was all her own. Even before she called out "Griffon, show yourself," a man came from the group along the edge to face her.

"Did you want me, milady?"

He did not bow to her and asked the question in a neutral voice that still managed to suggest something carnal.

"Never in a thousand years." Lucy Brevier spoke the words slowly with low-voiced venom and walked toward him.

Mariel gripped Edward's arm even tighter but did not look away from the drama.

The lady in black moved a few steps closer to Griffon until there was no more than three feet separating them. She opened the bag she was carrying. Turning it inside out, she let the coins fall to the floor, the clatter echoing in a discordant ringing until silence fell once again.

They stared at each other for a long, wordless moment.

Lord Griffon ignored the coins at his feet. He had nerve enough to smile. Edward wondered if he was the only one who recognized it as a sign of defeat and perhaps respect. When Griffon spoke, it was a whisper that still carried through the room. "In a thousand years, Lucy, I will still want you."

Several women sighed at the thought, but Lucy Brevier did not react with so much as a blush. She threw the bag down with the coins, turned, and fled the room.

Silence held the crowd until the sound of the door closing woke everyone from the spell. Lord Griffon still ignored the coins thrown at his feet and turned to his hostess. Several servants came forward to collect them.

Mariel turned to Edward, her hand at her throat. "Oh, dear heaven, Edward."

"No one will forget this party, and we no longer need wonder who will be the subject of tomorrow's gossip."

He took the hand she had raised to her throat and nodded toward the servants. "Do you think if we ask they will give us the money back and let us try again?"

"It is not funny, Edward." She pulled her hand from his. "Did you see her? Her distress. Her pain. We were a part of that. How can you be so casual about something that changed her life? People are not like chess pieces. They should not be moved at whim and for our entertainment."

"We changed her life for the better, Mariel. Why does that upset you?"

"Because there is something between them."

"Yes, two hundred guineas."

"No, it is more than the money. Matthew told us as much. Why would she make such a spectacle of paying the debt? Why would he pretend it is unimportant?" She looked away from him and shut her eyes. "It was wrong of us to play with someone's life that way."

Edward looked at Lord Griffon. "Griffon is flirting outrageously with Lady Heslop. He is either a very good actor or not suffering from a broken heart."

Everyone was watching Griffon, some more overtly than others. After a quick glance, Mariel turned from him completely. "It meant something to her, then, perhaps only to her."

"We gave her the money without stipulation, Mariel. We did not tell her how to use it."

"You are right." She admitted it, but only grudgingly. "It is only that she looked so"—Mariel looked down at the floor and paused a moment as if choosing her word carefully— "she looked so alone."

He stepped so close that there was no more than a breath between them. "And that, my darling, we can do nothing about. But I can see why it would have upset you."

She looked up into his face, his eyes. "I am not alone anymore, Edward. I do know that."

The music began again, and they melted into each other's arms. This was as intimate as their world could be for the next few hours, and they made the most of the dance that let them touch each other, hold each other, and dream.

As the night deepened toward dawn, the groups grew smaller until there were fewer couples dancing or seated à deux in the dining room. By four, when he suggested that they make their farewells, the crowd had thinned considerably.

He settled her in the coach with a warm brick at her feet. The rain left a chill in the air, and he sat close to her, a gesture she welcomed by nestling even closer. "It was fun, Edward. Except for Lady Brevier's distress, it was all fun. How long do you think the duke and Lady Godmersham will continue angry with each other?"

"I wonder if Griffon and Lady Helsop's liaison lasts longer than one night?"

She shook her head, and her smile was tinged with sadness.

"Lady Brevier's loneliness still haunts me."

She looked up at him, raised her face to his, and he understood the invitation. He whispered, "Loneliness is a specter that haunts us as well, Mariel." He kissed her. "Come home with me." He whispered the words between small, intense kisses. "Come home with me." The kisses underscored the urgency of his asking. "Come home with me now."

His lips, his hands, his body pressed into hers, made the invitation irresistible. Her body wanted the touch, her heart longed for the connection, her mind was a muddled confusion. She gave in to the moment, the erotic indulgence, until reason faded and his last murmured "Come home with me" was more than she could resist.

It was only a few blocks farther, and their fevered kisses made the distance shorter. The house was dark but for a light in the entry hall. They stepped from the carriage. He escorted her up the steps, his arm around her, holding her as close as movement would allow. He paused at the door to pull her hood more firmly around her face.

It was the smallest gesture, but it robbed the moment of a fraction of its sweetness. Neither one of them wanted anyone to know they were to be lovers.

The door swung open, but there was no porter or butler to be seen. They began making their way up the stairs, the house as silent, as secret, as they were. Another bit of certainty was chipped away.

His room was empty as well. No valet, but a robe left on the bed, which had been turned down in welcome. He removed her cloak and draped it over the chair. He took her in his arms and kissed her with such overwhelming passion that she felt the pleasure beat through her as tantalizing as the act of love itself. His kisses trailed down her neck to end at the crest of her bosom, where it met the fabric of her gown.

It was so exactly the right thing to do that her own confidence evaporated. Had he done this so many times that he knew exactly what would draw her need forward, bury any doubt? She would have preferred awkwardness; a little of it would have made her believe that this was different, that this would last.

She began to shiver. Her breath came in a long, jagged gasp and she shook her head. He closed his own eyes, but she saw his anguish and frustration.

"I'm sorry, I'm so sorry. I thought this was what I wanted. Now I think not."

He was still silent, but led her to the chair near the fire. He sat her in it, pulled a shawl from the back of it, and wrapped it around her.

He drew an upholstered footstool a little away from the chair and sat on it so that he could look up into her face. They sat silent until she was calm and could draw a deep breath. She gave him a smile that was as close to apology as she could come.

He held her hand, running his own hand up her arm and then down again, as if warming her.

There was nothing erotic about his touch. Or very little.

She sat still, abandoning herself to the comfort he offered, knowing it was selfish, knowing he wanted more, but in such desperate need herself that she took and did not think to give to him.

When he did speak, it was softly. "From the first moment, we knew, did we not? In the graveyard in Cashton."

She nodded.

"When I did not know you at all but still knew you well enough to share myself."

"I knew you well enough to understand the question that was all in one gesture."

"Life is short. You heard that and answered it with one long, slow nod that carried understanding, agreement, consolation all at once."

She nodded again.

"Each misunderstanding, each perfect understanding, each kiss, each meeting, has brought us here tonight. Only I did not know until a moment ago that this is about love and not sex."

She sighed deeply. "How can you be so noble?"

"My nobility is every bit a challenge, have no doubt of that, but I would be more of a rake than Griffon and more like a lecher if I pressed the advantage when the lady who holds my heart is still unsure."

"You must think me such a tease."

He laughed, that intimate sound she so loved. "Not at all. It was the kisses, you see. They seduced both of us when only one of us understood their power."

She stood up and stepped away from him. "Do stop being so nice about this, Edward. It is a hideous disappointment. Admit it."

He moved between her and the door before he answered. "An argument would make this so much easier, would it not?"

"I am not trying to start an argument."

He ignored the lie. "I can be patient because I have hopes for the future. An argument would only slow progress. A progress toward something that we both truly want." When she looked skeptical he added, "By your own admission."

"I may never be ready."

"Only if you lie to yourself as well as to me." He let her stand up. "Then I will be hideously disappointed."

He picked up her cloak and draped it over her shoulders,

barely touching her. But when she turned to face him, he took her into his arms and looked deeply into her eyes.

"This is a beginning. This is not an end. This is the first step in finding what we truly both want from the other. Something more than friendship, something more than a partnership to do good, something that will last beyond the ballroom and carry us into the night, the two of us alone and together."

He did not move to kiss her, and she understood that initiative must come from her. Her acceptance of this promise, this prospect, this possibility. She kissed him cautiously and then lost the caution in the flame of desire.

He escorted her home. In the coach they sat across from each other, aware that proximity was temptation.

"You know all my secrets now, Edward. But I know none of yours." She reached over and traced the scar above his eyebrow.

"How did you come by that?"

He looked almost relived at the question, and she wondered if he had secrets that he would not want to share. She refused to let the notion ruin her evening.

"This scar? It was nothing really." He moved over to sit next to her. "It happened, I think, the first or second year I was in town. It was at a balloon ascension, one of the first. Everyone was there, and I do mean everyone."

"My grandmother remembers it."

"You see. And she did not tell you what happened?"

"No, we were talking of other things. You had yet to be the subject of enduring interest that you are now."

"That does put me in my place. But I will mention that my scar is hardly the usual sort of thing one discusses with one's grandparent."

"I was curious and only a very little interested then. I described you to her." She smiled. "It does seem a very long time ago."

They were silent a minute; no words passed between them.

Still, she knew what he was thinking. Long ago in a day's measure but even longer in the time the heart counts.

"I was determined to be part of the adventure of this launch and joined a group of young men to help hold the ropes. It was quite a thrill. The balloon drifted off, and as it floated up, the aeronaut raised the customary glass of champagne to toast."

Mariel nodded, wondering what they toasted: the crowd left behind, the success of the launch, their own pride, but she did not ask.

"Then of a sudden the champagne bottle came plummeting to the ground. I remember wondering if we could have used balloons to drop bombs would we have lost the war with America, and a second later I realized our group of rope handlers was in the direct line of this particular missile."

"Oh, dear." Mariel raised her hand to her throat.

"Yes." He reached up and took her hand. "I pushed Lockwood away and was almost fast enough myself, but some small part of the bottle nipped my head, right along the eyebrow. It bled impressively, but you can see that it is the veriest scratch."

She reached to caress the spot once again. "But you came so close to worse, Edward."

"Yes, I did."

He was very matter-of-fact about it. She shivered, not as sanguine as he was.

"I think that is where my reputation for being lucky began. It was also the point at which I decided that I would find more excitement, albeit intellectual excitement, in a game of chess."

She prayed for him then. Closed her eyes and prayed that his luck would never end. She reached up and kissed the small scar as though the gesture would guarantee his safety.

"Those adventures are behind me, Mariel. I now find my entertainments in much quieter places." And proceeded to show her what he meant. It felt so right to be in his arms that she wondered at his patience and her hesitation.

The first quiet light of dawn was easing the dark when they reached Hale House.

Mariel knew that nothing had ended tonight. Though nothing had really begun yet either. "Hyde Park tomorrow at five o'clock?"

"I count the hours, Mariel."

# Seventeen

The sky was leaden, but Hyde Park was crowded with open carriages and people on horseback nonetheless, as if daring the bad weather to return. Too many rain-soaked days made them all willing to run the risk of ruined bonnets and dampened cravats if it meant the chance to share and observe the latest news.

Word had passed regarding their dance at the Bentleys, their obvious fascination with each other. Mariel would swear that every one of their acquaintance was stopping to see if the attachment was visible.

It was. Mariel knew by the satisfied nods of the women and the knowing smiles of the gentlemen. She hardly objected, but wondered what made it so obvious. Was it because they sat closer than absolutely necessary? Or was it that they were more interested in what each other had to say than in the *on-dits* of the men and women who greeted them? She looked at him and he at her, and they knew their mutual smiles beamed a message hard to ignore.

They managed a staccato conversation of their own in between meeting and greeting the ton, who paraded in pairs and solo.

"I have composed a message for James and will send it first thing in the morning," Mariel said.

They paused to greet two gentlemen. Edward introduced them to Mariel. When they rode off, Edward picked up the conversation as though merely seconds had passed.

"Excellent, and wise of you not to delay the meeting. It

will be better for the two of you to meet privately for the first time than at some rout or Venetian breakfast."

Mrs. Bentley pulled her curricle to a stop and asked if they were interested in joining them in their box at the theater.

Edward pleaded a previous engagement. She rode off after noting that Lord Griffon and Lady Heslop were not here either together or separately. Edward and Mariel exchanged glances but forebore to comment on how the two might be entertaining themselves today.

"Yes, I would hate it if I ran into James before the whole ton. These last few minutes show you why."

A couple they had met the night before rode past, but paused only long enough to exchange greetings.

"I wish I knew what to say to him. How to start. Edward, I play the meeting in my head and it seems forced and awkward."

"It may well be."

Two more carriages slowed as they passed, and the conversation centered around the latest gossip, Lady Brevier's surprise appearance at the Bentleys' party.

Mariel felt compelled to interfere. "She did not throw a glass of champagne in his face after she threw the money at him. He did not say he would have her no matter what the cost."

When they were alone again, she turned to Edward. "Honestly, gossip is bad enough, but at least they should tell the story as it happened."

"That is asking more than man is capable of. You must admit that even you and I saw the event differently. You were convinced there was something between them and I thought not."

"Yes, I wish I understood how it can be that a room full of people can see the same event and proceed to describe it in an entirely different way."

"Because in the telling they become part of the story, and adding another changes how it is told. This meeting with

James and his new wife will appear different to everyone involved. You think it will be awkward and he may see it another way entirely. You have the same father and he treated you both badly. But beyond that you have a secret you have never shared, the story of William, and he must have his own ghosts to haunt him."

The mention of William let her see the truth of that.

The Harbisons rode together and stopped their horses and waved. "We are looking forward to seeing you tonight."

Mariel nodded. "It should prove interesting, and I am flattered that you would think I am among the best whist players in London."

"No question of it. There will be ten tables in all." Harbison appeared delighted at the prospect of losing more money. "It is an impressive response for so short a notice, eh? For you must know the idea came to me only when we saw you with Matthew."

"Who else did you consult on the guest list?"

Edward's question seemed rather rude to Mariel, but when Letty said, "Besides the ones you suggested?" Mariel understood his interest and her lack of offense.

Harbison picked up the explanation. "We asked the Earl Tilbury to suggest some names, for he is always at a table somewhere, and Letty checked with some of the ladies to make sure the female side of the list was complete. It makes for an interesting group. "Lord Morgan will be there, Mariel."

"Oh, wonderful." She had not wanted to ask and had been hoping for it.

"Yes, indeed," Letty chirped with all the pride of a hostess who has achieved a coup. "It appears that Christiana is going to spend the evening awaiting the arrival of her new sister-in-law. Morgan refused so tame an entertainment and considers himself free to attend."

Even as she spoke, Letty's face reddened. She must have just realized that Christiana's new sister-in-law was also

Mariel's. She knew as well as anyone that no one other than Morgan had ever called in Cashton.

Mariel reached out and patted her sleeve. "I will be seeing Viscount Crandall myself tomorrow, Letty."

"Oh, Mariel, that is wonderful." Her disquiet disappeared. "I know it will be such a relief for both of you to heal the breach."

The horses showed their displeasure at the long pause, and Harbison interrupted. "We must move on, my dear." He raised his crop in farewell. "We will see you tonight."

When they were gone, Edward moved his horses on and they began the return circuit. "Very well done. The word is out, and no matter how the meeting goes, all that you have to do is be seen in James's company once or twice and all will think that, as Letty said, 'the breach is healed.'"

"Or that we are barely speaking, or that I am going to live at Braemoor, or that I think his wife a darling or a devil. In other words, the ton will think what it will. I am not doing this for them. I am doing it for Grandmère, for Anna, for my mother's memory, and, I suppose, for myself."

"And for James and his children and your grandchildren."

"Oh, dear, you are making me sound far more virtuous than I feel."

Before he could reassure her further, they were joined by Willy Gates astride his newest horse. He held the spirited animal only long enough to thank Edward for making the purchase possible.

"Gates, all I did was encourage you to try. Hardly anything more."

"Playing it too humble, Hadley. Why, if you weren't so generous, you could have bought the two horses and sold them yourself. If you had not been there urging me, I would have missed this fellow completely. You are responsible for the whole event."

His horse decided it was time to leave, and Edward had no opportunity for disavowal.

"I do believe half of London thinks you have the ear of the angels, Edward. If not God himself."

He shook his head but did not deny it.

" 'Tis good that they do not know of your generosity to Lady Brevier, Edward. What would they make of that?"

"The ton would find an explanation. Pure generosity is beyond their understanding." He waved to a friend who was discreet enough not to stop. "And my part in it was not purely altruistic. I hoped it would enable me to see more of you, to have you know me better, to bring us close to the confidence we share now. I do believe it was more the act of a selfish man than a generous one."

"You will never convince me that you are self-seeking."

He smiled. It was a sweet, gentle smile, as though what she had said was foolish. "You say what every lover longs to hear. I worry that it is the conceit of new affection, though I thank you a thousand times for the compliment."

"Do you not want me to defend you, Edward, even from yourself? Why does my trust label me as naive?"

"Not naive, Mariel, dearest, but tender feelings do gloss over failings. Perhaps I am not selfish, but I am self-indulgent. I want you to know that I see myself more clearly than you do."

"And how do you see me?" Even she heard the fear in her voice. "Dare I ask when you are in so frank a mood?"

He laughed so loud that several heads turned their way. She tried to smile so that the crowd would know that it was a shared joke, not that she was the brunt of it.

"No one ever will accuse you of being coy and, oh, how I treasure that. You are strong, direct, honest, intelligent. Your failing: too strong an inclination to see things in stark terms, honest or dishonest, selfish or unselfish." He took her hand and kissed it.

She was flattered, for not one of the qualities he cited offended her. She was hardly fool enough to press him for more negative traits. In time he would know her even better, and that would be the true test of their friendship. Would he still laugh so heartily when her directness seemed more insensitive than honest?

Before she could ask or Edward could continue, a late arrival slowed them to a stop. His cousin Estelle greeted them as though they were the answer to her prayers.

"Please, Hadley, can I go home with you?"

"You've arrived only this minute, Estelle."

"Because Gregori had to borrow this equipage and the horse is slow and the carriage not at all reliable." She spoke as though her companion did not understand English or would, at least, not take offense at her complaint.

Gregori gave a long-suffering sigh and bowed to them. "Someday I will buy my own horses and show my love what an Italian horseman is capable of."

"May I please come with you?" Estelle begged. "Then there may be some chance that I will be ready for the rout tonight."

It meant an end to the last of their privacy, but they could hardly say no. The curricle's seat was not meant for three, and they spent an amused few moments contriving a fit. Hale House was only a few blocks from the park, and by the time they reached the front entrance, the three had managed themselves quite neatly into a space meant for two. That meant that Mariel was sitting closer to Edward than most would consider proper. She did not complain.

"Are we here already?" Mariel glanced at him, and with that hint he proceeded to ignore the familiar door and circle the square once again.

"Edward, what are you doing?" Estelle asked in complete ignorance.

"If you have to ask, Estelle, then I wonder at Gregori's attentions. I am enjoying a few more moments of this delightful crush."

A small, breathy "Oh" was all Estelle answered. She apparently missed the message completely, because she moved closer to the edge of the seat. As if they *wanted* more room between them.

"I really must talk to Gregori." Edward shook his head and took a corner rather sharply so that Mariel was almost in his lap. "At least the two of us are of the same mind."

Mariel laughed, and was still laughing when he left her at Hale House a few moments later.

Edward found Lockwood waiting for him in the library, drinking the wine his butler had provided.

"Knew it would rain again."

"It started only this moment, Lockwood. The park was filled, as crowded as Parliament on opening day. You missed a most entertaining hour."

"Just as entertaining here, waiting for you. Besides, you can tell me what is worth knowing."

Edward moved to pour himself a drink. Lockwood turned in his chair and spoke before he joined him.

"Do you think Chartwell will be there tonight? He has to be one of the best whist players around."

"I doubt it, Lockwood. He's good, I'll give you that, but hardly a part of the ton. Have you ever seen him at a ball or rout or even in a box at the theater?"

"He was at one of Signora Rouselli's concerts. Made me wonder if he was the one who brought her here."

"All the less likely for him to be at the Harbisons'."

"But you know Tilbury. It is all skill and no matter the pedigree with him."

"You want him to be there, is that it? Still feeling sore over that marathon?"

"I won, I tell you. No matter he was called away by some message from the Admiralty."

"Yes, yes. I know." Edward shook his head. "Don't entertain the idea that you will reprise that marathon if he comes tonight. Our hosts have said that this will be a test of expertise but nothing more than a friendly game for modest stakes."

"Tell Chartwell." He spoke testily.

"Lockwood, he will not be there." The man looked so disappointed that Edward relented. "But if he is, you can prove your mettle against him easily. He will be away from his usual milieu, certain to be a little uncomfortable in such unfamiliar surroundings."

Lockwood turned thoughtful. "Yes, you're right. I can beat him if the partners and the cards cooperate." Then he added, "And you will be there with your good luck and all that."

Edward did not mention that half the people there would consider him *their* own personal good luck charm. He sat in his favorite chair and stretched his legs out in front of him.

"That chair is an eyesore, Hadley." Lockwood looked around him. "The rest of this room is perfect, but that . . ." He waved his hand at the offending chair and let his voice trail off, as though no adjective were vile enough to describe it accurately.

"No, it is this chair that is perfect. I have given my aunt orders that it is not to be touched. It might be old, but it fits me as well as one of Weston's coats. Why would I allow someone to tamper with something so comfortable?"

"Your aunt may take direction, but I suspect that it will be the first thing your wife will change."

Edward stilled, his glass halfway to his mouth. "What wife is that, Lockwood?"

"Mrs. Whitlow. I did not need to be in the park today to know that. The two of you were as close as peas in a pod at the Bentleys', but come morning she was at Hale House. Holding out for marriage, I'd wager."

Edward set his glass down. "Gerald Lockwood, do not even consider an entry in the betting book. You would surely lose."

"Does that mean no wedding bells?"

"It means that what happens between Mrs. Whitlow and Edward Hadley is ours alone. Not anyone else's, not even a friend of such long standing as you."

"Oh, ho, Hadley. You may count most of the ton as owing

you a favor for one thing or another, but no one is so grateful to you that they will ignore this bit of news. It's what gives their own boring lives interest."

"There is no news." Edward unclenched his jaw and forced what he hoped was a nonchalant smile.

Lockwood slapped his hand on his thigh. Edward knew the gesture. He was trying to decide how to proceed.

"I am serious about protecting our privacy." He almost added that it mattered to Mariel and so to him, but closed his mouth on words he was sure would only fuel the interest.

Lockwood nodded. Edward noted he did not agree to keep silent. He tried one more time.

"Lockwood, I have known you longer than almost anyone in town. Do not give me cause to distrust you."

"No need to threaten me, Hadley." He spoke with a stiff edge to his voice.

Edward laughed. "Not a threat, not at all. Besides, I can't recall an antic of yours that is not common knowledge." He sobered. "I want you to understand that my friendship with Mrs. Whitlow proceeds as we wish and not as society dictates."

This time Lockwood stood up. He held out his hand to him and Edward rose too. "I promise you, Hadley, no one will hear speculation from me."

They shook on it, then Lockwood said, "But I want to be the first to know."

His comment was a way to regain the balance between them, nothing more. Edward knew that and chose not to react at all.

Lockwood did not regain his seat but brushed invisible wrinkles from his coat. "Must be off to change for the card party. Looking forward to it."

Edward sat down again, this time in the rarely used chair Lockwood had vacated. The stiff, damask-covered horsehair suited his less than comfortable thoughts.

He would be hard pressed to count the number of affairs

that had filled his London Seasons. Not that he regarded it as an accomplishment, but he enjoyed companionship and women enjoyed him. Yet, no one had ever suggested he was a rake, and he wondered why.

How was he different from Lord Griffon? Everyone knew that Griffon did not care at all what society thought of him. That his conquests included more than one woman who should have been left alone. Like Lucy Brevier.

Edward thought back and realized that his lovers had always been notably available. He had never once had to guess if they would be interested, or talk them round to accepting his company. Until Mariel Whitlow.

Of course he could argue that the talking round he had to do with her was the result of a series of misunderstandings starting with Estelle's stupid comment about discussing wedding plans with her mother. Or even further back than that, when he had received the interfering and confusing note from Mariel's far from stupid grandmother.

No matter, he had spent the first part of their time together trying to convince her to give him a chance. She must be the first woman not to fall in his arms at his first hint of interest. Or at least the first since he had inherited on his father's death. That made her unique in yet another way.

Charm and wealth had not won her. It was his mind. He laughed to himself, but it was true. They liked sharing ideas more stimulating than views on the weather and the current fashion. And they had fun together. He stood, picked up his glass, and considered what he would wear to the Harbisons'. They had fun together, and he hoped they would continue that adventure for weeks, even months to come. He had not said a word about marriage.

# Eighteen

"This will be so much fun."

Edward returned her grin. He would never hear the word again without thinking of her, of how she had made the most of this Season and found fun in a dozen places.

"I have played whist often enough these last weeks to know who is clever, who can count the cards, who is willing to risk it all."

She was animated and restless and obviously in high spirits. "It does make me feel much more secure than I did at first."

Her enthusiasm was the exact antidote he needed. She was no more thinking of marriage than he was. All she was thinking about this evening was playing cards and winning.

Tomorrow, next week, even next month, she would come to him with as much fervor as she felt at this moment. It would be worth the wait. He reached over and took her hands, as though examining them for some cardplayer's trick.

He raised one, moved the glove aside, and pressed a kiss to her wrist. She was warm and smelled both sweet and sensual. Is that how she would be in bed? The thought warmed him in a more carnal way, and he let her draw her hands back into her lap.

"You are as mercurial as our spring weather, Mariel. I never know what will catch your fancy. Balloon ascensions, whist, Mrs. Linwood's awful needle painting, evenings at the Society of Sacred Music, your harp, finding new charities to support, new dresses, or discussions of any kind as long as they are not arguments. They have nothing in common but that they all make you smile."

She was quiet a moment and then said, "They all mean more when I share them with you."

The carriage swayed to a stop several houses away from the Harbisons'. They would have to wait until the other carriages let off their passengers.

She was the one who leaned closer this time and pressed her lips to his mouth. Reaching out, he pulled her onto his lap, and the kiss became more than the meeting of lips. Passion jolted through him, and he could feel her own rise in response. Kissing was not enough, but it was all they had for now. There was nothing sweet about it, the urgency was mutual, the wanting shared, the promise exchanged. Soon, very soon.

They moved apart as the house lights brightened the interior of the coach and it was their turn to alight. They spent a moment arranging their clothes, and then each smiled at the other. Mariel reached out to straighten his hat, and he reached and placed a finger on her lips. She kissed it.

The footman might have seen the gesture when he opened the door but was too well trained to react in any way.

Edward followed her from the carriage and wondered if he would be able to concentrate on cards at all tonight.

Mariel was grateful that the cards would distract her. At least she hoped they would. If she spent the next few hours reliving that kiss, she would be so eager for his touch that the carriage might be bed enough. She accepted Letty's invitation to use the ladies' withdrawing room to freshen up and wondered if the kiss showed.

Staring into the mirror, alone in the room, she knew that the kiss was as much a caution as an enticement. The question muted the hunger awakened by the embrace: The time had come to decide if this was what she wanted.

She trembled, wanting as fully as her passion would allow.

Her head ached as she tried to separate rational thought from the ache that only sex could ease.

She stopped staring at herself and looked down at her hands. Neither one of them had said "I love you." Oh, they had spoken of it that day at Matthew's office, but neither had said the three words that would change their world, their lives. At least she had thought them. Had Edward?

By the time she came down the stairs to join the small crowd in the front salon, she was no less calm but in better control. He had said that he would let her set the pace, but how could she know her thoughts when his kisses so thoroughly reminded her of what she could have with him? He was master enough to color her judgment with temptation. And she was so willing to be persuaded.

As she came down the steps, the knocker sounded and the hall porter opened it to a gust of soggy London air and a large gentleman who moved through the door as quickly as he could.

Mariel waited a few steps from the ground floor until the door was closed, hoping to avoid the chill, damp air.

The man swept off his cloak with practiced grace and handed his hat and walking stick to the porter. All in silence.

He turned toward the salon but did not see her waiting on the stairs.

Mariel froze in shock. James. Her brother James was standing in front of her.

It was her worst fear.

That they should meet first in some public place.

And it was happening.

She gasped, but at that moment before his gaze was drawn to her, Mariel was able to look at James, the half brother she had not seen since he was in his early twenties.

He had changed. It was more than the inch or so he had added over the years. His hair was still blond, but it was bleached almost white by the same sun that had darkened his skin. Morgan had not mentioned that he had spent much time at sea or out of doors, but James had the look of a man more accustomed to riding his horse across the Downs than sitting in drawing rooms.

He had the same air, a reserve that had settled on him long before most acquired it. They had each found their own way to evade their father's wrath, and James had done it by withdrawing somewhere deep inside himself. He looked like that now, even though this was a social gathering that could in no way be threatening.

His eyes met hers, the same clear gray that could be warm or cold as steel. At the moment he wore a polite expression that was less than a smile.

"Beg pardon, ma'am. Are you my hostess, Mrs. Harbison?"

He stood on the other side of the balustrade, and she came down one step until their eyes were level and the wall sconce let him see her face more clearly. How could he not recognize her?

"James? It's Mariel."

The polite twist of his lips disappeared. He was going to snub her. She could only be grateful that there was no one else in the hall.

He bowed to her. "I beg your pardon, ma'am, but we have not met."

She raised her hand to her throat. "Not in ten years. Please, James, don't do this. Did you not say that you wanted us to meet again, that you wanted to put the past behind us?"

She could see his embarrassment winning out over the veneer of gentleman's manners. "I am not James, madam. My name is Chartwell."

"But that cannot be." It was an inane thing to say. Of course he would know his own name. Confusion overrode her anxiety. She came down the last of the steps and rounded the corner so that she stood in front of him. She could do no more than shake her head as she tried to order her thoughts.

"I assure you, Chartwell is my name. Captain William Chartwell of His Majesty's Navy, at your service." He had mastered his irritation, his look patronizing, as though he were humoring a woman lost to dementia.

This given name was an even greater shock. "William?" She felt as though she would faint.

"Yes." He said the one word brusquely and then reached for her arm as she swayed

Just then Letty Harbison came out into the hall. She left the door open, and the sound of guests spilled into the deadly quiet of the hallway.

"Captain Chartwell . . . ?" she began, and then saw Mariel leaning on his arm. "Mariel, what is it? Shall I call Hadley or your brother?" She looked at the tall man all but holding her. "Perhaps not Edward. Yes, let me get your brother. Let one Braedon care for another."

She swirled around, leaving them alone once again. Mariel heard her calling Morgan's name, and even as she did, two or three of the more curious came into the hall to see what had upset the usually unflappable Letty Harbison.

Chartwell stiffened, his expression changed. If he had been detached before, he was the opposite now. His expression was so fierce that Mariel looked around wondering what the insult had been. It was not the people watching, for his back was to them. "What is it?" she asked.

He let go of her arm and looked down at her. "Are you a Braedon?" He all but hissed the question.

She cringed from the malevolence in his voice and heard one gentleman's "Say there, Chartwell" in her defense.

More puzzled than frightened, she ignored the growing crowd and answered, "I was. Then Mariel Whitlow. I still am Mrs. Whitlow and this past two years a widow."

With wooden politeness, completely at odds with his anger, he led her to a chair. He would have had her sit, but she was not about to give him the advantage of towering over her.

She refused the chair, but he turned from her anyway. He went to the porter and took the cloak he had handed into his care only a minute before.

"Wait! Wait! You must stay. Please wait. I have to know." She knew she sounded nearly incoherent, but how could you ask a man if he was your long-lost brother without sounding like something from a stage farce?

"Madam, if you are indeed of the Braedons who are the children of Marquis Straeford, then I have no desire to meet you or your brother. Your family represents everything I detest."

Someone in the crowd hissed, and low-voiced comments rippled through the group.

He turned to the porter. "Please extend my regrets to the Harbisons. I have no wish to be part of a company that welcomes them."

"You will wait. You must." She hurried up to him and grabbed his cloak-draped arm. "You are as much a Bracdon as we are, William. As legitimate as James or Morgan or me. I know that. I can convince them."

He turned back toward her, and she breathed a sigh of relief.

"Please, tell me where you are living, sir. I want to—I need to—talk with you. Why do you call yourself Chartwell?" It was the first of a thousand questions and the least important.

"My name is Chartwell because any name would be better than Braedon, milady."

Even as she tried to make sense of this rejection, she heard Edward's voice.

"Chartwell, wait a minute more. Give Mrs. Whitlow a chance to explain."

Chartwell shook his head. "This was your doing, was it not? I wondered at the invitation. You arranged it. You're nothing more than an interfering old woman." He took his hat from the porter. "I am gone from London tonight and hope never to see any Braedon again."

With that he ignored the porter, opened the door, and passed into the rainswept night.

Mariel did swoon then. All the energy drained from her body. William come back from the dead and now lost to them again. It could be that she was the only one who cared, and if so, then her heart would break for all of them.

She would have fallen if Edward had not been there. He reached for her even as one thought surfaced among the confusion of her sensibilities. "You knew he would be here?"

She sank into a chair and began to sob.

This was too much even for the gossip-curious, and the crowd melted back into the drawing room. Morgan closed the doors, but a moment later Letty Harbison came into the hall and left them open once again.

"I am so sorry, Mariel, Edward, Morgan." She addressed all three, not at all sure to whom she should apologize, or why.

Mariel took a deep breath and stood up. "Thank you, Letty, but how could you have known that Captain Chartwell was anything to us?" She looked at Morgan and realized when he looked as confused as Letty that he had no idea what she was talking about.

"He is our brother, our half brother actually. He is Annabelle's son born after she eloped to France. But he is a true Braedon, Father's son as much as you and James."

"By all the gods of Hades, how can he be here in England and we know nothing of it?"

"There is no time for explanations now. Go after him, Morgan. See if you can find out where he lives, where he is going."

He accepted her direction without question. Before he could do more than ask the porter for his cloak and cane, Edward said, "He is at the Falcon."

Morgan nodded and was out the door.

"You *do* know him!" Mariel looked at Edward through teary eyes. He looked worried. Or was it guilty.

"Yes, I've seen him several times and wondered at his likeness to your brother."

"You knew about William?" Her heart ached. "You knew about this man when I told you the story?"

"I thought the odds of him being your brother were remote at best. You never told me his given name, never that he was in the navy or even that he had survived to adulthood. Like you, it never occurred to me that he would change his last name."

A spark of anger came to life. It felt so much better than the ache of loss. "So you arranged this debacle? You are the one who had him put on the guest list tonight?"

"No. I had another plan."

"Another plan? If this one failed, then you have another plan? Spare me your kindness." She all but spit the words at him. "Who do you think you are?" Anger consumed her, a fine rage that he had fully earned. "Why would you do this to anyone?"

She waved to the hall behind them, where a small group watched with avid interest. "In so public a place. It will be all over London tomorrow."

He looked over his shoulder, and Letty Harbison encouraged the group to return to the salon. The empty hall did nothing to allay her anger.

"Do you think you are God, Edward? That you can play with people's lives for your own amusement? Give the footman ten guineas, help the penniless woman rid herself of debt, give Mariel the brother she wishes for. Do you not understand that your arrogant, frivolous choices ruin lives. Who else have you toyed with this way?"

Suddenly it occurred to her, and she stepped closer and whispered with white-hot anger, "The Burketts' daughter in Cashton and her hundred pounds. The dressmaker from Wales.

"Dear God, it's true, is it not? You have meddled in all their lives and dozens more for all I know. This is how you entertain yourself when the Season grows boring? You make a choice, give out the money, and then watch and see what happens."

He was speechless. Which only made her more angry. She had not thought that was possible.

She turned from him. "You use people for your amusement, like chess pieces come to life and you the player who can manipulate them at will. And you mask it all with your fabled charm and a smile." She turned from him and walked to the porter. "I will not be toyed with. I will not be a pawn on your human chessboard. I never want to see you again, Edward Hadley. Never."

# Nineteen

The card party went on, one table short. Chartwell, Mariel, and Morgan were gone already. Edward spent a few moments circulating among the guests but found their questions fueled rather than quelled the gossip. He excused himself, found his carriage, and made his way home with nothing but guilt for company.

The scent of roses and passion was still in the air. A crumpled handkerchief lay on the coach floor, and he remembered they had traveled together and yes, of course, she would have had to use his coach to return to her grandmother's.

He rapped on the ceiling, and when the coachman leaned down, he changed his direction, calling out, "Hale House." When he arrived he only stepped from the cab and stared up at the grand facade. A few windows were alight. Not everyone had gone to bed. Mariel was assuredly still awake.

His big mistake had been in not telling her about Chartwell when she had confided in him initially. At the very least he should have told her more about him, but who would have thought that the two of them would meet before he had a chance to advise Crandall. Who would have thought that a navy captain named Chartwell would indeed be the brother born in France more than thirty years before?

He climbed down from the coach unaided but did no more than stand before the door. Two hours earlier the house had looked much the same. Oh, if he could only recall time and start the evening over again.

If he were honest, he would have to go back further than

that to assuage her anger. Even before the moment he had decided not to mention Chartwell to Mariel.

She had accused him of playing God, including herself in the list of people he had helped over the years. Playing God? Hardly, but to banish that charge he would have to change his reaction that first time he had seen a beggar and reached for a coin. On a whim he decided to give the man whatever coin he should touch first. Of course, it was a guinea. The old man blessed him endlessly even as he walked on down the street and ended with "This will change my life, sir."

A guinea could change a man's life? He had almost walked back to ask how.

Or to the time when a misdirected champagne bottle had left him with a scar and could have, but for an inch or two, ended his life. It was at that moment that he grasped fully what a game of chance life was.

"You mask it all with your fabled charm and a smile." If he wanted to change that, then he would have go back to when he was all of five years old and first realized that his smile influenced people as surely as his father's wealth.

There it was. To satisfy her he would have to change who he was. He would have to change so much that his friends would not recognize him. If he changed to that extent, his life would be remade to some false model that was her ideal but not truly him. She might forgive him, but the forgiveness would be based on a lie.

Which was worse, arrogance or dishonesty? There was a question he would like to throw at her feet. Indeed, he raised his hand for the knocker, but sense overcame his anger. He turned and went back down the steps, climbed into the carriage, and sat there, trying to decide what to do. He loved her as much as he had ever loved anyone, but to give her what she wanted would make him hate himself.

A moment later the carriage started moving, making his decision for him.

\* \* \*

"Leave Morgan alone, Mariel." Her grandmother spoke calmly. Indeed, she was the only person who seemed to be at all at ease with the situation. "His eye is only blackened. It will heal well enough. The cold compress is all the medicine he needs."

"He hit you? William hit you?" Mariel stepped away as her grandmother wished, but it was more difficult to control her anger.

Morgan nodded. "I should have known better than to try to reason with him. He did do his best to control his temper. But when I said that he had responsibilities, well, that set him off like a call to arms."

"He's gone, then?"

"By daylight he will be."

"What will we tell James?"

"The truth, Mariel. That we found William quite by accident and he wants nothing to do with us."

Mariel leaned her head against the post at the foot of her grandmother's bed.

"Come here, girl." Her grandmother raised a hand from the bedcovers and gestured for her to sit down.

When she sat in the chair closest to the bed, the old lady took her hand and patted it with a slow, comforting motion.

Mariel looked at Morgan. "We did not find him by accident."

He had put his head back on the chair but straightened when she spoke. "What?"

"I did not meet Captain Chartwell by accident. Edward Hadley arranged for him to be there tonight. He had met him before and thought that he might be some connection." Had he said he thought Chartwell could be her brother? She could not recall every detail of the conversation, but it did not matter in the face of his calculated behavior.

"Sounds like something he would do, but surely that was in all innocence. For no one outside the family knows about

William." Morgan put his head back again but kept on talking. "A few years ago there were some rumors, and James came to town. It was the year I met Christiana." He smiled a little and then winced as the grin wrinkled his eyes, surely making his injured eye hurt all the more. "James came to town and we accompanied him to some gaming hell. Chartwell never saw us. He did look very like James, but we decided he was some relative we would prefer not to know. He never approached us and James let it go. He had more demanding problems to deal with then."

"Now we know why he ignored you."

"I'm not even sure Rhys knows about our missing brother, for I found out only when Marguerite gave me some journals that Mother wrote." A thought occurred to him. "You've not seen those journals. How did you know about him, Mariel?"

"Mother told me. When she was sick. She told me all about him and bade me keep it a secret. But that if he ever came forward, I was to know that he was no pretender."

"You've known for better than fifteen years and never told anyone?"

Morgan did not look angry so much as surprised.

"I am not going to apologize for doing what Mama asked when she was on her deathbed. I did tell Grandmère years ago." She looked away from her audience. "And last week I told Edward Hadley."

"I see," Morgan said, and Mariel thought that he saw a great deal more than the simple telling of the tale of William Braedon.

"Yes, and Edward betrayed me."

"I would hardly go that far, Mariel." This from her grandmother. "He could not be sure."

"He could have warned me. He said nothing. It was almost as though he wanted to embarrass me."

She was mortified that her family should be sitting here with her, witnessing the end of a dream. She stood up. "I am going to rest. Sleep may be too much to hope for."

She was almost to the door, when a pressing thought struck her. She turned back to her brother. "Morgan, I have written a note for James, asking for a meeting. Would you deliver it for me? Please let him know that I very much want to see him, wherever and whenever he wishes."

Grandmère's whispered "Thank God, Mariel" distracted her only a little.

She smiled at her grandmother, or at least tried to smile. A surfeit of emotion made it difficult. "Morgan, there is something else. We must consider what we are going to tell him about William."

"Everything," Morgan said. "And if you cannot, then I will."

Sleep did come, but only after another hour of anger that gave way to heartache. She was disgusted at the thought that last night's incident, precipitated by her behavior, would be all over town this morning. By dinnertime there would be a hundred different versions. She wondered bitterly if Rowlandson would do another cartoon of her.

At every appearance from here on, people would watch to see how she treated Hadley and who each of them next took up with. For her part, they could watch for months to no effect. She had every intention of returning to Cashton at the end of the Season with her heart as whole as she could make it.

She could give Anna more attention, and her charity work would keep her occupied as well. She drifted off to sleep finally, planning a new life, one that was devoid of men and their machinations.

Her dreams were not happy ones.

The next morning, word was waiting that James was as eager as she was for a meeting. Morgan would call for her as soon as she was able and willing.

With the meeting set for noon, Mariel dressed with some care, but in the most comfortable of her new gowns. She changed her hairstyle twice and was about to have her maid dress it again, when Spreen came to tell her that Morgan had come from the Braedon town house to escort her back to the family reunion.

She thought about stopping to see her grandmother but did not want to keep Morgan waiting. She sent a message with Spreen and promised a report as soon as she returned.

He bowed rather formally and then took her hands in his. "By all the gods of beauty, you do look lovely, Mariel."

"Your eye looks better." If he could lie, then so could she. His black eye was even more colorful than it had been the night before. She might not have a damaged eye, but she knew she had circles under hers, that her hairstyle was definitely behind the times, and she had just noticed a spot on the long sleeve of her gown.

"Shall we go, Mariel? Christiana is waiting with James and Marguerite in the drawing room that was Mama's favorite."

Mariel nodded, all at once too nervous to speak. They traveled in silence.

It was childish, but she had avoided the square since her return to London. The town house looked the same—the facade wide and windowed, the front door at the top of twin staircases that curved gracefully around a statue of Zeus and pots of spring flowers.

Brixton was still the butler, his hair thinned and his face more lined. He bowed to her. "Welcome home, milady."

She was touched by this departure from his usual formality. At the end of the front hall the door was cracked, and she could see two or three familiar faces peeking through. Mrs. Brixton was the only one she recognized, and the housekeeper raised her hand slightly in greeting while she dabbed at her eyes with a handkerchief.

She knew that Brixton would disapprove of that familiarity, so she did no more than return the same small wave, but the sweetness of the staff bolstered her courage.

She hurried up the stairs with Morgan following her, then stopped abruptly. Turning to him, she asked, "Is he the same? Is there anything I should know?"

Morgan shrugged. "He is the same and completely different."

"That is no help at all, Morgan." She welcomed the irritation raised by his totally inadequate answer. It was better than the nerves that had been growing the nearer they came to the meeting.

"Go in, Mariel. You'll see." He moved ahead of her and opened the door, and then stepped back so that she could enter first.

James was standing by the fireplace. When she came through the door he moved to the center of the room.

Morgan was wrong. He did not look the same at all. He was fully grown in more ways than height and strength of face. He was handsomer than he had been at twenty-three, when they had last met.

He did look like William, though if they stood together one could easily tell them apart, and not only because William's hair was whiter and his skin darker. Despite the difference, no one could deny that they were brothers.

"Welcome home, Mariel."

Even standing still he radiated a power that few men could equal. That reminded her so strongly of her father that her confidence faltered and she did no more than nod.

His somber expression eased a little, his expression gentler. "Mariel, you are not the only person I have hurt in my misguided effort to win the marquis's approval. I ask your forgiveness, and wish we could find as much closeness in the next ten years as we have estrangement in the past ten."

His humility made her uneasy. In fact, he seemed more comfortable with it than she did. "Thank you, James. To be included in the family again will mean more to me than you can know."

It was a carefully orchestrated exchange for both of them, but the next gesture was not. He took a step toward her and, without the slightest hesitation, drew her closer. The fierce hug was so unexpected that she did not at first respond.

It was this gesture more than anything else that convinced her that James was not a copy of their father. Mariel could not recall the marquis ever touching her, much less hugging her with such desperate apology. Or was it welcome?

He let her go but still held her at an arm's length as though he were examining her as closely as she had previously studied him.

"I thought it would be easier," James admitted, ducking his head a little in a gesture she recalled from childhood. "Making amends is something I have been doing a good bit of this last year. But none of those other apologies have meant as much to me as this."

"Or to me."

A woman Mariel did not know came forward. Petite and pretty, this must be James's wife, Marguerite.

The introductions were made quickly and, without hesitation, Marguerite greeted her in the French way with a kiss on both cheeks. She then grinned at her husband.

"At last the family is complete," Marguerite said. "Except for Anna, who we will meet later, and of course Rhys, who is still away, but he will come back and then he must apologize to you, James, for none of that stupid argument was your fault. Then we will be complete. It is as perfect as it can be for now, and we should celebrate with champagne, should we not?"

Mariel looked from Marguerite to Morgan and Christiana and then at James.

"But of course." James spoke with absurd indulgence. "Champagne for breakfast, lunch, and dinner, today and every day."

"No, not every day," Marguerite said. "If we did that, then it would not be special."

"I'm still learning, you see." He spoke to Mariel, but he watched his wife cross the room with a possessive affection that was as amusing as it was touching.

This was so much easier than she had feared it would be.

That was one thing for which she could thank Edward. If it had not been for his insight, she would have come to this meeting, if she had come at all, with her resentment still very much intact. If he was here. . . But it hurt too much to think of him, of that, so she pushed him from her mind.

While they waited for Brixton to bring the champagne, her brothers and their wives sat together on the two settees facing each other.

It was Morgan who brought up William. "While I do believe that champagne is in order, we must think of something else to drink to, for the family is not complete."

Mariel turned to James and Marguerite. "Last night we found William."

James was silent. Marguerite fired a dozen questions at them. Finally James turned to her. Mariel could not see his expression, but Marguerite stopped abruptly and then said, "I knew he was alive!" before moving closer to James and settling to silence.

Between them, Morgan and Mariel recounted the evening, leaving out her argument with Edward. James and Marguerite listened intently. Even Christiana did not move, and Mariel was certain she must have heard the story already.

Morgan explained his black eye, and Marguerite straightened, radiating indignation. *"Mon Dieu,* how could he? You are his brother."

"Clearly he does not agree with us on this."

When Marguerite would have gone on, James took her hand. "We will wait if we must." He glanced at his wife and spoke to her in French. The fact that they all could speak the language did nothing to diminish the intimacy of his words. "I know it will be difficult, but in time it will be made right." He raised her hand and kissed it. The gesture did more than express affection. It sealed a promise.

Marguerite nodded and Mariel could see her outrage fade.

The champagne came then, and they spent some few minutes popping the cork, pouring the foaming liquid, and toasting one another, their good fortune, the future, and, of course, the new Braemoor, which was already under construction.

"The architect is there alone while we are here. I only hope that Mrs. Lanning reminds him to eat and to wear a hat and coat." James laughed. "He is the most forgetful man I have ever met and yet manages to hold the entire design of the house in his head."

"He is a genius." Marguerite made that sound as though that were the only excuse he needed. "You will come to Braemoor to visit us and bring Anna? We are in the dower house, and it is small, it is true, but there is a very nice suite on the ground floor. You will both be comfortable there."

"Thank you, Marguerite. Shall we come for Michaelmas?" She refused to think of what she had hoped to be doing in September.

"Yes, it is a lovely time of year in Sussex."

Morgan set his glass down, took the bottle, and poured the last of the champagne into everyone's glasses. He set the bottle down but remained standing. "There is one other decision that we must make."

They all turned to him, and Christiana nodded. Clearly this is something that they had already discussed.

"We know we are one family again, but I think we must find a way to announce it to the ton. Besides making it known that we are one, it will accomplish something else. More clearly than anything else, it will tell the world that James is head of the family and that we are united behind him."

They all drank the toast implied, and Marguerite turned to Christiana. "Are there any balls in the next day or so?"

Christiana nodded thoughtfully. "There are three this week alone as well as a masquerade." She glanced at Morgan, and they exchanged a secret smile. "Not the masquerade. Our lives are confusing enough already."

Christiana might have meant it as a joke, but none of them laughed.

Marguerite stood up. "You choose the ball, Christiana, but not tonight, I think. We need some time to be a family."

James nodded. "Dinner together, at the least."

They all looked at Mariel, and she nodded, adding, "With Grandmère as well."

"She is well enough?" James asked.

"She has longed for this moment for years, James. You might not actually be her grandchild, but she has always considered you as one. She would not miss this reunion, but I will ask Mrs. Dayhull if it would be too much of a strain."

*"Eh bien,"* Marguerite continued. "Tonight we have a plan. When Christiana decides what ball we will attend, we will all go. We will arrive together. We will be introduced together, and you, Mariel, this once if that is all you wish, you will be introduced as Lady Mariel Braedon Whitlow. When they hear that and see us together, that will tell everyone all they need to know."

She turned to her husband, certain of his approval.

"She is no longer a housekeeper," James explained, "and is forever looking for something else to manage. I am so happy that it is not only me she is managing that I think it an excellent idea."

Marguerite turned to Mariel yet again. "What are you going to wear?"

# Twenty

The group split on the heels of that question. Christiana and Marguerite decided to accompany Mariel back to Hale House in order to report to the dowager duchess on the success of the meeting, see if she wished to join them for dinner, and to look through Mariel's wardrobe for something suitable for the upcoming ball.

Morgan would accompany James to Whites so he could visit with as many of his acquaintances as a short town sojourn would allow. They had all agreed that if Grandmère were well enough, they would meet again at Hale House for dinner.

The dowager duchess heard the news of the reunion with a satisfied smile and only one small sniff of emotion. She insisted that she would welcome the company for dinner. Mariel let Mrs. Dayhull's enthusiasm measure the true state of affairs. Her nod and smile were all the reassurance needed.

"Come back and tell me which dress you decide on. If I am to come down for dinner, then I must rest for an hour."

They all kissed the old lady and then hurried down the hall and up one flight of stairs to Mariel's suite of rooms.

Marguerite seated herself in the chair nearest the fire, explaining, "When it comes to fashion, I trust Christiana completely. I come so late to the ton that I know more of wool and bombazine than ball gowns."

Mariel wondered at how frankly she spoke of her past. She had no idea of the details, but they hardly mattered in the light of James's obvious happiness.

"You do understand that I was housekeeper at Braemoor before we married?" Marguerite asked.

"You are so frank about it. Do you not mind the possibility of gossip?"

"Gossip? What is there to gossip about if one does not keep secrets? If you are open and honest, then it is only the snide and mean-spirited who will make gossip of it. And they would hardly count as friends."

Mariel could not decide if Marguerite spoke with wisdom or naïveté.

"Besides"—the new viscountess grinned a wicked little smile—"James would not tolerate mean words of me any more than I would of him."

Ah, thought Mariel, she spoke with the confidence of someone loved. Someone who trusted her lover completely. Someone who knew that she would never be betrayed.

It only proved that there were so many different kinds of love. The love she and Edward had come close to was neither deep nor true, if it had been love at all.

She realized that the silence had lengthened and both Marguerite and Christiana were watching her with concern.

"I am so happy for you and James, Marguerite. That you both have found something deep and lasting."

"You will find love again, Mariel. I am sure of it."

"I have known love once, Marguerite. That is more than many people are given."

"Nonsense. Is it that Hadley person who has hurt you?"

"I already told her, Mariel." Christiana spoke from the door of the dressing room.

"Yes." Mariel spoke with barely controlled vehemence. This was one group she could trust. "My heart was unguarded. I thought what we shared meant I could trust him as you trust James. I was wrong. In the end he treated me as he treats all the rest of the ton. As people who exist for his amusement."

"He is charming?" Marguerite asked as if that would explain everything.

"Yes, he is quite irresistible. I even—" She stopped. There was no need to admit that she had been to his bedroom. They did not need to know every detail of her stupidity. She began again. "He is quite persuasive, but I must have known that he could not be trusted."

She saw Marguerite glance at Christiana, but was too intent on controlling her emotions to try to decipher what was passing between them.

"What is this gown, Mariel? I was not with you when you purchased this material, was I?"

"No, I went back and chose two more."

"But this is remarkable fabric." Christiana pulled the gown from its muslin wrapper and draped it over a chair.

"And an absurd indulgence. It was much too expensive. Who was I trying to impress?" She knew the answer to that and was sure that her sisters-in-law did too. "It hardly matters anymore."

"Oh, it matters still." Marguerite regarded the gown with some wonder. "And he *will* be impressed." With a decisive nod of conviction she sealed his fate. "When he sees you dressed in that, he will know what he has lost and wish to die for the pain of it."

"Oh, dear, that is rather more revenge than I should want, is it not?" She actually felt a little sorry for him. All this support was very heartening, but did not bode well for Edward Hadley.

"To know you and love you and then test that love in so stupid a way. Pain is what the fool deserves."


Edward fingered the chess piece. The ivory was cool against his fingers but warmed quickly. He set it back on the board and considered the rest of the pieces, each in place and ready, waiting for two players to give them life.

So much easier to be a pawn or a knight and let your life be at the command of some casual gamester. So much easier to start, finish, and begin again. That was the salvation of chess.

The pieces had no feelings, their ordered presence renewed at the end of each game, with the silent invitation to try again.

Nothing like life. Nothing. A stupid move in life meant more than failure.

He threw the piece back on the board, ruining the careful order of the two rows of white pieces.

If the move was bad enough, it could steep one in heartache and regret, and strip life of its meaning.

He took one edge of the board and flipped it. The pieces fell to the carpet in a quiet cascade, the noise barely loud enough to be noticed. Edward watched the pieces and wondered what he could throw, how loud a noise it would take to erase the sound of her fury.

*Arrogant and frivolous. Arrogant and frivolous.* For the first three days after her dismissal, those words were a mantra that did anything but calm him. They did, however, become the focus of his life.

He made the round of the usual parties with his longtime friends until those two words would have been a compliment. He drank more than he should, gambled, and lost more than was wise, then left twenty guineas in a coach for anyone to find and stopped his slow descent to damnation only when he found himself at the bedroom door of the ton's favored brothel.

The whore, the name she used was Chloe, laughed when he asked what she would do with a fortune. "Set myself up with a house of my own, of course. With my own girls and no one to tell me how many to entertain or how to do it."

He left her with something more than the fee she had not earned and wondered what she would say if she knew how close she had come to that fantasy fortune. It was the first time in his life that he had ever felt as though he had played God. With that one question he had decided her life. Or was it her answer that had decided it?

He bent down and picked up the chessboard, relieved to see that nothing was broken. Sitting on the footstool, he began to pick up each piece and set it back in place.

Thank God he had not taken what comfort he could from Chloe. If he had, he would have debased the love that was still there, despite anger and misunderstanding.

If Mariel's beauty and grace drew him like a magnet, it was her honor and honesty that held him to her. If he gave her that same honesty, could they reclaim what they had? He was willing to try. He laughed. He was more than willing to try. He was desperate. Her presence breathed substance into his life. Meaning. Purpose.

Virtues he had never known he was looking for until that moment in a graveyard when their hearts first met.

When they met again he would have proof that his personal charity was more than a game for his amusement. Matthew could compile a list. He had never intended to play God. He only hoped he could prove it and that she would believe him. That she would not expect changes that would be impossible for him to make.

The chess pieces were all in place except for the king and queen. He placed them in the middle of the board, without support, facing each other. The queen able to move in any direction and any distance. The king able to move only one space at a time. It hardly mattered in which direction he moved, for the only move that made any difference was the one step closer. She could run from him, and if she did, he would have to accept that it was over. But he had to at least try.


She looked spectacular. Edward watched Mariel from the edge of the crowd. She was dancing with the Duke of Redmond, who was virtually ignoring the figures in favor of their discussion—of the Mongolfier balloon, no doubt.

Her dress caught the light each time she turned. It was a blue gown, a dark blue but it was shadowed with gold. As she moved in the steps of the dance, the gown would shimmer with golden highlights. It was magic and she looked magical in it.

He had come late and missed the Braedon family entrance. Nevertheless, he felt as though he had been there, for at least three people had recounted it to him. The way the whole room paused when they appeared before their hosts and how the crowd had reacted when "the Lady Mariel Braedon Whitlow" was announced. There was even some applause, at least that is what one of his informants had insisted. At the sound, people had hurried in from the other rooms, too late to enjoy the spectacle.

Oh, how he wished he could have seen it, and then reminded himself that "nonchalance" was his byword for tonight.

If he was hoping for reconciliation, it was clear that she was not. She never once searched the room for him. If their ability to communicate without words was real, surely she would know that he was here. If she was willing to listen to him, she would at least acknowledge him.

She was done with him.

Indeed, the man she claimed to love was not the true Edward Hadley. He had wondered for a while if the true Hadley might not be the man he was when they were together. But if that was so, then his whole life had been a farce, or at the least a game in which he had been the loser.

No. He had made choices and found ways to cure his boredom, that was all. If she thought that was playing God, then it only showed how conventional she was. They would not suit at all.

Still, he wanted that one additional conversation with her, if only a short one. He wanted her to know that he had not been the one to invite Chartwell to the Harbisons' card party. That he would never have deliberately put her in such a difficult situation.

It was Chartwell who had accused him of arranging the meeting. He did not care a fig if Chartwell ever knew the truth, but more than anything else he wanted Mariel to know it had been chance, ugly chance, that had brought the two Braedons together and not a plan of his devising.

He realized that he was still watching her, and then noticed almost everyone else was too. She was the center of attention. Tonight the young girls did not stand a chance against the beauty and wisdom of Mariel Whitlow. This was neither the time nor place for that one last conversation.

Remaining in the ballroom was a torture he need not continue. He would find conversation somewhere. Or perhaps he would find the card room. This was enough of a crush that he could be here for hours and not run into her.

Every room on the ground floor had been opened up to accommodate the crowd. He passed through two salons, where there was hardly room enough to breathe and then found the library. It was quieter here, one couple about to begin a game of chess. They invited him to observe, but Edward declined. It would be a good while before he could enjoy chess again.

There was another group seated near the empty fireplace, engaged in an earnest discussion on the increase of novels by women.

"It is hardly a new phenomenon. It began before my father was born."

Another agreed. "It is known these days only because women are allowed to name themselves as authors."

"More socially acceptable," someone else added.

"And publishers are paying more," Edward said.

The whole group looked at him. Mrs. Burris shook her head. "Money is hardly the subject under discussion here, Mr. Hadley."

"Oh, yes, it is." This from a man he did not know. "He is right. Money is as strong an inducement to create as is the urge to share a thought."

The idea did not seem to sit well with the rest of the crowd. The stranger continued. "Have you read the poetry of Isolde Geddes?"

Most of them nodded.

"Did you not read the advertisement where she credits her success to an unknown benefactor who gave her the money on which to live while she was writing and then waiting for her book to sell enough to convince the publisher that she was a success?"

"It was a lover."

"No, I think not."

Edward left them debating the morals of a woman they had never met. Even an intellectual discussion could descend to gossip. But Edward knew the truth. It had not been a lover who had made Isolde Geddes self-sufficient. It had been him.

Leaving the group had hardly been necessary. No one there even hinted at his philanthropy. He had worried since his and Mariel's argument. Worried that now everyone would know of his absurd hobby. But no one did. It was some small gift that part of their argument had been for their understanding alone.

Or else the ton was so agog at the revelation of Chartwell's connection to the Braedons or his and Mariel's loss of composure that they remembered nothing else.

No matter the reason, he was grateful. Life was misery enough without having to deal with the questions and curious looks that would come if they all knew that he had been sharing his fortune with complete strangers. Not to mention the number who would ask for a loan.

None of them were half as deserving as Isolde Geddes. When he had seen her acting as companion to some miserable old lady, he had no idea that she longed to write poetry. His gift of money had been a lifeline. He had rescued her, dammit. He had not played God.

He was making his way down the front hall, when he all but ran into a petite, dark-haired bundle of energy he recognized as Viscount Crandall's wife.

"Mr. Hadley, how lovely to see you again."

He was sure they had never been introduced, but he was not about to say so.

"My pleasure, my lady."

She leaned a little closer to him. "I am in need of some air. Could you give me your arm? There is a lovely garden that

our hostess has set up with table and chairs for supper al-
fresco." She took his arm even though he had not offered it.

"My sister, Lady Morgan, tells me that the Westbournes
started this theme and that each hostess has interpreted it in
her own way." She moved toward the terrace doors, definitely
the one in charge.

Edward looked around for her husband, not certain that this
was a wise idea.

"James will meet us there," she whispered. "He was going
to come find you, but I have saved him the trouble."

"If the viscount wishes to speak with me, would it not be
better for us to meet at your town house. This could attract
unwanted attention."

"And I was told that you ignored gossip. Have you turned
decorous? Whose influence is that?" She asked the question
without the flirtatious edge the question implied. She asked
as though she already knew the answer. "We will hardly be
noticed, Mr. Hadley. Lord Griffon has this moment arrived
with someone no one recognizes. That will hold their interest
for long enough."

One would think that the viscountess had arranged with
Griffon to provide the distraction. Edward looked more carefully at her. She had the air of someone planning a serious
campaign and decided it was entirely possible for her to have
enlisted Griffon's aid.

Crandall rose when the two joined them, seeming not at all
surprised that his wife had come back with him as a prize. But
then, he had the ability to mask his feelings to an uncanny de-
gree. As did William Chartwell. Did he know about William?
Did he care? Was this the time to speak to him of it?

Both gentlemen waited until Lady Crandall was seated and
then seated themselves.

"Thank you for meeting us, Hadley. I have some questions
that I believe you can answer, but I also think that if we are
seen to be on speaking terms, it will ease any gossip regarding you and my sister."

Edward noted the small smile that accompanied the two words "my sister" and wanted to take some credit for it. "I suppose it could ease gossip, my lord, unless they think that I am asking you for permission to court her."

James laughed. "Then perhaps I should have said it will confuse the ton."

"Do you wish to court her?" Lady Crandall asked the question with such sudden and eager interest that Edward considered his words carefully.

"I believe that she made her feelings toward me very clear at the Harbisons' card party."

"And what did she say to you?"

"As if you have not already heard every word of it, my lady." He kept smiling, but anger was just below the surface. He shifted in his seat.

"Ah, but what you heard is what matters the most."

"Give him some privacy, my dear." James spoke with asperity despite the endearment, and his wife turned to him.

"Would you find some champagne for me?"

Her tone, if not the order, implied his interference was not welcome.

"And miss this entertainment. Never." Crandall sat back, crossed his arms, and gave Hadley a look that said "I tried." Edward suspected that they would have words later. It did not seem to bother Crandall's wife at all. Nor did it spare him this inquisition. "What did she say to you, Mr. Hadley?"

"She said that I played God. That all my efforts to help people were nothing more than playing God."

"But most assuredly that is not so."

He was so taken aback by her defense that he could not control his surprise. "You have only just met me, my lady. How can you know that?"

"Yes, I have known you for only a few moments, but I have known God all my life."

Edward almost laughed at the presumption. He looked at James, whose smile was an outright grin. He raised his hands in denial. "She does not mean that I am God. Besides, we have known each other for only two years."

"If you want to meet someone who thought he was God, then you must go to Wales and talk to James's father." Marguerite shuddered. "More in league with the devil, that man is."

The viscountess spoke with such a bitter edge that her husband reached over and put an arm on her shoulder, his own amusement gone.

She did not turn to look at him, but his touch did calm her and redirect the discussion to him.

"You are neither God nor Satan, Mr. Hadley. You are a man. I know from personal experience how hard it is for a man to let his feelings show."

She turned to face her husband, took his hand from her shoulder, and kissed it. His usually masked feelings showed now as he looked at her, Edward thought. He was discomfited at the intensity that shimmered between them. Embarrassed and envious.

She turned back, all business once again. "If you want another chance, then you must write to her, tell her exactly how you feel."

And risk having his heart stomped on? He shook his head.

She looked away for a moment. "Did you see her tonight?"

"Yes," he answered cautiously, suspecting a trick question. Marguerite said nothing, the silence growing until he felt compelled to add, "She looked beautiful."

"But a little sad, I think."

"Not when I saw her. She was laughing with Redmond over something and spent an absurd amount of time admiring some fop's gaudy waistcoat."

Marguerite smiled. "Indeed."

He realized how neatly he had fallen into that trap and all but swore.

"When you were watching her tonight your true feelings showed. You will try one more time. You must." She leaned forward. "You will do it because you love her."

"That is quite enough, Marguerite. You are going too far." This time James spoke with authority. "I want my sister's happiness as much as you. But this man cannot be expected to bare his soul at a party so that you can determine if theirs is a match to be supported. It is their business."

"Thank you, Crandall." Edward hoped that would put an end to the discussion. The viscountess looked as though a yelling argument was one of her favorite things. Indeed, knowing Crandall, it might well be a requirement for a happy marriage or at least one where her wishes were understood.

*"Eh bien,* two against one are not good odds, are they, Mr. Hadley? I will concede." She nodded to her husband. "But not give up."

"I am forewarned." Crandall bowed from his seat and turned to him. "As are you, Hadley."

Who had who wrapped around their finger? he wondered. Or was *that* the secret of a good marriage? Each knew how far to go and how much to give. And how long had been considering what made a marriage worth the effort?

"Please, Mr. Hadley." She looked at her husband, who gave her the slightest nod of approval. The newest member of the Braedon family leaned closer. "I have helped you and Mariel."

Is that what that had been? It felt more like the attack of an Amazon than Cupid at work.

"Now you can help us. We would like you to tell us everything that you know of the man who calls himself William Chartwell."

# Twenty-one

"When we asked him about William last night, Mr. Hadley said that he had nothing to do with the captain's invitation to the card party."

Marguerite made the announcement to the room in general: the duchess, Mrs. Dayhull, Christiana, and Mariel.

Then she turned to Mariel. "I think he would very much like an opportunity to talk to you."

"You are telling me that Edward had no idea that William would be at the party?" Mariel's heavy heart lightened.

"It changes things, does it not?" Marguerite said.

Mariel thought of the note that had arrived that morning. The note she had yet to read. When she did not answer, Marguerite continued.

"He told us that the captain accused him of it and you drew your own conclusion from that."

"That could be," Mariel conceded. "The whole episode is a jumble in my memory. The most vivid details are how he looked and how I felt." She thought a moment. "Hideous" was her one-word description.

She looked around her. "It is not something I care to discuss, even with people as dear to me as all of you."

"But I do." Her grandmother turned to Marguerite. "Go on, dear girl."

"Grandmère," Mariel pleaded, "surely there is something better to talk about than Edward Hadley and William Chartwell."

Her grandmother waved her hand dismissively, already intent on the story Marguerite was recounting.

Mariel listened a moment, then turned away from the bed and walked to the window. A few moments later, Marguerite came to stand next to her.

"Mariel no longer seems convinced of his charm," she said.

"Eh, look at me when you talk, child, or I can't hear you."

Marguerite walked back toward the bed and the duchess.

Mariel stayed at the window, apart from the group, even though she was the center of it. "It sounds as though the rest of you are quite captivated with him." That sounded shrewish, if not downright jealous. She tried again. "I felt a fool last night, trying to avoid him."

"Why did you?" Christiana spoke for the first time.

"Because I was still furious with him."

"Do you feel different now that you know that he did not plan the meeting?" Christiana asked.

"He is guilty of worse. Edward Hadley is charming. We all have experience of that, do we not?" Mariel looked around the room, and even Mrs. Dayhull nodded.

"Oh, stop being nonsensical, girl. Charm is never a fault."

Mariel flushed and was about to reply, when Christiana interrupted.

"I think what Mariel means is that Hadley has come to rely on his charm to help excuse his more thoughtless behavior."

Mariel nodded.

With faint apology Christiana continued. "And she is afraid that she is still much too susceptible to it."

"Yes." Mariel could feel a blush rising but ignored it. "But that will change. I plan to spend the rest of the Season ignoring him. I have not spent as much time with Anna as I would have liked. And there are a number of musicales that I will enjoy. Then we'll go back to Cashton." July seemed a lifetime away.

"So there is something besides his supposed interference with William that offended you?" Marguerite did not wait for a reply. "Mr. Hadley told me that you accused him of playing God."

"Yes." Mariel refused to back down from the accusation.

"He does. He uses his wealth and his charm to meddle in people's lives."

"He did not seem that arrogant to me."

"Arrogant?" the duchess said. "Of course he is arrogant. It is the one trait each member of the ton can claim. Including you, Mariel."

"'Overconfident' might be a better word," Christiana said. "The world is his to command." She turned to Marguerite. "It is not quite as bad as Mariel and Grandmère make it sound." Christiana added, "The *ton* calls him their lucky charm. We could tell you any number of stories of people whose fortunes have been changed, and they insist it is because of Edward Hadley. Willy Gates for one, and Gerald Lockwood's winning the card marathon."

Christiana looked at Mariel, who nodded and thought, *Lucy Brevier and the modiste from Wales*. She was not ever going to tell that story, no matter how estranged they were.

"I heard of the marathon last night." Marguerite paused. "And only the day before, someone was telling me that Mr. Hadley told her of an antiquity being sold by some impoverished earl." She was silent and then shook her head. "But you cannot call that playing God. Most assuredly it is not." Marguerite leaned forward a little. "It is not that Mr. Hadley is playing God. It is that God is playing with Mr. Hadley."

Mariel noticed that the others looked as confused as she did. Marguerite saw it, too, and explained further. "God is using him, do you not see?"

"Edward as a divine messenger?" Mariel asked.

"Edward Hadley is hardly an angel." The duchess raised her eyebrows as she spoke.

Mariel realized that she was not the only one who knew stories Edward would as soon keep quiet. Though Mariel suspected Grandmère's stories had nothing to do with giving away ridiculous sums of money.

"One need not be an angel. Oh, no. God uses Edward Hadley in the same way he uses all of us. As he used Simon Marfield when I was offered the position at Braemoor."

Mariel understood but must have still looked skeptical, for Marguerite continued her explanation.

"Even as he used the marquis when he forced you, Mariel, to make a choice between your family and your husband. For God does not always make the choices easy or the consequences comfortable."

"It is attributing far too noble a motive to much of his behavior. I may have been too strong in my accusation, but at the very least he is frivolous and wastcful."

"God uses us whether we are saint or sinner," Marguerite insisted.

The duchess laughed. "I suppose that even now you would say that God is using you to mend the rift between Mariel and Edward."

"It is up to you how you choose to behave." Marguerite shrugged. "God does not tell us what choices to make."

The duchess turned her full attention to her granddaughter. "See how skillfully she moves from Edward's behavior to forgiving him? Marguerite, next you will be writing sermons for the bishop."

"Not I, your grace." Marguerite's tone was filled with humility that was completely eroded by a mischievous smile. "James will tell you that I do believe in forgiveness for even the most stupid behavior, but only after some suffering. And that sort of revenge is hardly the belief of a truly angelic spirit."

"Edward was unforgivably meddlesome."

"He is as miserable as you are." Marguerite spoke with conviction. "I would beg that you at least listen to him."

"If I do, it is as Christiana says, he will charm his way into my good graces yet again." Mariel folded her arms across her chest.

"If it is that easy for him to charm you, Mariel," the duchess said, "then it is only your strong will keeping you apart." A small coughing spasm followed the duchess's pronouncement, and Mariel knew that she must rest soon.

"Since when has this become a subject for debate?" Mariel moved toward the door. "Grandmère, it is my pleasure to entertain you, but I think it is time for you to rest."

"You are not as happy as you could be, Mariel." Christiana spoke, completely ignoring Mariel's suggestion. "You tried last night. You looked lovely and I am sure almost everyone was fooled. But your smile never quite reached your eyes and you never once laughed."

"Mariel." Her grandmother summed it up. "We all have noticed and do not find your heartache entertaining at all."

Christiana stood up and began to cross the room as she continued. "We know that being part of the family again has brought you some joy. But being without Edward has brought shadows to your eyes. Your face is sad, too sad."

Christiana walked closer to Mariel as though the words were for her alone, but she did not lower her voice. "It may be that he is not the lover you hoped him to be, and if that is true, then we are all so sorry. You seemed so well suited. As though one of you completed the other. He gave you laughter. You gave him purpose."

"Mariel, it could be that you failed him as well." Her grandmother waited until she came closer. "Ah, yes, I see that makes you angry."

"I hate it that my personal life is set out for all of you to discuss."

"But only because your family loves you and will care for you." This from Mrs. Dayhull, who spoke so rarely that Mariel had to count it as the truth. This could never be gossip. She smiled at the woman who was so much an observer and wondered what she would have done with independent means.

"I know you all care, Mrs. Dayhull. I never thought anything less, but I thank you for the reminder." Mariel turned to her grandmother. "How did I fail him, Grandmère?"

"By not listening. By not giving him a chance to explain."

Mariel nodded, remembering the note in her room.

"Indeed, granddaughter." The duchess reached for her hand and her attention. "If what our dear Marguerite says about the divine plan is true, then you must think of it this way."

All four of them gave her their complete attention.

"It could be that God is giving you the chance to make Edward see how much more fully life can be lived."

The coughing fit that followed Grandmère's announcement could not have been deliberate, but it was an effective end to the conversation. Mrs. Dayhull came to the side of the bed, her expression one of concern. It was enough of a message that within a minute they had made their good-byes and gone to freshen up for a tour of Hyde Park.

Her grandmother's words echoed through her even as Mariel left the others and went to her room. What had Grandmère meant by a life more fully lived?

Something more than the physical completion they could give each other. The memory of their kisses, even the memory of holding his hand, had her longing for his touch despite her anger. She missed that as much as she missed the way their minds would share the same thought with nothing more than a glance.

As much as her grandmother had loved her long-dead husband, Mariel was sure she had meant more than physical union. And if God had any part in this, then surely he did too.

She walked over to her desk and sat down, picking up the folded paper that had been delivered with her morning chocolate.

She resisted the urge to smell the paper, but she did rub her fingers over the wax seal, imagining his fingers there, imagining his touch.

It had taken him five days to send it. Was that because he had been angry too? Had he tried, and failed as she had, to forget? To forget the way it felt when they were together.

As she opened the message, she consoled herself with the

thought that at least this small part of her life was private. The decision to open the note. The decision to act on the message. Both were hers alone.

He did have the worst handwriting, as though he were testing her to find out how ardently she wished to hear from him. Even if it had been written in Russian, she would have found a way to read it.

> *Mariel, my dear,*
>     *Signor Ponto would be honored to see you at the cello program at the Academy of Ancient Music Thursday evening. So would I. Please do not disappoint us.*
>                                                     *Your Edward*

Her heart ached. *Your Edward.* Did he really mean that? Did he still hold out hope that he could win her to his way of thinking, charm her into his good graces? If the two words *Your Edward* could touch her so, there was little doubt that seeing him would have an even more potent effect.

Then another thought struck her. When Signor Ponto had brought them together at their second meeting, the maestro had exclaimed, "He has a true appreciation of the cello."

Mariel knew that was patently untrue. By his own admission, the only music Edward enjoyed at all was the harp, and that only because he associated it with his family and happy days.

He appreciated the cello because Signor Ponto's prize pupil was another of Edward's beneficiaries. Of course he was, she thought.

Did he follow all of them to see what they did with his gift? How often was the money used for good? How often was it wasted?

And were Marguerite and Grandmère right? Was she in his life to give it more meaning, to cure his boredom? He had shown her how to have fun. Could it be that she had something equally important to give him?

She closed her eyes and prayed, the note held against her breast. Her heart that had ached with emptiness now eased with hope.

# Twenty-two

Mariel raised a hand to greet Signor Ponto. She had arrived at the very last moment. The decision to come had been
made hours before, but her uncertainty about every other aspect of this meeting had her too tense for any sort of
conversation. So tense that she had to hold her hands tightly
to still their shaking.

She scanned the room as if assessing the size of the crowd.
Edward was not in sight. She moved mechanically toward a
seat only two rows from the back and insisted to herself that
even if he did not make an appearance, the music would be
compensation enough.

For a horrifying moment she thought she would cry. If he
did not come, she would not care a whit for the music no matter how fine it was. She had not even arranged for someone
to collect her here. It had been his invitation. Of course he
would come.

In an effort to distract herself, she surveyed the room once
again. The crowd was thin. One or two people nodded to her,
and she gave them polite nods. A smile was too much to ask.

She smoothed the skirt of her copper-colored gown. It
was the last of her new ones, and she was contemplating
ordering one or two more. Foolish, she decided. A waste
of money better spent other ways. The Season would be
over in a few weeks.

Already people were drifting from town. They might blame
it on the wet weather or the pall that remained after Prime

Minister Spenser's assassination in May, but she knew it was none of those.

It was boredom that sent them packing. The beau monde would disperse to their homes for the summer months until ennui settled again. In the fall or the spring they would race back to London, hoping to find something to end the monotony.

Something or someone.

She was no different. Without Edward beside her, the entertainments were no more than a way to escape her own low spirits. *I miss him.*

It was the smallest of admissions, made so quietly that she was able to ignore it as Signor Ponto called attention to the front of the hall.

As he made his introduction, she decided that perhaps she would leave for Cashton sooner than originally planned. Once there, she would have more time to spend with Anna. She could turn her attention to the charity that had been so long a dream. Helping others had given her life meaning before she met Edward Hadley. It would again.

There was polite applause after Ponto's introduction. She was so lost in thought that the sound startled her.

She forced her full attention on the stage. The young man who had looked so nervous in Dover now exuded confidence. He bowed to the audience, showed no disappointment at the small crowd, and then seated himself.

The cello was the exact opposite of the harp. The harp played on the surface of emotion, tempting and teasing. The cello went at once to the core of being, its deeper string sound less ephemeral and more visceral.

He began with the same piece he had played in Dover, and Mariel was instantly transported back to the second time she had seen Edward Hadley, leaning against a wall, watching her. This was where it had begun, and she could not stand the reminder a moment longer.

Rising from her seat, she turned to see if she could reach

the door before her heart would break, and saw Edward leaning against the wall as he had that first time.

He smiled at her. *Hello, darling, I've missed you. Never lie. Tell me you missed me too.*

She sat down abruptly, furious. Furious with him for putting her through this. Tears trickled down her cheeks. Only one or two, but more were sure to follow. She knew herself well enough to realize that the fury was a substitute for fear.

She thought of her grandmother's words, of what Marguerite and Christiana had urged, but knew that Edward himself had given her the best advice of all when he had urged her to meet James.

Open your heart. Abandon your grudge. Give life a chance. She could at least sit with him. Listen to him and try to rediscover the perfect fit that had made them feel so complete together. If that was too much to ask, then she would have the satisfaction of knowing she had tried. She could not be lonelier than she already was.

She turned around again, and he did not wait for a further invitation. He gave up the wall and took the seat on the aisle next to her.

"Thank you for claiming this seat for me."

It was the silliest thing for him to say when there were twenty other empty chairs. But it was true. The place next to her had been empty for a sennight, and no one had come close to filling his place. No one ever would.

She raised her hand to her throat and two more tears traced their way down her cheeks. She heard a whispered "Mariel!" He took her hand. "Oh, God, don't cry."

She tried to stop; indeed, she was barely crying but could not speak for fear two tears would become a sob.

He pulled her from her seat and urged her to the door as though it were normal to leave after three bars of music had been played. The action so surprised her that the tears evaporated before they had reached the foyer.

The porter was assisting two late arrivals, and with a most

ungentlemanly curse Edward pushed open a door and pulled her into a room that might have been an office.

She drew a deep breath and was about to speak, when he pressed a finger to her open lips.

"This first." He kissed her. He made it a dozen little kisses, his lips taking the smallest sweet sampling of hers. How could a kiss be an apology? But that was what it felt like. Until she could stand the tantalizing touch no more and opened her mouth to him.

If the first had been apology, this was passion, built up and then banked as a fire on a cold night. Now it sprang to life and consumed both of them. When they drew apart, his hair was disheveled, the sleeve of her dress pushed from her shoulder.

"Is there a bed in this room, do you think," Edward whispered. He kissed her neck and moved his mouth closer to her aching breasts. She could feel her nipples tighten, and when his hand touched her through her dress, she sighed, one long, slow release of restraint that had been a part of her for two years.

"We hardly need a bed, Edward." She reached for some semblance of control. One moment more and the floor would serve the purpose. "We must talk first. It would be too easy to let our hunger for each other overcome our differences."

She knew that was exactly what he wanted. If he could show her the deepest pleasure of his company, then he hoped all their differences would melt away.

"As you wish, Mariel." He leaned his forehead against hers as he whispered the words. "But make no mistake, I want you more than my next breath."

"And I want more than a casual lover."

"I love you, Mariel. Yes, I want the pleasure of your company in every way, but I want more than that. I want your equally beautiful mind and heart, and all the goodness that makes you what you are."

"Then we will talk, Edward. We must talk."

He let go of her and she took a small step back.

"Talking is something we do almost as well as kissing." He spoke on that intimate laugh that was all for her. "I'll have the porter call for my carriage."

He was at the door and she stopped him, raising a hand to smooth his hair. He took the hand and kissed it. "Wait here, Mariel, I will bring your cloak."

It seemed a good suggestion. Her disarray was not as easily put right. Was that a tear in her gown at the shoulder? She looked around the office. She would never view a desk and chairs in exactly the same way. What an odd place to say "I love you."

He waved the postillion off and opened the carriage door himself, calling out "Hale House" to the coachman.

His direction stopped her. She put a hand on his arm to stay him as he was about to hand her into the carriage. "Hale House?"

He understood. "The choice is always yours, Mariel." Then he shrugged. "And my aunt and cousin are at home tonight."

"Ah, then Hale House it is." She allowed herself to be handed into the carriage and seated before either of them spoke again.

"Edward, what is it about an office that makes you so willing to say 'I love you'?"

He laughed out loud. "That is hardly the question I thought you would start with."

"The first time you used the word was in Mr. Matthew's office. Do you remember?"

"Oh, yes." He spoke as if she had just reawakened that memory. "I know exactly why. That first time it seemed a safe place. I knew that in such staid surroundings it would sound less of a commitment. I had never spoken the words before and was afraid of how they would sound in too intimate a spot."

He pulled her close and whispered, "And the second time, I spoke in such staid surroundings because I could not wait one moment more."

He had told her; now he did his best to convince her. His lips, his hands, his whole being, breathed the words into her until the truth of it settled in her heart.

He held her close to him. She rested her hand inside his jacket, against the starched smoothness of his shirt. She could feel the rapid beat of his heart, his breathing harsh enough to convince her that self-control was an effort.

She straightened and he seemed to relax. The silence lengthened. "I'm sure it was an excellent concert." It was a banal bit of conversation, but she needed to do something to distract herself from the thought of all the empty beds at Hale House.

"I have no doubt he will play to perfection." There was a long beat of silence before he added, "He is one of mine, you know."

He made the confession as though testing this bit of honesty before committing to more.

"Of course he is." She straightened her cloak and pushed the hood off her head. "He is on my list."

"You've made a list?"

"Oh, yes. It is a short one, but I have no doubt that not only London but the entire country is littered with your beneficiaries."

"Who did you guess?" he asked with boyish curiosity as though delighted to finally be able to share the game.

"The modiste from Wales, the Burketts' daughter."

"The Burketts' daughter?" Edward's questioning lasted only a second. "Oh, you mean the waitress at the pub in Cashton."

"Yes." She hesitated. "And I thought perhaps Signora Rouselli."

"Mariel, I will think you are a witch."

"Aha. I thought so. How could no one know? All of the ton speculated for weeks when she arrived from Europe with only the vaguest explanation of her travels."

"No one guessed because I did not actually have a hand in her journey, and I could prove that. I only provided the money. You would be amazed at how much can happen if only you provide the means. In Signora Rouselli's case, the man who arranged for her journey had no idea where the funds came from."

Mariel nodded her understanding.

"I am ahead of myself." He sat back but did not let go of her hands. "Sometimes I gave the money on impulse, sometimes because I thought there was a need. Sometimes I had a fair idea of how it would be used, but, Mariel, I gave the money with no expectations." He looked at her, trying not to sound anything but honest. "This is important for you to know, to believe."

"I do. I do believe you, Edward. How is it that no one has ever guessed at this until me, until now?"

"Because no one has known me as well as you do. No one has ever been as close or even begun to understand me." He raised the hand still in his and kissed it. "But I must have a perverse mind, for even you are not in perfect understanding. I have gone to Matthew for a list—"

She cut him off with a surprised "Matthew is part of this?"

"Well, yes. I was not nearly as partial as you are to witnessing the actual presentation of the gift. Matthew has been my man of business and my father's before me. I trusted him to handle all the details. He even made one or two suggestions himself."

"Like Lucy Brevier." A dozen small questions were answered. One large one remained. "Why, Edward?"

"Why Lady Brevier?"

"Why any of them?"

The carriage drew to a stop and the postillion jumped down to open the door. The question hung in the air between them and Mariel wished they could keep on driving until all her questions were answered. The dark made confidences so much easier.

* * *

The rain had started again, and Edward welcomed the light and warmth of the foyer. With it, uncertainty returned. He loved this woman, but could he give her what she demanded, or would she ask too much of him. What was too much?

She led the way to the music room. "It is the only room where I am sure there is a fire and candles."

He supposed that could be true, but he further hoped that she chose it because it was the first place they had kissed and, he hoped, the next.

She did not turn to him when they entered, but walked to the fireplace to warm her hands. He could have warmed her much more thoroughly, but he knew she was right. The echo of her in his arms clouded his judgment. There was some comfort that if he was distracted, then she was as well.

Without turning around she began. "Before you answer my question, Edward, it is my turn to explain. I must apologize for behaving like a fishwife in a public place. It was so very wrong of me, and my only explanation is that I was both shocked and upset by William's animosity and by what I thought was your hand in bringing us together.

She turned now and looked at him. "Marguerite explained that you were not part of that at all. But for those few moments, Edward, perhaps even for the next few days, before she talked to me, I felt as though my entire world were nothing more than a house of cards collapsing before me."

"I am so sorry." He shook his head. "If ever four words were inadequate, it is those. They cannot possibly convey how horrified I was to see Chartwell there."

She did smile now. "As I recall, you were speechless."

"It's not funny. You liken it to a house of cards collapsing; for me it was like watching you being tortured, causing the torture and then unable to stop it." He shuddered. "My explanation is not nearly as simple as yours, Mariel."

He walked to where she stood. When he would have taken her hands, she shook her head and put them behind her back.

"I mean no insult, Edward." She was smiling again. "I cannot touch you and listen with an impartial mind."

That was almost as much a comfort as holding her hands would have been. He put one of his hands on the fireplace mantel and looked down into the quiet flame for a moment. "I came after you that night."

"You did?"

"I was undone by your pain. I stood at your door, considering what had happened, what you had accused me of." He looked at her. "I left without knocking, as angry at you as you were at me. Angry at you for making me question all the choices I had made with my life. For making me see them as something bad, if not evil, when they were well meant, if ill conceived."

He reached out and cradled her cheek with his hand. He did not pull her close. He wanted the contact only so she would know that he was no longer angry and to reassure himself that her heart was not still bruised. He let his hand fall even as she pressed her cheek into his touch.

"You accused me of playing God. I have never played God, Mariel. Never." He shook his head, and knew his expression was as aloof as it was apologetic.

She opened her mouth and then merely nodded.

"I never played God. Mariel, it never once occurred to me that I could." He looked away from her thoughtful eyes and then back again. "You must believe that or we have no future."

"Of course I do, Edward."

"I suppose I can thank Lady Crandall for that. I expect she gave you the same lecture in theology that she gave me."

"Yes," she did. Now they were both smiling. Surely that was a good sign.

"You asked why I did it. Why I give money away." He took a deep breath and wondered at the phrase that confession was good for the soul. He felt as though he were exposing his heart and handing her a knife.

"There is no one reason, either virtuous or suspect. I did it because I was bored. That is the simplest explanation. I did it because the only thing my mother ever asked is that we be kind to one another. I did it because it made me feel good. I did it because giving money away and watching what happened was fun."

"I suspect, Edward, that your behavior is more like the gods of Rome and Greece than our Christian God."

He was not sure if that was an insult, not until she added, "But you are kinder, Edward, so much kinder than I have ever understood those gods to be."

"That is generous of you, for there was at least one occasion when I was not. To this moment I cannot explain why I did not tell you about Chartwell, especially after you told me of your missing half brother. I had every intention of telling Crandall and letting him pursue it. If he had chosen to ignore it, I like to think that I would have told you." He paused. "Eventually."

"Oh, you would have, I am sure of that. What we share will never brook deceit." She put that before him, and he did not mistake the mandate in it.

"We know that now if we did not before, Mariel. It is the lesson I learned at the Harbisons', and I hope never to have to learn one as harshly again."

"Edward, I think you have spent so many years immersed in your role as a secret champion that you thought to treat me as the others and present the prize of my brother as a gift."

He looked abashed. He knew he did. "To that end I must tell you that I have contacted Matthew and asked him to find your brother William. I will not trust Crandall in this when I know how important it is to you to have the chance to speak with him again."

Her smile was all the thanks he needed.

"I will always treat you with love and respect, Mariel." He paused, for here was the heart of the matter. "But I cannot promise to change, that I even want to change as you might wish."

"Why should I want you to be any less than the generous, free-spirited man I have come to know? I may not approve of all your choices, but it is only those that I wish we could change. I thoroughly approve of you."

*And love.* Why did she not add those two words? They were what he most needed to hear.

"I do know you, Edward, as well, I think, as you know me. We have spent as much time in the discussion of ideas as in more intimate amusement."

He laughed at that. "This is the most cerebral affair I have ever had. In fact, I might point out that with the exception of a very few kisses, it has been *entirely* cerebral."

"Oh, dear, Edward," she said, laughing. "I love you, truly I do."

Relief poured through him. "Say it again."

"I love you. I love you. I love you." She paused a moment and then added, "Just as you are, Edward." When he shook his head, she explained. She showed him with a kiss that was tender and loving. Then she turned cautious. "I do have some small hope that you and I, together, can find good works that meet both our needs. And that in time our needs will become the same."

*This kind of sharing makes a good marriage.* And as he gave himself up to the joy that she offered, he realized why he had so recently been considering the elements of a good marriage.

When she drew away, he let her go until she was at arm's length. "You said that you have never had a shouting row in your life. Well, now we have, and it was enough for a lifetime. It might clear the air, but when hearts are involved, it is too painful to be enjoyed."

She nodded. "We can make up now." She kissed him lightly on the lips, a habit he could grow used to. "I promise that making up will be far more satisfying than the argument."

"More than fun?"

"Much more." She proceeded to show him and then suggested the bedroom.

He refused, and the passion-fogged part of his brain called him insane. "Marry me, Mariel. Please say you will."

That sobered her. Did she have to think about her answer?

"Edward, do you think that you can stand to be married to a strong willed, opinionated woman who—"

He cut her off by raising his fingers, pressing them against her lips, and then finished the sentence. "—who will light up my life and help me do good."

"I will be a wife who needs endless lessons in how to have fun."

"Who will eliminate the word 'bored' from my vocabulary."

"I bring a daughter and a family quite inclined to scandal."

"Who has learned the value of love and the cost of heartache, I hope for the last time."

"Of course I will marry you." She smiled. "But not yet."

His smile died.

"I have never had a lover before. And every woman should have *one.*" She reached up and kissed him again, this time on the corner of his mouth. "Don't you think it will be fun?"

# AUTHOR'S NOTE

William Chartwell, a Braedon by birth if not by name, promises to be an intriguing hero. What kind of woman would appeal to a man raised with so little feminine influence? His mother died at his birth. He was raised far from his family and, at the age of ten, was sent to sea by his uncaring father.

While I am helping William find the love of his life, I hope you enjoy reading Mariel and Edward's story, as well as the previous two books in the Braedon family series.

I write from my home near the Chesapeake Bay, an hour's drive from the nation's capital but as different from it as London is from the Dover coast. The cliffs near me rise up ninety feet from the bay and are filled with fossils dating back millions of years. They are readily found on the beach, one of the places that I spend time when I am not writing. Our house boasts a collection of sea treasures that includes shark teeth, ancient scallop shells, and driftwood in all shapes and sizes.

I can be reached by e-mail at MaryBlayney@aol.com.

# More Regency Romance
# From Zebra